HAUNTED MICHIGAN

3

MICHIGAN

T0159362

HAUNTED MICHIGAN

MICHIGAN

The Haunting Continues...

Rev. Gerald S. Hunter B.A., MDiv.

THUNDER BAY
—— PRESS ——

West Branch, Michigan

Haunted Michigan 3: The Haunting Continues...
Copyright © 2013 Rev. Gerald S. Hunter B.A., MDiv.

All rights reserved. No part of this book may be reproduced or transmitted in any form or by any means, electronic or mechanical, including photocopying, recording, or by any information storage or retrieval system without written permission from the publisher, except for the inclusion of brief quotations in a review.

Published by
Thunder Bay Press
West Branch, Michigan 48661

ISBN: 978-1-933272-37-5

Library of Congress Control Number: 2013937537

Notice

Although Thunder Bay Press and the author have exhaustively researched all sources to ensure the accuracy and completeness of the information contained in this book, we assume no responsibility for errors, inaccuracies, omissions, or any inconsistency herein. Special care was taken to preserve respect for the deceased and any slights of people or organizations are unintentional.

Haunted?

If you would like to share your own haunted Michigan experiences with Rev. Hunter, you may contact him by e-mail at thunderbaypressmichigan@gmail.com. We request that you respect Rev. Hunter's privacy and refrain from attempting to reach him at his home or work.

Printed in the United States of America

Table of Contents

Preface vii

Glossary of Terms. xiv

It Begins. 1

    Chapter 1 The Haunted Tavern. 2

    Chapter 2 Maggie Can Be A Bit Testy 11

    Chapter 3 Dealing With The Dead. 22

    Chapter 4 Legislative Spirits 32

    Chapter 5 Battle Alley. 39

    Chapter 6 Upscale Ghostly Dining. 49

    Chapter 7 Cross in the Dirt 60

    Chapter 8 Hanging Out At Hank's 74

    Chapter 9 Ghosts of Fairlane. 89

    Chapter 10 The Whistler 97

    Chapter 11 Messy and Mean 105

    Chapter 12 The "King," the Books, and the Spirits. 119

    Chapter 13 Hissing Hag. 123

    Chapter 14 The Historic Fort Wayne 132

    Chapter 15 Salvation Army Spooks 151

    Chapter 16 Who's That Peeking Around the Corner?. . . . 156

    Chapter 17 An Old Fashioned Haunting. 169

    Chapter 18 Mr. Bastard 185

    Chapter 19 The Bedtime People 196

    Chapter 20 Roadhouse Ghosts 203

    Chapter 21 Cold, Clammy Babysitter. 214

    Chapter 22 The Lumber Baron 225

    Chapter 23 The One that Started it All. 238

Encore, Encore! The Ghosts of the Michigan Theatre. 272

About the Author. 286

Preface

It is said that the past is prologue. That is certainly a true statement. Individuals, communities, and even countries are shaped by the events of their histories. The past always has a role in what we experience and how we understand who we are. While we can learn from our past history, we cannot remove it or go back and change any of it. In short, we may be finished with the past, but the past is never finished with us.

It's the same way for ghosts. The past has shaped not only who they continue to be, but often creates within them the strong desire to remain where they are. Some earthbound spirits, I believe, hang around because they are so emotionally attached to a particular place—a home, a business or some other place which remains meaningful to them. Others cling tenaciously to a particular person, such as a loved one who still walks the earth, or an enemy against whom they harbor a deep desire for revenge. Still others refuse to go because they simply don't know they're dead, having perhaps died suddenly, tragically, or unexpectedly. Then there are those who refuse to cross over to the next sphere of existence because of the strong religious belief in a god of retribution. In other words, they're afraid of eternal punishment.

In researching the nature of hauntings, I've run up against ghosts who fit into all of the above categories, and even more. For instance, there are ghosts who have crossed over just fine, but for whatever reason return every once in a while. Maybe they do so to bring comfort to a living loved one, or to offer assurance, or pronounce an important message. Those ghosts, it would seem, can pretty much come and go as they please. But the spirits which intrigue me most are the ones who may or may not know they are dead, can see all the life being lived amongst them, but can't participate in it. Many of them will try to return to the land of the living by doing the only thing they can, namely, inhabit the bodies of the living. Of course, this comes with a pretty large price tag attached to those they end up tormenting, often causing psychological problems for their hosts.

I say all this just to tell you how fascinating it is to experience a ghost. And a ghostly encounter allows us to understand there is much more to life than the singular existence we now experience, and that it is certainly possible to tap into the realm of the paranormal and run into a ghost or two. For me, it's been a lot of fun seeking out and being sought by the spirits of the dead. And admittedly, that fun has sometimes found itself mixed in with a few scares along the way.

As a result of writing my three books about haunted places in Michigan, I've had the opportunity to meet hundreds of people. I've met them in their homes, their workplaces, their vacation cottages, in graveyards, and in various other assorted locales. Many of those I've encountered in settings where I have lectured about my books and during my adventures hunting down or seeking out ghosts. Many times, I'm asked about things in which I have zero expertise, experience, or belief. I cannot tell you how often, after speaking about ghosts for a couple of hours at some library or community center, that people have asked me where I stand on UFOs or Bigfoot or some secret underground cave in Kentucky which leads to an alien world hidden beneath the outermost layer of the earth's crust. Usually, I just smile and let them know those things hold no interest for me and wish them well. Often, I am secretly hoping someone will come along and toss a net over them, or maybe just take away their voter registration cards.

One of the topics I've been more than skeptical about has to do with those folks who claim to be "psychic."

I've had, for the most part, pretty disappointing luck when checking these folks out as far as authenticity is concerned. I've always looked upon them with a somewhat jaundiced eye—until I met two of them who impressed me well beyond my skepticism and raised my eyebrows if not my hackles. One of them you'll meet in one of the stories in this book, and you'll read about how she impressed me. The other I will tell you a little bit about right now.

I will only say, by way of identification, that her name is Darcy, that she is quite well educated, youngish, and rather pulchritudinous. She has also convinced me she is extremely gifted as a psychic, asserting that she was born with her abilities, and they are as natural to her as breathing is to the rest of us.

I first met Darcy at a gathering where I hadn't met, or spoken with, any of the persons in attendance. After I gave a presentation, there was a time of conversation laced with libations—in other words, we enjoyed a happy hour. After my first bourbon on the rocks, she was introduced to me as a psychic. Well, when I meet a person purported to be tuned into a different frequency than the rest of us, I rather slyly lay out challenges for that individual to impress me. In short, I put them to the test.

Darcy and I spoke about her "gift" for several minutes, and she began speaking about spirit guides. Now, I know all about this theory, but I played dumb about the subject. I asked her if she could actually see spirit guides, and she answered in the affirmative. Then I asked her if she could see my spirit guide, and she said that not only could she see my spirit guide, but she had been watching it all afternoon. I asked if my guide happened to be a man or a woman, and she said it was a man, and that he was always with me, and was standing just behind me at that very moment. Intrigued because I couldn't smell his aftershave, I asked Darcy if she knew his name—I was really pushing the envelope, or so I thought. She paused for a few seconds, and then said, "Yes, it begins with an "r," but it's an old name, something you don't hear very often. It's Raul—no wait! It's Reuben, and you've been wondering why you never see him, but it's because he only speaks to you in your dreams. The two of you were at one time soldiers together."

At Darcy's comments, I literally fell back a few steps, stunned by what I had heard. Only two weeks prior to this conversation I had experienced a dream wherein a Civil War soldier named Reuben appeared to me, offering me information about a book I was supposed to write. The dream was so vivid I knew it was more than "just" a dream among dreams, and I actually began researching the book. As if that weren't enough to send the waiter for another round of distilled support, she went on to tell me I was suffering from a kidney problem, and that it would intermittently bleed profusely, causing me great discomfort and lost days in the hospital. She told me the doctors were puzzled, and didn't have an explanation for my malady. Again, she was spot on. I had gotten out of the hospital only two months prior to meeting Darcy, having yet another kidney flare up meeting exactly her description.

By now I was fascinated. I asked her if she had any idea about why I had been suffering from this ailment for so many years. She thought for a very brief moment, then said, "I see you in an old uniform, inside a trench. Reuben is with you, and the enemy is overwhelming you. The two of you are trying to get out of the trench, and as you are climbing out you are stabbed in the back by a man with a bayonet. It pierces your left kidney (that's the one, all right), and he basically eviscerated you. It was a terribly traumatic event, one you didn't even see coming. The psychic trauma is still with you, and is the reason why your kidney bleeds."

Intrigued? Well, Darcy then went on to tell me exactly where in my kidney the bleeding comes from.

She actually drew a picture of my kidney, with such finesse that it matched exactly where one of my MRIs had pinpointed the location of the bleeding. She explained I have small veins which rupture and cannot be cured by medicine but can be relieved through what she called "psychic healing."

Well, why did I just ramble on to you about this incident? Because it taught me that I need to pay attention even to those things I believe to be impossible. It taught me there is much more to who we are, and what we can do as human beings, than we ever imagined.

I've enjoyed writing about the ghosts of Michigan. That's obvious by the fact that this is my third book about them. I've enjoyed, and still enjoy, meeting them, catching glimpses of them by eye and by use of video equipment, and listening to them as they speak to me or to others or to one another. I've actually had the opportunity to catch some of their voices on my digital recorders, where they have acknowledged my presence, and even regaled me with poetic recitations from time to time.

I've also enjoyed meeting the vast variety of people who have claimed to have had a ghostly encounter. Many are some of the brightest and most professional people you can meet, while others are just ordinary folks like most of us. Among those who have confided in me concerning their interactions with ghosts have been engineers, morticians, attorneys, civil rights investigators, special education teachers, airline pilots (now there's a vivid thought), assembly line workers, restaurant wait staff, and people from every walk of life in between—except politicians, but that's understandable, as most of them already live in a world of their own, and create a certain spookiness all around them that the rest of us will never completely understand.

Michigan is a huge expanse of territory surrounded by a massive system of fresh water lakes. Within its boundaries are large concrete cities, pastoral

towns, quaint villages and rural pastures dotted with homesteads. And all of these places can be haunted. Every one of them. And more people admit that they believe in ghosts than you would ever expect. They've seen them or heard them or have sensed them lingering in the halls of life all around them.

Anyone can encounter what we refer to as a "ghost." It's not all that difficult, it just takes a bit of discipline and a measure of luck. When I'm asked how it's done, I suggest they simply sit quietly where you expect ghosts to be, and run some audio or video equipment. The hard part is being patient and quiet. An even harder, yet more effective way, is to learn how to meditate. It takes some practice, but it's well worth the effort. Just close your pie hole, pull out the ear buds, find a comfortable position in a quiet spot, and then concentrate on your breathing. If your mind starts to wander, which is the result of living in a world fraught with activity and noise, don't become discouraged, but bring yourself back to task.

I don't know if there will be a fourth book dealing with haunted places in Michigan. It's a lot of work, and takes a great deal of time and effort. And there are other projects I'd like to attempt before I exit this terrestrial ball of ours. But I'm thankful for the folks who have made these books popular, and appreciative of the friends who have accompanied me on many a ghost hunt—some productive and some downright fruitless. And I'm thankful for the woman I call my Darling Pretty—my wonderful wife and soul mate Tracey, who puts up with more from me when I'm involved in these excursions than you can imagine.

So, read and enjoy. The pleasure has been all mine.

Glossary of Terms

Due to the sudden, nationwide fascination with things paranormal, there seems to be some argument amongst ghost lovers about certain words used to describe these phenomena. This is simply my attempt to define the words ghost hunters bounce off one another as they write, speak, or think about all of the strange things we really don't fully understand in the first place.

Apparition: The sudden, strange and unexplained appearance of a person or a ghost. Since I believe ghosts are people to begin with, it sounds like doublespeak, but it isn't. Look at it this way: an apparition can be a living person who suddenly shows up in one place when he/she is already in a different place, which is weird enough but has certainly happened. Or it can be a dead person appearing in your midst, which happens more than most folks will ever admit.

Ghost: The spirit or soul of a person which manifests itself after that person's death. It is the term most used to describe an encounter with a dead person. It is proper to use both the terms "ghost" and "apparition" interchangeably, and I do so within the pages of my books.

Spirit/Soul: Now things get cloudy, depending upon any religious belief you may entertain, and even if you don't have any particular religious beliefs. If you're a Christian, you're going to discover there is disagreement about how to define these terms. For instance, the Apostle Paul implies a difference between the two, but the official teaching of the Catholic Church is that these terms are interchangeable. However, there are other denominations which speak of a difference. Sometimes the word soul is used to describe a living individual. Other times, it's used to refer to that which gives the spark of life to all things. And then we see where "soul" is used to describe that which is fashioned in the image of God, and which lives forever. Whew.

Spirit, on the other hand, or "ruauch" in Hebrew and "pneuma" in Greek (both of which appear many times in the Hebrew and Christian Bibles, can mean "wind," or the breath that animates living beings. Also the word "spirit" is used to describe God, who isn't understood as a physical being at all. Theologically, "spirit" can refer to a person's attitude or state of mind.

Confused? Yeah, me too. And I'm not even qualified to address these terms outside the Christian community.

Place Memory: A place memory resembles a haunting, but it really isn't. A place memory is perhaps best described as residual energy of a person or an event in which a person has participated that repeats itself over and over again. Let me offer an example. Let's say that from time to time when you enter your living room, you see an elderly woman sitting in a rocking chair next to a roaring fireplace, and she's working on a quilt. Each time you see her, she's always doing the same thing. And let's say you don't even own a rocking chair and that the fireplace has long been bricked up. Along with all that, while you watch her, she is absolutely oblivious to you. In other words, it's like watching the *Andy Griffith Show* reruns. They're always the same, and while you may react to seeing them, they don't react to seeing you. An example of a place memory appears in at least one story in this book and deals with a young man in a mechanics jumpsuit who is always seen walking down some stairs and exiting the house on his way to work. He's not real, it's just his energy playing itself out over and over again out of habit.

Haunting: This is the term generally used when a ghost or apparition interacts with a place or a person. Whenever I use the term, it's to describe ghostly activities that include the living. A ghost may or may not know you are there, but many times you will know they are there. They are the continuing life force of the dead. A place or a person may be haunted by a ghost or ghosts.

Paranormal: Those events and/or situations which are outside the "norm" of human existence. The term fascinates me because it implies something "other" than the way the world works. However, whatever occurs in human existence would seem, to me, to be a part of what is normal. Therefore, aren't paranormal events really normal? Some folks would argue that the paranormal events of life aren't rational, and therefore stand outside the realm of the normal. Well, all I can say to that is this—I've seen enough of the "normal" in life to make a good argument that it isn't all that rational.

Demons/Demonic: Some folks believe there are demons who come from the bowels of hell at the behest of Satan, and that they do demonic things. While I believe some people can be "demonic" (Hitler was certainly one) in the sense that their actions are unspeakably cruel, I don't buy into the whole demon stuff. In fact, it's interesting how one can trace the evolution of the "Devil" in what we refer to as the Old and New Testaments. He doesn't even appear until the book of Job, where he only serves as God's prosecuting attorney, unable to do anything to anyone without God's permission. From that starting point, religious thought begins to run rampant, and pretty soon he's got all the powers of Superman without the conscience needed to go with them.

The Haunt Meter

Once again, I offer my system of rating a haunted place by attaching a number of stars (*) to each story. The more stars, the more obvious the haunting.

It Begins

Chapter 1
The Haunted Tavern

Place Visited: The New Hudson Inn, a tavern and eatery located at 56870 Grand River Avenue in New Hudson, Michigan.

Period of Haunting: The joint is full of spirits, both the kind you drink and the sort who float around the place entertaining the patrons.

Date of Investigation: Initial visit July 2002. Recent visit November 2009.

Description of Location: The New Hudson Inn is the oldest continuously operated tavern in Michigan, having first opened its doors to travelers in 1831. A large, two story wood structure, it was built as a place of respite for weary travelers making the journey between Detroit and Lansing. The main floor is a rather raucous "L" shaped bar area which is extremely popular with the locals. During the summer, it is often crowded with Harley-Davidson motorcyclists of an interesting demeanor. The upper level of the inn, which in years past served as individual hotel rooms, is no longer in use except for storage and is accessible only by climbing a step ladder and hoisting oneself up through a hatch in the ceiling of the kitchen. The inn-bar-tavern or whatever you wish to call it is host to a very long wooden bar. How long? Well, that bar used to be a bowling lane. When it was delivered to the tavern many years back, it wouldn't fit through the doors, so, rather than cut the piece to fit, the staff cut a hole in the side of the building and moved it into place. The decor is rustic, rough, and not exactly the kind of place you'd take Mom for Mother's Day. Some of the walls are covered with photographs of patrons in various forms of inebriation, all of whom seem to be having an inordinate amount of fun. The booze is cheap and the burgers are great. This is an old-time bar for adults and not for the weak of heart. The staff is friendly and outgoing. If you're looking for a watering hole undiluted by political correctness and reminiscent of the glory days of yore, look no further. It is located just off the I-96 expressway about 6 miles from Novi to the east and US-23 to the west. Take the New Hudson exit off I-96, head south just past the Wal-Mart and turn left onto Grand River Avenue. Look immediately to your left and you'll see the famous old structure.

Haunt Meter: * * ½

THE NEW HUDSON INN is one of those places that, if it wasn't already haunted, ghosts would be inexplicably drawn toward it. Just walking inside the place can be an unsettling experience for sensitive folks, as the atmosphere feels, well... close. If you've ever stepped inside a place and immediately felt as though the spirits were watching you, then you know what I mean. Add to that the fact that the interior hasn't changed but a smidgen in the past seventy years or so, and you know in an unusual place.

The paranormal stories about this place are abundant, so in the interest of space I will touch on only a select few, beginning with that of a local painter who was hired to spruce up the outside of the establishment a few years back. Seeking anonymity because he still drinks there, I shall herein refer to him as Tom, and this is his story:

It was an ordinary July day, and I was hired to caulk and paint the windows on the outside of the upper level. That level hadn't been used in decades and was pretty run down—you know, wallpaper peeling off the walls, the linoleum flooring split and worn through, that sort of thing. I'd already worked on a couple of the windows and had gone down the ladder to grab a beer at the bar. After that I went back outside, moved my ladder to the next window, and climbed on up. I was just getting ready to scrape around the window frame when movement inside caught my eye. Man, I couldn't freakin' believe what I was seeing. The room, which a few minutes ago was bare and filthy, was now clean and filled with antique furniture just like a hotel room from way back in time. And there was a man standing in front of a dresser buttoning up a uniform coat. He looked like he was from the Civil War or something. He had one of those longish goatees and his hair was slicked back. He was looking into the mirror, and I could see his reflection. I looked around the room and there were pictures on the walls hanging by wires attached to nails. The bed was small and had a blanket folded up near the foot, and there was a small wooden stand with a wash bowl and pitcher on it. It didn't sink in right away that this wasn't normal, but in a few seconds it dawned on me that I must be looking back in time. Man, I slid down that ladder and headed back to the bar. I was shaking so badly the lady behind the bar asked me if I was okay. When I told her what I saw, she thought I was playing a joke on her. She didn't take me seriously until I told her I was through and went outside to pack up my stuff.

These sorts of stories are almost legendary in this neck of the woods. The inn has long been reputed to be haunted by various spirits, with some of the locals being true believers and others chalking up the spirits to the extreme ingestion of 100-proof spirits. All I know is that the ghosts seem to have the run of the place, as they have been sighted all through it.

As New Hudson is still one of those places where everyone knows everyone else, many people have their stories, but most people don't want their real names exposed in print. My next tale of other-worldly contact comes from a patron I shall call Tina.

Tina is a rather petite woman who nonetheless looks as though she could handle herself in any barroom situation. Still, there was one situation she'd never dreamed of encountering at the old inn, and in a place she'd least expected—the ladies room.

The restrooms of the establishment are themselves located in an unusual spot, right smack dab in the middle of the joint, between the barroom and the kitchen. They are therefore small, windowless, and not designed to impress the patrons. The idea is to relieve yourself and get back to the bar to refill your bladder, challenge your kidneys, and further damage your liver. Tina was doing just that on a winter's evening when darkness was deep and the bar traffic was slow. While in a posture not conducive to defending oneself, the knob on the restroom door began to turn. Since she hadn't locked the door, she raised her voice to announce the space was occupied. That didn't seem to matter, as the door silently slid open to reveal a man who, shall we say, didn't fit in with the decor. As Tina said:

> I looked up ready to do battle with this jerk; I mean, he was invading private territory. But just when I was about to tell him to get the hell out, I sort of just froze. I mean, this guy was kind of see-through. It's hard to explain; he was solid enough to have form, but I could still sort of see through him. He was really short and stocky and was wearing clothes

with no shape to them, they were all just sort of messy looking. He looked like a farmer out of one of those movies about the Depression. He needed a shave, and his hands were really big with thick fingers and all cracked and dirty. About the time I realized he wasn't real, he started fading away. The impression I got was that he never really saw me, but I sure as hell saw him, and it was a long time before I ever went back in there to pee.

I have a select crew of folks who accompany me whenever I'm asked to check out a haunted dwelling. When the New Hudson Inn invited me to stay after closing and see what was up, I brought along my gang of ghosters and all our equipment, i.e., digital cameras, infrared camera, several recorders (digital and tape), thermometers, EMF meters etc., and we entered and locked ourselves inside this dispensary of tasty libations for several hours.

We broke into teams of two, with two employees joining us for security reasons. The plan was for each team to find a place to sit while quietly observing the surroundings and making use of our equipment. Every forty-five minutes we would switch locations, so that each team would have a shot at a new location.

For the first couple of hours, everything was quiet to the point of bordering on disappointment. But as anyone who has ever sat in a haunted dwelling can attest, these things often take time and patience. Still, it wasn't until the second changing of the guard that anything out of the ordinary was encountered.

I took up a new position with my buddy Glenn, a professional administrator for the Livonia School system, at the far end of that bowling lane bar. We positioned our cameras to look down the length of the bar and to include in their frames the large mirror behind the bar. From that vantage point we could use our infrared thermometers to check out temperatures from as close as a few inches to as far away as thirty feet. Still, nothing ethereal emerged in our midst, and none of our readings were anything other than run-of-the-mill, ordinary. At least, that's how it was until I put my sonic ear equipment on and turned up the volume. The sonic ear tremendously amplifies the slightest nuance of sound while listening through a set of earphones.

While pointing the sensitive microphone down the length of the bar and cranking up the volume, I almost immediately picked up several voices. At first, it was as though I was listening to a conversation through a wall, the voices muffled but nonetheless evident. Then I began to hear distinct short sentences, none of which were altogether friendly. The first was a man's voice saying, "just leave," several times. Then I picked up a distinctly older man's tone as he chipped in with, "we don't want you." Neither voice showed up on our recorders, and nothing appeared in our videos. Just those voices passing from my amplified headset into my ears.. Later, when I let Sarah, a church secretary and fellow ghost aficionado use the equipment, she also heard faint voices, as though several women were having a distant conversation.

Before I continue with the description of my next ghostly encounter at the inn, let me offer the following tidbit of information. I have often had people send me photos they have taken of purportedly haunted places, both indoors and outdoors. They point out to me the "orbs," the little opaque circles which sometimes appear in a photograph, and maintain they are proof of the presence of spirits. Some folks say these orbs are energy given off by spirits, and others say they are spirits trying to fully manifest themselves, but falling a bit short. Others maintain they are proof only of moisture or dust in the air or on the lens of the camera. The latter explanation was the one I always adhered to, as it is my belief one ought to enter a supposedly haunted place with an open mind and without any preconceived notions. I must admit my mind was changed, if not entirely then at least to a good degree, by an experience I had in a haunted restaurant in Jackson, Michigan. I won't go into detail about the encounter here, but you can find it in another chapter of this book. Suffice it to say, I no longer dismiss these opaque circles out of hand.

At any rate, after having spent a tour of duty in every location of the inn, I decided to go way up to the attic. That entailed my climbing the step ladder on the first floor, pulling myself up through the hatch, and then making my way over to the attic entry doorway at the far west end of the second level. No one had checked out the attic, as it was suggested to us by the owner that it wasn't the safest place in the building to traverse. Curiosity had me in its steely grip, so I opened the door and gently trekked up the ancient worn steps, a flashlight providing my only source of illumination.

Reaching the top of the stairs, I scanned the interior of the attic, which spread the entire length of the building, with my flashlight. It was easy to get an idea of just how old this building truly is. The original rough-hewn beams, thick and solid, were still there, held in place by wooded pegs. There was no flooring, just cross beams, so I remained on the top step and began to shoot photos with my digital Sony. I shut off my flashlight and turned on the camera's flash feature. Then I examined each shot on the camera's screen for any anomalies. There were none—at first, that is.

I had taken about a dozen shots of the rugged attic area, and after getting no ghostly results, I used a little trick a fellow ghost hunter had given me a few years before. She told me that if I wanted to take a photo of ghosts, I should at least have the courtesy of asking permission first. After all, she says, ghosts are just people and you are in their space. So, I asked out loud if there was anyone present and if they'd allow me to photograph them. From that point on my photos had the presence of orbs. Lots of orbs. Dozens if not hundreds of them.

Having seemingly struck apparitional gold, my partner and I decided to use the same technique on the second floor, which is still separated into individual rooms. The same thing happened. When we asked, we got results. When we didn't ask, we didn't get results. It was somewhat gratifying to feel as though we were politely communicating with the spirits therein.

We were tying up loose ends at the close of our adventure, and all of us were seated at the bar (no, we don't allow drinking on our excursions) discussing the night's events. About half my crew was disappointed, as they hadn't encountered even the slightest sense of a spiritual presence, while the other half felt at least somewhat satisfied the place had spirits wandering the halls, the barroom, and even the ladies indoor privy. That's also when one of the employees, a no nonsense college student who earned tuition money tending bar, spoke up with her story.

Angie (not her real name) related that several times in the past few months she had seen the apparition of a man walk from the end of the bar and into the adjoining room. Each time, she said, it was late at night and few customers were present. The man, always dressed the same in dungarees and a work shirt, could be seen for anywhere from a second or two to about half a minute. She maintains that one time she had seen him standing at the end of the bar watching her as she sat with a customer smoking a cigarette. She nudged her client and gently pointed to the end of the bar. He looked at the guy, and then asked, "When did he come in?" Then, the man turned away from them and walked into the back room of the bar and out of sight. They both got up, hurried over to that area, and found it empty. There are no exit doors, so he had no escape route. Whether out of courage or inebriation, the two of them shared a laugh and another beer before closing up shop and going home.

Aside from these incidents, the New Hudson Inn is host to the garden variety paranormal activity. Doors that were closed and locked are found open, lights that have been switched on will turn off, and footsteps are often heard above the heads of the patrons, as though the ghosts of yesteryear are still rambling about on the second floor, unpacking their satchels for the night as they await the next coach or train. And one of those ghosts will play games with the help from time to time, moving cases of empty beer bottles from one part of the back storage area to another.

Planning a Visit? The folks at the New Hudson Inn are friendly and approachable. Just call ahead and ask for the manager in charge, but call during the daytime when they aren't swamped with customers. If you belong to a ghost investigation team, they'll most likely warm right up to you and make arrangements for your visit. Be prepared to arrive late, just as they close. Sometimes they're open until the last legally-mandated hour, and sometimes they close up shop early, it all depends upon the volume of business. And don't let this old historic building mislead you. This place is ancient by Michigan standards and not a lot of restoration has been done to the place. It's easy, therefore, to mistake creaking noises and wind through the windows as something else entirely.

Still Haunted? Biker babes and locals alike will assure you the ghosts are still actively carousing around the place.

Chapter 2
Maggie Can Be A Bit Testy

Place Visited: A private dwelling in Redford, Michigan, an immediate suburb of Detroit.

Period of Haunting: This haunting seems to have begun in the late 1950s, when a resident of the house committed suicide. It continues to this day.

Date of Investigation: Summer of 2008

Description of Location: A single story, working class home in an older suburb of Redford, Michigan. At the time of its construction, the neighborhood, as well as Redford in general, was comprised of mostly blue collar folks involved in some manner with the automobile industry. The home is located on the stretch of Sumner Street, just a block or so south of 7 Mile Road and just before Allison Park. By today's standards the homes in Redford are small, with postage stamp yards to match. In many cases, not much more than a driveway separates the side of one house from the side of another. Redford boasts a population of just over 50,000 living souls, but it's anyone's guess how many disembodied beings aren't on the census rolls. From the south you can take Grand River to 7 Mile and turn left. Get ready right away for another left turn onto Sumner. The house is on the left-hand side, a few doors before you get to the park. If you're coming from the west or north, find M-5 on your Michigan map and follow it southeasterly until you get to 7 Mile and then turn right. At this point you can follow the above directions. From there, dear ghost hunter, you're on your own, as the residents strongly prefer no uninvited guests. If you want to feast on good grub and wash it all down with your choice of spirits, may I suggest the White Rhino Pub, about a mile west of Sumner Street on 7 Mile Road. Good food and drink in a good sports bar atmosphere. No ghost adventure is complete without good grub and a brew or two, especially if you're visiting a home like the one in this chapter.

Haunt Meter: * * * *

THIS IS A SEEMINGLY ORDINARY HOME on an ordinary street which boasts ordinary people. It's what's inside this ordinary home that is extraordinary. And more than a little bit frightening.

Dan and Liz Cowden (not their real names) bought the home in the mid 1990s, not long after their marriage a couple years earlier. The price met their somewhat strapped budget, and the location was near where they worked, she as a waitress and he at a small factory a couple miles away. After taking possession they moved right in and set up housekeeping in their single story home with a full, yet unfinished, basement. Right away, they noticed something was not quite conducive to suburban bliss.

As with most folks who purchase a home, the first order of business was to make the place feel like it was theirs. Hence, Dan and Liz decided the kitchen needed some cosmetic surgery. The appliances were old, and when they moved them out for new ones, they discovered the refrigerator had been leaking over the years, soaking into the floorboards and warping them. So, they decided it was time to replace the flooring and lay down new tile. Of course, one thing normally leads to another when a project begins in an older home, and the realization soon descended upon them that they may as well go ahead and do a complete kitchen make-over. Handy with tools and with patience to spare, Dan took to the project like a kid takes to a new computer game. After moving the stove and refrigerator to a temporary setting in the dining room, he began tearing up the old flooring. Now, if you have any education in things paranormal, you already know that remodeling a haunted home doesn't always score points with the resident spectres. They sometimes become a tad testy and begin to express their discontent in ways that tend to gain your attention. Dan discovered this soon after he had torn up the old flooring.

I was working on the floor late on a Friday night because I didn't have to get up early for work the next day. It was probably around 11:30 and Liz was in the bathroom getting ready for bed. I was scooting around on my hands and knees laying the sub-flooring so I could get it ready for the tile. I had been drinking a lot of coffee that night so I'd stay alert, and when I reached for my cup, which had been just a foot or so away, it wasn't there. I looked around the kitchen floor and didn't see it. I just figured maybe I'd set it on the counter, so I stood up to look but it wasn't there either. Now, I had just poured that cup and it was still pretty hot, so I know it had to be close by. Just about then I heard what sounded like glass breaking in the next room—the dining room—and I stepped in there to see if something fell. My coffee cup was on the dining room table in pieces, and coffee was spilled all over Liz's white tablecloth. I had a helluva time explaining that one to her because I didn't want to tell her I hadn't even been in the dining room and didn't know how my coffee had gotten in there. I didn't want to scare her, so I just took the heat, cleaned up the mess and went to bed.

It's easy to chalk up a strange experience to fatigue, and that's what Dan tried to do. He told himself he must have been too tired to remember going into the dining room with his steamy brew. What he couldn't explain was how the cup managed to break, but sometimes it's better to live in the state of denial than the state of reality and face the notion that there are things happening in our midst which transcend what we consider to be "normal."

The work continued without unforeseen disturbances most of that weekend. Dan had a friend come over to help finish the sub-flooring and assist with the prep work for laying the tile. The job took all day Saturday and most of Sunday. Sunday evening, the last tile was in place and Dan had placed dining room chairs in both kitchen doorways to prevent anyone from walking on the freshly laid tile until it was seasoned. Then he sat at the dining room table, popped the top on a cold beer and began scanning a hunting magazine.

The night sky had fully descended by then, and ambient light was no longer sufficient, so Dan reached over and switched on the overhead chandelier. It was then he noticed someone standing on his newly tiled floor, threatening the integrity of the carefully spaced tiles.

I slammed my beer down and stood up to tell Liz to get the hell off the tile, only it wasn't Liz. Instead, it was some skinny old lady with scraggly gray hair. She was standing barefooted right smack in the middle of the kitchen just glaring at me. Man, if looks could kill I'd have been dead on the spot. She looked to be in her eighties, with sort of sunken cheeks that made her eyes look too big for her face. I didn't have a clue who she was or how she got there, and I just stood there staring back at her. I remember the room got really cold, and it stunk like garbage all around me. Then she raised her right arm and pointed a finger at me and said, "stop it." That's all she said, "stop it." It was like a warning. Then she turned away from me and started walking across the kitchen to the door leading into the living room. About the time she got to where I had stacked the chairs, she sort of melted away.

If Dan had any reservations about keeping this encounter from Liz, they never rose to the surface. Instead, he headed out of the dining room looking for her—Liz that is, not the uninvited scold. He found her in the bedroom folding clothes. He asked if she had heard or seen "anything weird," and that question naturally led to a full description of what he had just experienced. As he finished his strange tale, he expected her to either laugh and accuse him of drinking one beer over the threshold of sobriety, which he hadn't, or yell at him to stop trying to frighten her. She didn't do either. In fact, she offered something strange herself. She said she was just getting ready to go tell him to stop playing games, and that this was actually the second time she was folding her clothes. She went on to say she had removed her things from the dryer, taken them to the bedroom, and folded them. She had left the room to look for a sock she thought she had dropped along the way, and when she had returned to the bedroom, the clothes were scattered all over the place. Hence, it wasn't such a stretch for her to believe Dan was telling the truth.

The next few days were a bit nerve-wracking for Dan and Liz, not because they had more strange encounters, but because they were afraid they were going to have more encounters. Every unfamiliar creak, squeak, and shadow made their pulses quicken, and they felt as though they were walking on eggs instead of a new kitchen floor. But things were actually quiet, and their lives seemed to be getting back to normal. Until, of course, Dan began refacing the kitchen cabinets. That's when he once again ran unexpectedly into the same old woman.

> I thought living in a house that may have a ghost in it was scary enough, but when I checked into the price of new cabinets I thought I was going to go into shock. That's when we decided to reface the old cabinets—you know, replace the old doors and reface the trim. I had spent an entire morning removing the old doors and taking off the hardware. Since I had plans to build some storage cabinets for the garage, I decided to store them in the basement, where I had set up a little workshop. I carried the first load down, set them next to the workbench and turned around to go back for another load. That's when I saw movement out of the corner of my eye. My brain was saying not to look, but my eyes had already glanced over. Off in the corner was that same old lady, only this time she wasn't standing there scowling and pointing a finger at me. She was hanging from one of the old cast iron water pipes.

If you've ever watched a television show or a movie wherein a character has committed suicide by hanging, you've probably been misled about the appearance of it all. Hollywood tends to tone it down, leaving the recently deceased to appear no different in death as they did in life, except for that nasty rope looped around the neck. It wasn't that way for Dan.

> It was one of those situations where you were frozen, like you couldn't move. You didn't want to look, but you didn't have the strength to look away, either. And it was one nasty-assed sight to behold. Her neck looked way too long for the rest of her body, and the skin

around where the rope was looked all dark blue or black. Her eyes weren't completely shut, and her tongue was sticking out of her mouth. It was huge and black. As soon as the initial shock wore off, which took all of about a couple seconds, I flew up those stairs and out into the back yard.

Why the back yard? Because that's where Liz was. If I've learned anything at all during my years listening to the stories of those who encounter ghosts, it's that a man will run to a woman if he's scared and one's around. In this case, Liz was in the back yard working in her little vegetable garden.

Visibly shaken, Dan poured out the details of his trip to the basement not withholding any of the gruesome details. The end result was that two terrified people now stood in the back yard, staring at the little home they had purchased together and where they had intended to spend many years of marital bliss. As Dan relates:

> We pulled some folding chairs from out of the garage and sat in the yard for a couple hours, talking about what we should do or what we thought might be going on. We both needed a beer, but neither one of us was about to go into the house and get one. After a while we calmed down and started to wonder how anything so strange could be happening on such a nice day. We both decided to go together downstairs and check it out. We didn't find anything, but the rest of the trips to the basement with those cabinet doors were made by the two of us, me carrying the doors and Liz tagging along for courage.

Over the next several months the hanging lady was no longer seen swinging from a water pipe in the basement. In fact, everything calmed down quite a bit, and the Cowden's couldn't have been more pleased. The kitchen remodeling went off without any more hitches, as did the family bathroom. Everything seemed to be normal, and not a word was mentioned to any friends or relatives about the old lady hanging in the basement.

It was late October when the activity picked up a bit. The happy couple began noticing how light bulbs would suddenly start to burn brighter and just as suddenly burn out. Then the television would turn itself on, turn itself off, change channels, or even adjust volume all by itself. As if these things weren't enough, every once in a while they would hear a kitchen cabinet door slam, or they would smell a putrid odor in the kitchen. These little things led them to believe bigger things were on the way, and they were right.

It was just a few nights before Thanksgiving when their resident spirit made yet another appearance. The Cowden's were fast asleep in their small but well-appointed bedroom when Liz suddenly awakened. She didn't know what had tossed her back into consciousness, but she found herself wide awake and, as she puts it, "scared as hell."

> It was like my unconscious mind had told me to wake up, that something wasn't right. It took a minute for my eyes to adjust, and when they did I saw someone standing in the bedroom doorway, looking at us. It was the old woman Dan had been seeing. Dan had begun referring to her as the "scowling lady," and I can see why. She was giving us one of those looks like we were disgusting to her. I squinted my eyes to get a better look at her, and when I did she started walking toward the bed, pointing a finger at me. I knew she was going to say something, I could just feel it, but I didn't want to hear, so I quickly

grabbed my pillow and threw it at her, and she disappeared.

This seemed to be the beginning of several sightings between Thanksgiving and Christmas. Who knows, maybe the old girl wanted the holidays to herself. At any rate, Liz and Dan started running into her, almost literally some times, regularly. She was seen in the bedroom closet once when Liz opened the door to get her work clothes; she showed up one morning standing in the bathroom when Dan went in to take his shower; and she made an uninvited appearance when the two of them were eating dinner one evening, standing in the doorway of the dining room, once again scowling.

Liz and Dan finally decided to let some good friends of theirs in on what was going on in their home, and it was suggested by them that they get on the internet and try to search old news items to see if anything strange had ever happened in the house, like someone hanging in the basement with her tongue sticking out. So, off to the library they trekked one evening to do just that. In that setting they could look through old newspaper stories if the internet search didn't pan out, thereby making best use of their time. As it turned out, they struck gold. Well, if not gold, at least silver.

It seems that in the late '50s (Notice how I didn't give the specific year? I am well aware of the skills of ghost hunters, and don't wish to reveal this location.) an elderly woman had committed suicide at their address. The Cowden's now had a piece of history to connect to their haunting.

Inspired by what they had found, and realizing that knowledge brings a sense of control, they decided to bounce the story off one of their elderly neighbors, in hopes of further confirmation. Again, the effort was fruitful. "Old Wade," as he was referred to by long-time residents, was an elderly gent who had lived longer in the neighborhood than any of the rest. And yes, he did have at least an interesting tidbit to add to what the Cowden's had already discovered. There indeed had been a woman who had committed suicide in the home. No one in the neighborhood liked her, and the kids all called her "Maggie the Witch" because she was so mean to them. Furthermore, she had hanged herself in the basement for some unknown reason. But what the Cowden's didn't know was that one of the neighbors way back then, a friendly old chap who looked out for the old girl, had entered the home after not having seen her for a couple days. As the story goes, this old boy found Maggie hanging from the water pipe, cut her down, and carried her upstairs into the kitchen. That's the location where his heart decided to go into vapor lock, and he dropped dead on the spot of a massive coronary. Old Wade went on to say that legend around the neighborhood for years was that the two of them lay there in friendly bliss for several days before they were found, and that to this day a thick stench can be smelled in association with that home from time to time.

The story struck a realistic chord with the Cowden's. Especially that stench, which they had encountered more than once. Armed with their new information, they felt a bit more at ease about their home. At least now they knew who she was and why she was still hanging around (no pun intended, really). All this newborn confidence helped dissipate some of their fear, and now they take every opportunity to study the nature of hauntings in general, and their past haunting in particular. They make use of cameras and recorders, and even keep a "ghost journal," jotting down with great interest those incidents which years before had kept them awake all night.

It was soon discovered that not everything about Maggie the Witch was bad. Many times the Cowden's returned home from a night out to find the kitchen swimming with the scent of freshly baked bread or apple pie. Dan says it smells so good you'd wish the old hag would leave a piece for him on the kitchen counter.

So, maybe Maggie is getting used to the new residents taking up space in her home. Maybe if we can adapt to ghosts, they can adapt to us. Who knows?

The haunting of the Cowden home continues. Footsteps are heard as the old woman's bare feet slap across the kitchen tile, the television still dances the funky chicken, and the figure of the slight lady is seen from time to time roaming the house, still behaving as though it's hers.

Planning a Visit? Don't. If you can't respect my wishes, then respect theirs.

Still Haunted? Most certainly. In fact, Dan and Liz have become quite the ghost enthusiasts, joining one of the many ghost hunting groups which seem to be popping up all over Michigan. Their group has spent many nights in their home, watching and listening for Maggie and, so they say, sometimes making contact with her.

Chapter 3
Dealing With The Dead

Place Visited: A metro Detroit funeral home.

Period of Haunting: The spirits of the dead have roamed around the living—and the dead—for several years now.

Date of Investigation: September–October, 2007

Description of Location: Oh, the horror of it all! This one twists my literary ethics into knots, as I so much want to divulge the location, but have actually been told in no uncertain terms it would be in my best interests not to do so. This is a funeral home with deep roots in its community, having served several generations of families throughout its history. It is located in a rather upscale suburb of Detroit, and the best I can offer you is to think north instead of south. I had to swear my team (we call our group The Bogles) to secrecy before I even revealed the location to any of them. Be advised that all the information herein is accurate except for the names of those folks involved.

Haunt Meter: * * * * *

IF YOU THINK FUNERAL HOMES are creepy enough when you have to pay your last respects to someone, just add the extra dimension of ghosts skulking about and you've got a real reason to keep looking over your shoulder.

I was contacted by the general manager of the funeral home, an amiable young woman named Chloe, after she had read my two previous books about haunted places throughout Michigan. She expressed some reservation about even speaking with me over the phone, but when I assured her I would never break confidence, she agreed to meet me in person. Over coffee at a Big Boy Restaurant miles from her place of business, we hit it off quite well, and she finally opened the doors of the funeral home to me and my crew.

It's not easy to set a scheduled time to visit a funeral home, because they never know when business will drop in on them. So, the only way to have guaranteed access is to visit after they are closed. Which means going into the place after dark, and being locked inside. These are not conditions for the faint of heart, but there's a certain appeal in it all to a certified ghost hunter.

We arrived, four of us, with our gear neatly nestled within our backpacks at 10 p.m., after having followed previous instructions to park our cars behind the home in the far back corner of the lot where passing cars wouldn't see them. We entered through an employee only entrance in the back and were ushered to one of the front offices where families meet with a funeral director to plan a loved one's service. After introductions all around, we were told there were currently no families being served, which is polite undertaker talk meaning there were no stiffs laying around anywhere. You could actually hear the sighs of relief skirting through the room.

Chloe, a trim and more than attractive woman with chestnut hair and a cherubic face, breaks the stereotypical mold of what a funeral director is supposed to look like. In fact, she doesn't break that mold, she shatters it. At any rate, before we drifted into the bowels of that uncomfortably comfortable home of death, Chloe filled us in on her latest ghostly experience before.

Several things have happened since I began working here, but at first I just kept my mouth shut. It's not like you can talk about these things without it hurting your career chances. After a while I discovered that just about everyone who worked here at one time or another has had stories to tell. I have several, but I'll just tell you about the most recent one.

About three weeks ago we went out on a call to pick up a little girl who died from leukemia. She was about seven years old, and the family was pretty upset, as you can imagine. She passed away at home, and when we arrived we let the parents and other relatives and friends spend all the time they wanted with her before we made the removal. Then we took her to our facility and the next morning she was embalmed. Later we met with the family to make arrangements. At that time they gave us a beautiful yellow dress with white polka-dots for the viewing.

Later that day we had visitation for another family, an elderly man with a lot of children and grandchildren, so the place was full and we were quite busy. Well, with lots of people coming and going, our staff keeps a check on the door to make sure no youngsters go outside alone or wander off in the building where they shouldn't go. Clarence, one of our attendants, was working that evening, and he's really good about those things. He's a retired professional who works part time for us. Well, Clarence said that at least three times he saw a little girl standing off by herself down the hallway past the chapel where visitation was taking place. The first two times he saw her, he said he was distracted by guests coming in or going out and couldn't go and deal with her, and that each time he had looked back she would be gone.

The third time he saw her, she was way back down the hall again, all by herself just watching everybody. He found it strange that she was always alone and was concerned because she looked frightened. So, this time, he headed down the hall to check things out. He said he walked up to her and asked her where her mom and dad were, but she didn't answer, she just looked at him. Then he said he took his eyes off her for just a second to check on the front door, and when he looked down again she was gone. It shook him up a lot because there was no place she could have disappeared to that fast. He didn't see her again the rest of the evening.

The next day we had visitation all afternoon and evening for the little girl, and the place was really full. Whenever there's the death of a child, we're generally very busy. We had two staff members available, and I was working the visitation, too. We always have a licensed funeral director on duty in case the family needs something. Anyway, I came out of my office once and passed by the chapel as a couple with a little boy was coming out. I heard the little boy, who couldn't have been any more than four or five, say, "She's wearing a yellow dress just like Emma's," which was the name of the deceased. The parents asked who he was talking about, and the kid just kept pointing down the hallway and said, "It's her, over there," but there wasn't any little girl down there. That sort of gave me the willies because of what Clarence had told me had happened to him the night before.

It's not altogether unusual for a child to see things we adults can't. Their minds are still unpolluted by rational thought and very open to seeing a dimension of life we're taught to ignore or deny as we grow up. In this case, Chloe was sure the little fella was seeing the dead girl, and she said he even stared back at the hallway as he was carried out, and waved. For her part, Chloe was too busy to spend much time thinking about it, or maybe she just used how busy she was to keep from thinking about it. It doesn't really matter, though, because what happened the next day, the day of the funeral service, made her not only think about it, it made her deal with it.

We had visitation for an hour the next morning, just before the service was to begin. The place was packed and it was really a sad time for everybody. We had been busy setting up extra chairs and making sure everything was in order, and we were finally able to take a break when the minister began the service. At that time we close the chapel doors and listen to the service until it's time to go back in and give final instructions.

Everything was finished and the family and friends had exited to their cars for the procession to the cemetery. We were in the chapel closing the casket when our office manager, Barb, walked in. Barb never does this, but she asked if she could view the body before we removed it to the hearse. The casket wasn't closed, so she stepped up and looked inside. Then she started to tremble all over and walked out really fast. We thought maybe she knew the girl, or maybe because it was someone so young it played back some sad memory she had, so we let it go.

When we got back from the cemetery, Barb was in my office waiting for me. She was still visibly shaken, and she told me she couldn't work here any longer, and that she was giving us her two weeks' notice. When I asked her what was wrong, she told me that all during the minister's service the little girl lying in the casket was standing next to her desk, watching her. She said she knew the girl wasn't real, and she tried to avoid looking directly at her, but that she stayed right there through the whole service, and she could see her out of the corner of her eye. She was wearing a yellow dress with white polka-dots, and just standing there quietly watching.

Chloe said she tried to talk Barb out of leaving because she had been such a faithful employee for several years. Then Barb told her that this hadn't been the only time she had seen the dead wandering about the funeral home. In the past, though, they had never invaded the sanctity of her office. She had caught glimpses of others from time to time as she went about her business elsewhere in the establishment, but she was able to endure because she spent most of her time in her office with the door shut. This time, things had gotten a little too up-close and personal, and she was leaving, not so much for greener pastures as for those where the dead don't ramble around.

Primed by Chloe's preamble to the evening's excursion, our team divided up into twos and set up our equipment. One team settled into one visitation room while the other set up equipment in the second visitation room. (Notice I didn't refer to these rooms as "chapels" as funeral directors tend to do. The minister in me insists on pointing out that churches have chapels, funeral homes have visitation rooms.)

Each team remained in their places for over an hour, recording, snapping photos, taking measurements and simply observing and listening. When time was up, we met in the arrangement room to decide where to go next. It was determined one team would take the selection room, where family members pick out a casket from the dozen or so on display, while the other would settle in to the prep room, where the bodies are actually embalmed. *Please note: while there doesn't appear to be any law forbidding the public to enter the prep room, almost all funeral directors won't allow it. They site sanitary and safety reasons.*

Chloe escorted two of us down into the prep room and answered any questions we had about all the strange looking equipment. After she had answered, we were both sorry we had been curious enough to ask. After all, it's not the most comfortable place to spend your time, and it all looks rather cold and, well... antiseptically still. Nonetheless, we were determined to carry out our task, and so we set about performing the mission before us. Since we had been told not to touch anything—as if we'd enjoy playing with trocars, scalpels and suction machines—we were careful during our sequestered hour to respect that request.

We spent the first few minutes centering ourselves, which means we sat quietly and meditated while our video cameras recorded the room. Then we took measurements with our EMF (electromagnetic field) equipment and digital thermometers. While there didn't seem to be any unnatural response to our EMF readings, we noticed a sudden and significant drop in temperature several times in one particular part of the prep room. It was the area where personal effects of the deceased were kept, a cabinet across from the embalming table. At one point the temperature there dropped from about 67 degrees to just under 40 degrees in a matter of only a couple of seconds, and then bounded back up again just as quickly.

The rest of the night went much the same way we always spend them. We would switch areas with the other team, then visit new areas, stay there for an hour or so, and switch again. With the exception of having spent most of the night inside a building full of equipment used upon dead people, not much of interest took place. We finished up our visit to the funeral home around 2 a.m., and went to an all-night coffee shop down the road to bounce our initial reactions off one another. Two of us thought we heard faint voices a couple of times, and several photos had orbs in them, if you believe in such things as orbs. Just as we were getting ready to leave, we mentioned the drop in temperature in the prep room, and the other team mentioned they had gotten the same type of readings in the same place. That's when Chloe smiled and told us another tale about the dead making themselves known in her place of business.

Chloe said that for quite some time they had employed the services of a trade embalmer. This is a person who isn't an employee of any particular funeral home, but who is on call with several places to do all their embalming for them. It's a rather lucrative way to earn a living, but it's not for everyone. She said the man's name was Charles, and that he had been doing most of their embalming for a couple of years. After they had gotten to know one another quite well, they had lunch one day and Charles loosened up enough to ask her if anyone had ever noticed anything strange down inside the prep room. Intrigued, Chloe answered in the affirmative, and then invited Charles to share why he had brought the subject to light. He said that on a couple of occasions, while in the process of embalming, he caught sight of someone standing just a few feet away, watching what he was doing. Both times, he said, when he finally got the courage to look over, the person disappeared. The best he could do was describe the translucent visitor as a man, dressed in clothing that resembled either the 1930s or the 1940s. As to facial appearance, he sported a slicked hair cut popular to those decades and a well clipped, small mustache.

If that wasn't enough to add to Chloe's distress about the ghosts wandering about within her establishment, Charles had an even more disturbing tale to share. It seems that in the past couple of weeks he had been down in the prep room embalming a middle-aged man whose heart had suddenly refused to cooperate with the idea of sustaining life. While removing the natural bodily fluids in preparation to replace them with a more stable solution, the procedures were being examined by a man standing just a couple feet to his left, only this time the man watching was the same man being embalmed.

My team examined our tapes and photos, and aside from a couple of orbs in photos of the prep room, and a few lines our ears had picked up from faint disembodied voices, it was a rather uneventful evening—at least when compared to what others have experienced. We were able to make out one voice, that of a woman, softly uttering, "I want to go now." I don't blame her any, I'm not overly fond of hanging around funeral homes either.

As I mentioned earlier, this would have been a great place to go into detail about, including photos and real names and such. The provenance of the stories related to me are excellent, as most funeral directors I know are intimately acquainted with death and the idea of a hereafter, and not likely to make up such stories. Alas, what funeral director wants the public to know that the dead tend to hang around their halls of service even after the dirt's been tossed over that hole in the ground?

Author's note: In a conversation I recently had with a gifted psychic, whom you met in the prologue of this tome, I was informed that it is very, very unusual for the dead to hang around funeral homes and cemeteries. She said that when dead people see their own bodies, they generally accept the fact that it's over for them, and mosey on over to the next sphere of existence. She claims that most dead people hanging around have never seen their own corpse, and many times don't know they're dead. Hmmm, interesting.

Planning a Visit? Good luck, there are scads of funeral homes throughout metro Detroit, and I haven't given enough hints to enable you to pinpoint this location.

Still Haunted? Yup. Still haunted. Chloe, in a recent cell phone conversation told me images of the dead still wander the viewing rooms, and strange incidents still manifest themselves down in the prep room. Charles, she said, has recently reported embalming tools being rearranged while preparing bodies, and personal effects of the deceased that have been placed in one location have turned up in another.

Chapter 4
Legislative Spirits

Place Visited: The State of Michigan Capitol Building, Lansing, Michigan.

Period of Haunting: Apparently there's a long history of paranormal activity here.

Date of Investigation: October, 2008.

Description of Location: Since this is a book about haunted places in Michigan, I will assume the reader is aware of the location of our State Capitol and can find Lansing on a map. If that's not the case, then I would suggest a remedial course in local history at a local elementary school. Lansing is a city of about 120,000 animated and breathing souls, as well as its share of inanimate, non-breathing entities. The major employer used to be General Motors, where the former Oldsmobile auto was built. Now there are no more Oldsmobiles, and no more jobs. The downtown area is a mix of old and new, rich and poor, the important and the forgotten. Upscale men's shops (catering to state legislators and business lobbyists) share street space with homeless shelters, and trendy pubs reside near topless bars.

The Capitol Building recently underwent major reconstruction and restoration at a cost which raised the eyebrows of more than a few registered voters. The work was nothing less than stunning. The ground floor, which looks and feels like a basement level, has a glass ceiling, opaque and gorgeous. Schoolchildren on field trips enjoy lying on the floor and looking up at that ceiling. The main floor boasts a large, circular atrium rising four stories. The view from the higher floors downward is majestic. The second floor section of the atrium is ringed with the hand-painted portraits of every Michigan governor. No detail was missed during the renovation. Everything from the senate chamber to the men's rooms was painstakingly renewed to its former grandeur.

The Capitol Building is located, as one would expect, on Michigan Avenue in the heart of the downtown district. In fact, it interrupts Michigan Avenue, and one must drive around the building to proceed down the road. Due to the nature of the business it conducts, there are many fine places to dine, as well as fun places. I would suggest a couple of local favorites, Emil's and Clara's. Emil's is several blocks east of the Capitol and offers tasty Italian cuisine in a crowded—no, let's say intimate—setting. I cannot suggest a personal favorite, as I enjoy just about everything I've ever had there. It's not spacious, but it does retain a family feeling conducive to an enjoyable experience. Clara's, a short hop down from Emil's, is a former train depot finding new life as an eatery. It boasts two levels and an attached authentic railroad dining car in which you may dine. They offer everything from sandwiches to full meals. I particularly enjoyed their meatloaf dinner, but I've always been partial to meatloaf. Why do I nearly always mention food in my descriptions of haunted places? Because a good meal is comfort food for a busted investigation, or a great way to celebrate a successful ghost hunt.

Haunt Meter: * *

I BEGIN THIS STORY WITH AN APOLOGY for its brevity, as employees within these hallowed halls of legislative mischief are reluctant to talk. Therefore, I shall begin my tale, not with a history of the haunting, but with my experience there on another level.

The Capitol Building is, or rather, was, a popular place for weddings. I have been informed that they no longer allow these events. When they did, the activities coordinator would schedule these events to take place when no tours were being conducted, so that privacy and intimacy could better be guaranteed. It was under these circumstances I was privileged to officiate at a matrimonial event on a warm and inviting October evening in the year of our Lord, 2008.

I always make it a policy to arrive very early when I am officiating at a wedding ceremony. Why? Because I don't like officiating at weddings. I'd much rather be the officiant at a funeral service. If I mess up at a funeral service, it's really no big deal, as the dead generally don't mind. But if I mess up at a wedding—forget a cue or call the bride by the wrong name, or show up late—either my head or my rear (I've often been told that in my case they're rather interchangeable) will be handed to me on a platter. And I'd probably not be offered a piece of the wedding cake. At any rate, I always arrive early, and the Capitol Building ceremony was no exception.

With time on my hands, I met with the events coordinator to work out the logistics of the service. It would take place in the rotunda, already tastefully decorated and ringed with chairs for the guests. That out of the way, I asked if it was permissible to wander the hallowed halls and snap a few photos while people filtered in. Being a real history buff, I had brought along my digital Sony with a huge memory stick, which is more than I can say for my cognitive abilities. Permission was granted, and with a full hour before the festivities, I roamed each and every floor, peeping into closed rooms and snapping away.

The restoration work was indeed impressive, and I snapped photos of just about every area from just about every angle. I entered those rooms which weren't locked, and strode the ornate staircases from one floor to another. I even managed to get a few shots of the

Rotunda of the Capitol Building

senate chamber, but the door to the governor's office was, alas, locked up tighter than a republican tax cut. Original oils and carved busts filled the screen of my camera, as did the carved woodwork fashioned from Michigan lumber.

In short, I had taken many shots of the place before the wedding ceremony was to begin. I didn't have time to go through them right away, so I performed the ceremony, which went off without a hitch, ate a sumptuous meal at a nearby restaurant, then headed back home with the idea of taking a quick look at my photographic handiwork before heading off to bed for a sweet night of peaceful repose. Those intentions were dashed when I saw something unusual in one of my photos. I had taken a shot of a stairway connecting the first floor to the second. About halfway up the darkly stained wooden steps was what first appeared to be a red blotch. Interested in why it was there, I downloaded the shot, then played with the zoom button on my photo

Stairs to the second floor

program. What at first resembled a red blotch turned out to be a reddened face. And not just any face, but a rather macabre one. The mouth was open in what looked like some sort of painful grimace, as though that face had heard one too many filibusters, and the eyes were quite skeletal. Needless to say, I didn't get to bed as early as I had planned.

As I often do with phantom photos, I emailed it to several persons, some friends and some relatives. I gave no insight into the history or nature of the photo, I simply asked them to look at the shot and then get back with me with their observations. I never mentioned the anomaly within. Without exception, each individual identified the fact that there was a face hovering over the staircase about half way down. I didn't need the confirmation, but it never hurts to have it. One of the individuals, a decided skeptic, asked me if I had "photoshopped" the picture. I don't even know how to do that, as my generation finds it difficult to learn such things.

Armed with a printed copy of the mysterious photo, I traversed I-96 once again to Lansing. Once there, I found the events office but was told the coordinator was out that day. I showed the photo instead to a couple of the service staff, who found it quite odd, indeed. They suggested I speak with the custodial staff, as it was believed they had stories of their own to tell, so off I went in search of those folks who wander the halls after dark, wiping and shining, scrubbing and waxing, and all in an effort to wipe away the grime of broken campaign promises.

I was surprised when only one individual would speak to me about strange things that go bump in the night. But even this person, a custodian, wanted to remain anonymous. My impression was that the paid staff had been warned about speaking of such things. At any rate, Louis (not his real name, but he looked like a Louis) said that one time he had been buffing the marble floors outside the Senate chamber when he heard what he thought to be voices emanating through the entry doors. His first thought was that some folks were in there chatting, but then he realized not many people hang around for legislative conversations after two in the morning—those usually take place at one of the local watering holes.

By his own admission not a particularly brave man, Louis said he shut off his floor buffer and tiptoed to the doors. He listened as one voice, distant and somewhat oratorical in nature, seemed to echo softly within the chamber. He could only catch a detached word here and there, such as "peace" and "willow." Mustering up courage from whatever reserves he harbored, he said he unlocked the door and carefully opened it just enough to peek inside. Louis said he saw a man on the floor of the chamber, dressed in clothing from well over a hundred years earlier. He was somewhat misty from the waist down, but he sported a high collar and a long, black formal looking coat. Louis said he closed the door, locked it, and turned his buffing machine back on. He figured if he didn't disturb the orator, maybe the orator would leave him alone as well.

As I said earlier, no one seemed at ease to offer me any information about strange events, sounds, or sights within this historical building. Even the security staff, who normally check out anything of interest as a part of their job, basically told me that they weren't at liberty to discuss such goings-on, and suggested I keep moving on.

Planning a Visit? Why not, it's your Capitol Building, and your taxes pay for its upkeep. The place is open to the public, and the staff will inform you when you tread into forbidden territory. The best time to get there is during regular working hours (as if legislators actually work), which generally means between 9 a.m. and 5 p.m. Take your camera along, as you may get lucky and have something to show little kids before their field trips to Lansing.

Still Haunted? I don't see why not. I had only been there twice in 2008 and during one visit I got a pretty good photo that convinced me, so the way I figure it I'm hitting 50%, and that's pretty good for any ghost hunter.

Chapter 5
Battle Alley

Place Visited: The historic Holly Hotel. The exact address is 110 Battle Alley, Holly, Michigan. It is part of the National Historic Registry and is considered one of the most haunted places, not only in Michigan, but in the United States. Now, that's pretty impressive.

Period of Haunting: This place has a history of haunted experiences dating way back to its early days when it was the place to stay when passing through town.

Date of Investigation: Summer 2009.

Description of Location: The Holly Hotel is located in the town of Holly just a few miles east of US-23. It is not far from the city of Fenton, which is also on the US-23 corridor, and which also hosts its own haunted hotel, the Fenton Hotel, which I wrote about in my first book of haunted places. Holly is a small town, with the "small town feel" one would expect. It hosts some very nice antiques stores and specialty shops. There's no point in going into great detail to give driving directions, as my readers can simply use whatever computer map program which suits them to find the easiest route.

The Holly Hotel, or the "Historic Holly Hotel" as its front awning discloses, consists of four levels: the basement, main floor, and two upper floors. All but the upper level are open to the public and in use for various functions. All three operating levels have their own bar, so there's never a need to pine at great length for a libation whenever you need to slake your thirst. The street itself is named Battle Alley, not in part because the notorious prohibitionist Carrie Nation once wielded her famous hatchet within the walls of the Holly Hotel, chopping up the bar and scaring the holy hell out of both patrons and staff. But that was a good century ago.

The hotel found its incarnation in 1891, when it served as a place of repose for train travelers making their journey across Michigan. It was originally named the Hirst Hotel after the owner of the same name. It burned down in 1913, and many folks believe that is when the first ghosts began to appear, the hapless remains of some of the victims of that devastating fire. Mr. Hirst, it is said, was quite despondent over the tragedy and passed away in 1920. His ghost is also roaming the building, making itself known through the strong scent of cigar smoke from the stogies he notoriously enjoyed puffing upon.

The interior of the hotel is a sight to behold, restored to its former glory and ornately decorated. The entry walls are dotted with framed notes from celebrities ranging from Suzanne Somers to George H. W. Bush, all of whom have dined there. Original paintings and photos, some quite old, delight the eyes. The present owners are to some degree history buffs, and each year they hold a dinner called "The Titanic," wherein the staff dresses in period costume, and the meal served during that event matches in every detail the last formal dinner aboard the Titanic before it kissed up against the iceberg which sent it to its watery death.

Haunt Meter: * * * *

I REALIZE I AM BREAKING MY OWN RULE as I pen this tale of the haunted hotel. I had promised myself to write only about places that had never been written about before. The Holly Hotel has been investigated and written about on numerous occasions by many folks interested in the paranormal. However, my experiences there, along with those of my crew, were unique enough to give, I hope, a fresh face to an old haunting.

I first visited the hotel out of curiosity, with no intention of ever conducting an investigation or writing a story. But the place has a way of making you feel, well, attached to the haunting. It draws you into itself and practically cries out for attention. That being the case, I struck up a conversation with one of the assistant managers, a young and quite lovely woman with a vivacious personality named Samantha. She, as with the entire staff of the Holly, are quite willing to discuss the haunting, and they all have their own stories of encounters with spirits wandering the premises. She quickly consented to my request to investigate the place, and arrangements were made to spend some darkened hours alone with my crew inside the eatery.

We arrived early, before closing time, and made a cursory walk through the place, each of us simply wandering about on our own, snapping photos and soaking in the ambience. Then we gathered at the bar on the main floor and spent a while listening to Samantha as she gave us the lowdown on the history of the hotel and the nature of the strange and unsettling experiences she and others have had over the years. Here's the story in her words:

> The fire of 1913 took place in the cold of winter, and the place was gutted. It was operating as a hotel then, and it is said that a little girl died in the fire. She was a pretty girl with red hair, full of life and energy. People often see her at different places in the hotel, and it's clear she's a ghost from the clothes she wears and the way she shows up and then just disappears. She loves to play around with things in the kitchen and enjoys throwing tea cups and moving utensils. She's been seen on just about every floor, and sometimes you

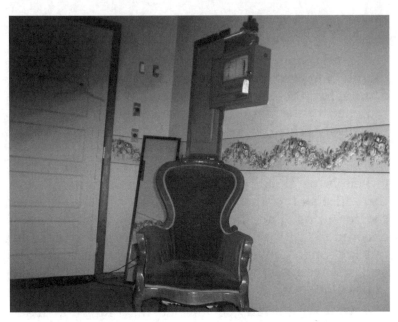

Bride's room where a ghost mist—see the shadow
in the top left corner—moved across the room

can hear her laughing. It's a little creepy to
hear when you're alone in the building.

The other ghost that's seen a lot is Nora
Kane. We have pictures of Nora, and she was
very beautiful. It's said she died in the hotel
as well, but we're not sure of the nature of
her death. She's a nice ghost, never trying to
upset anyone. It was once her hotel, and she
is still very attached to it. We see her a lot in
the bride's room upstairs (*Author's note: the
bride's room is a small room reserved for brides
to dress for their weddings, of which the hotel
hosts many*). We don't know why she chooses
that room, except that she loved weddings.
She's always dressed very beautifully and is
quite lovely to look at. Those who have seen
her say she's not in the least scary. I had my
own encounter with her a couple years ago. I

was in the bride's room getting myself ready for a wedding I was standing up in, and we were all wearing strapless dresses. I had my dress hanging on the back of the door on a metal hanger, and when I turned around to get it, it was off the hanger and lying across a chair several feet away. Then, after getting dressed, I opened the door to leave the room, and when I stepped into the hallway I felt someone grab my dress and pull it down to my waist. It was rather embarrassing to say the least as I was completely exposed for all to see from the waist up, and I jumped back into the room to cover myself. It was then I was told that Nora was a very modest woman, and wouldn't have approved of my bare shoulders. That didn't make much sense to me. I mean, if she didn't approve of bare shoulders then why would she bare my breasts for everyone to see?

Samantha continued to spin story after story of events to curdle the resolve of the strongest of ghost hunters. She spoke of a woman who accompanied her daughter to the restroom downstairs—there are no restrooms on the main floor—and was struck by the photograph of a woman hanging in the foyer of the ladies room. The woman in the photograph dates backward in time quite a way, and she's all fixed up in Victorian era clothing and hairstyle. She took her camera out of her purse and took a shot of the photo. She was not prepared for the added attraction of a second face mirrored in the glass of the framed photo. She showed the image to several staff members, and they are certain the second face belongs to Nora. Samantha says the lady spent nearly an hour trying to recreate the event by snapping several more shots of the photo, but to no avail. It seems ghosts are capricious, and show up when they wish.

Second floor where the ghosts of the old man with the
cigar and the young well dressed woman are seen

The Holly Hotel seems to have many spirits floating
about the place. Some with unfinished business, some
who are strongly attached to the place, and others who
may just be wandering through on their way to other
haunts. Some show up in the restrooms, others in the
kitchen, but most show up just about anywhere in the
building. One seems to enjoy the basement. Samantha is
somewhat of an artist with stained glass and is allowed
a work area in a storage room down there. Once, she
was working on a piece when she felt the need to take
a break. She went upstairs, enjoyed a cool drink, and
then returned to her work area, which she keeps locked,
only to find her metal dividing pieces, used to separate
the different colors of glass, all twisted and bent, and
some of her glass broken and strewn about the room. I
guess there's at least one ghost down there who fancies
himself an art critic.

Several patrons report striding up or down the carpeted staircases and passing a gentleman dressed in a riding jacket and a top hat, smoking a large cigar. He seems amiable enough, as he smiles at the guests, but on second glance, he's gone, slipped into thin air and leaving behind only the scent of his cigar. That, says the staff, is Mr. Hirst, the original owner of the hotel. Other patrons, as well as staff, report disembodied voices, slamming doors, strange scents, and all the other phenomena generally associated with haunted dwellings.

Oh, I nearly forgot. I was telling you about our experiences during our investigation. Let's get back to it.

There were six of us in our group that night, and we decided to break into three smaller groups, with each group taking up residence in a different part of the hotel. Our modus operandi was unchanged. Each team would record audio and video, snap digital photos and take readings from various instruments. Two of our members, along with Samantha, sat in an upstairs banquet room on plush divans. They picked up the faint sounds of a young girl, and one of our team members, quite sensitive to spirits, felt an overwhelming sense of sadness from her, as though she were looking for a loved one she was unable to find.

For most of the night that was pretty much all that we happened to encounter. That is, until Sarah, a member of my team, and I decided to stake out the bride's room. It's quite small and not all that comfortable. To be truthful, I don't know why bride's even use the room. It was originally one of the smaller guest rooms when the hotel was actually a hotel. There's just one door to the room and a single, lone window which looks out onto a rather bleak alley. It must have been cramped quarters back in the day. At any rate, Sarah and I entered, made ourselves as comfortable as possible, and sat in the darkness, meditating and snapping photos and recording.

Upstairs banquet room where the
Bogle team recorded voices

Not much happened until Sarah decided to go elsewhere. After she left the room, I sat in it alone, concentrating my thoughts upon whatever spirits were around. I was inviting them to make themselves known, and asking permission to take their photo. I then began shooting several photos only a couple of seconds apart, using my flash. I took several shots of the closed door, and in one of them there is a dark misty shadow floating near the top of the door. Intrigued, I began asking for further proof that someone other than myself was in the room. Suddenly, the entire room was engulfed by the acrid scent of garlic, enough to make my eyes water. It didn't waft in, it just suddenly appeared at full strength, as though someone were pressing it right in front of my face.

That excited my senses, and I needed validation, so I strode quickly out of the room and ran downstairs, where I ran into Samantha and Sarah talking by the bar. I didn't tell them why, I just told them to hurry up to the bride's room. They entered, and I asked if they could smell anything. They both immediately identified the scent as garlic. As if this weren't strange enough on its own, the scent was extremely localized. Inside the room it reeked of garlic. Sticking your head outside the doorway there was no scent at all. It filled the room, but could not be sensed even an inch outside the room. Then, as quickly as it had appeared, it disappeared. I thanked the spirits, and we left the room, feeling as though we had struck pay dirt, or at least pay garlic.

Everyone on my team had their own sense as to which section of the hotel was most haunted. One team felt the basement area where the comedy club is located was the creepiest, while another team was certain the second floor banquet area was hosting the most spirits. As for me, even though the bride's room gave me the verification I was looking for, I felt, on a purely subjective level, that the main floor was where the spirits most liked to roam.

Oh, did I mention the slap? I guess it slipped my mind. It seems everywhere I go, when people find out I write about haunted places in Michigan, they have their own stories to tell. Such a conversation came up at a local restaurant one evening, and the person I was speaking with asked me if I had ever checked out the Holly Hotel. I told her I was in the process of working on that chapter, and she piped in with her own tale. It seems she had a date with a young gentleman who took her there for dinner. He was a nice guy, and she was entertaining the thought of treating him to an amorous encounter after dessert. Here's her cute story.

> We had a really good dinner, candlelight and soft music with linen tablecloths and napkins, and I was really getting into this guy. I mean, it's a really romantic place with a really romantic atmosphere.

I excused myself to go to the ladies room to freshen up. I wanted to make everything just right for the ride back to my apartment. I was the only one in the restroom, the one downstairs, and I checked my hair and makeup, and then decided to remove a certain piece of intrusive underwear. I was thinking about "making love" (quotations indicate my change of her words for the benefit of our younger audience), and while removing my bra I all of a sudden got a hard smack across the face. I mean, it left a red mark. I got the hell out of there. I gotta tell you, it killed the mood.

Could this have been the prim and proper Nora? Who knows. Whoever it was didn't like the way this young woman was thinking and seemed to become, at least for the moment, a surrogate mother. Ah, a ghost with values and decorum, you gotta appreciate that.

Stories about the Holly Hotel abound. Nearly everyone seems to have had an encounter there. With this place, you don't have to be a detached reader of ghost stories, you can be a part of your own.

Planning a Visit? It's not a problem with this place. In fact, I highly recommend it. Make a supper reservation, or stop in for high tea in the afternoon, as it's a rare treat and a classy experience. The food is sumptuously prepared, the high tea is a rare treat, and the bar hosts some well blended cocktails. The staff is gracious, and will allow you to enjoy yourself as you walk around soaking in the decor.

Still Haunted? Is a bullfrog waterproof? Go ahead and drop in, but dress appropriately and keep your thoughts pure. Nora insists you practice clean living and proper etiquette.

Chapter 6
Upscale Ghostly Dining

Place Visited: The Bella Notte Restaurant, 137 West Michigan Avenue, Jackson, Michigan. The Bella Notte is as upscale as its name implies and is located in the center of downtown Jackson. It is a fine dining restaurant with a menu to make the most discriminating diner salivate in expectation of culinary delights. A great place for a romantic dinner or an intimate lunch. If you're checking this place out for ghosts, don't leave without trying out the food. The Bella Notte is owned and operated by Greg and Annette Walker, who have done a remarkable job with the restoration and promotion of this fine restaurant. Get on the net and check out their menu and drink offerings.

Period of Haunting: The ghosts have been yammering around this place for years and years, and I have no reason to believe they've stopped.

Date of Investigation: April, 2007.

Description of Location: The Bella Notte is a historic building, having been part of the original downtown area of Jackson. It is a multi-storied building, but the original second floor was removed, opening up the ground floor dining area to make a spacious and elegant place to dine. There is a balcony around the perimeter of the first floor, where folks enjoy private dining. The upper floors are for storage. Jackson is a favorite town of mine, since that's where I spend a lot of my time. It's located off the I-94 corridor between Ann Arbor and Battle Creek. If you can't find it on a map, then you were never meant to leave your driveway. Jackson is a somewhat eclectic city, given that upscale stores are mixed amongst thrift shops, and the elegant Bella Notte is right across the street from a popular topless bar. As I've written in one of my prior tomes, Jackson is home to The Parlour, the finest, bar none, ice cream shop in Michigan—huge portions not for the faint of heart.

Haunt Meter: * * * *

I DISCOVERED THE BELLA NOTTE one nice summer's day when I escorted my wife, Tracey, downtown for some mundane banking business. It looked like a classy place to take a classy woman, so I suggested we drop in for lunch. I'm glad we did, for more reasons than one. The food was excellent, she dining on the Michigan salad, and I on, what else for a man of my discriminating palate, a huge and juicy hamburger.

While dining, we soaked in the atmosphere, impressed by the classy bar and wait staff, white linens, and fine service. When the young woman serving us stopped by to offer us a shot at their desserts, I piped up, as I often do, and asked if they ever had any ghosts showing up around the place. Whenever I ask such a question, I prepare myself in advance for strange looks just in case, but things were different here. She indicated that the restaurant was host to many of them, and that most of the staff have experienced an encounter or two, some mild, some a little unsettling, and some outright frightening.

She and I carried on a tableside conversation until she needed to take care of other guests. I shall refer to her as Sally since I lost the set of notes I had taken which had her real name listed. She spoke of walking into the kitchen and watching a serving tray of silverware slide across the stainless steel counter and crash to the floor. That sort of thing was common, she said, as well as the occasional glass flying off a shelf and splintering itself on the floor. But the most aggravating thing to her was how often a large bowl of salad, replete with fresh and expensive greens and veggies, would simply turn itself upside down, spreading its contents across counter and floor. That would make her angry because she would have to clean it up. When you're dealing with ghosts, it's not like you can hold them responsible for tidying up their own messes.

Sally also filled me in about one night when business was particularly slow, and the evening was late. She was seated at the bar, enjoying a soft drink and chatting with the young woman tending the not-so-soft drink requests, when they beheld a young woman, dressed in what they took to be 1930's clothing, suddenly appear in the dining room, walk over to where a staircase used to be, and disappear as she ascended unseen steps. Sally said she would have graduated to hard liquor had she not been on duty. She also told me that they weren't the only ones to have seen this woman, that many customers have reported her making the scene as she skirted her way past the tables of customers.

I found Sally's stories interesting, as any ghost aficionado would, and informed her that I was the author of a book about haunted places. I asked if she thought the owners would be amenable to an investigation. She assured me that Annette Walker, who owns the place along with her husband, Greg, would be more than happy to speak with me about it since she had been privy to ghostly encounters of her own.

Annette is a free spirited woman, very pleasant and fun to be around. She truly enjoys her restaurant business and is quite involved in community events. She's one of those people flowing with excess energy, and we hit it off right away. She informed me that there are many spirits wandering about the place and that she has seen them quite often. She indicated that the ghost she most often encounters is that of a small girl who looks as though she dates from the early part of the twentieth century. She wanders the building and always appears to be sad, as though she is lonely and perhaps even frightened. Guests have seen her cowering in one of the back corners of the restaurant as though she's fearful of all the strange people around her.

Annette's conversation was stimulating to say the least. Just the sort of thing to fire up the sensibilities of any ghost hunter. So, I did what came naturally, I asked if my wife and I could tour the facility and get a feel for things. Permission was readily granted, and off we went in search of whatever spirit would be inclined to make our acquaintance.

There's a small, private room on the left balcony area of the first floor that's used for private lunch meetings and so forth. During our discussion, Annette had informed us that this somewhat sequestered room is where one of the spirits seems to hide out. There's a door on either end of the room and a large window looking down upon the dining area below. We went inside, totally unprepared to document our activities, closed the curtains to the window, shut the doors, and turned out the lights. It was wonderfully dark, which any ghost enthusiast enjoys, and we sat on chairs near the window and remained quiet and motionless. Sure enough, not five minutes later we both had a personal introduction to the ghost who calls that room home.

We watched in satisfied amazement as a blue, iridescent form materialized near the door to our left. It was the size of a human being, but not as humanly formed as one might expect. It's movement was fluid, yet it seemed to be emitting some sort of erratic, electric glow. It moved slowly at first, as though tentative of our presence, then a bit more quickly until it reached about halfway across the room, where it stopped. Although I have described it as shadowy, it still had form and depth. Intrigued, I stepped forward slowly until I was directly in front of it, about ten inches away. Then I cautiously extended my arm until my hand made contact of a sort. Placing my fingers within, I immediately felt electricity tingle through my arm, making the hair stand on end. When I withdrew my hand, the tingling ended, and the form moved slowly toward the opposite door where it seemed to seep through to the other side. Ah, the stuff of which a ghost hunter's dreams are made!

Pumped up from our encounter, I approached Annette, told her of our experience, and asked if I could bring my ghost hunters with me for an investigation. She assented, and I made arrangements to bring in my team the following week, on a weekday after closing. I told them nothing of what we had experienced, as I prefer my living companions encounter the dead without benefit of the power of suggestion.

We arrived at the Bella Notte just before 10 p.m., met with Annette around one of her dining tables, and drank soft drinks while everyone made her acquaintance. (I forbid the use of alcohol or drugs before or during our investigations.) Then, after the last bar patron strode out the door on loosely-jointed legs, we divided up into teams, chose our stakeout positions, and hauled our equipment into place. The lights went out when the kitchen staff left, and the hunt for apparitions began in earnest.

We had three teams that night. One team chose an upper storage floor, expansive and sparse, the second team chose the balcony area where I had experienced my run-in with the blue ghost, and the third team, which constituted myself and my special education/ghost hunting friend Glenn, took control over the entire main floor of the restaurant.

We hadn't been in position long when both Glenn and I thought we heard sounds not associated with the living. Uncertain as to where they were coming from, we decided to split up. He would check the enclosed stairway leading up to the second floor while I would check out the bar and right side of the dining area. With our missions completed, Glenn tiptoed over to me and whispered that there was something on the staircase I needed to see to believe. Grabbing my camera, I headed on over and peeked around the doorway to the stairs. My flashlight beam slowly climbed the stairs until I caught sight of something—a set of curvy female legs. Ever so slowly, I raised my beam until it illuminated... the face of Marilyn Monroe. Glenn, jokester that he has always been, had found a cardboard cutout of this screen siren and set it up on the steps. Regardless of what you're thinking at this moment, it helps to have someone with a sense of humor on your ghost hunting expeditions.

After another half hour or so, our three teams met down in the dining room for shift change. That's where we trade stakeout positions. While in the process, our team which had been on the upper floor reported the distinct sounds of footsteps. From time to time those footsteps seemed to shuffle. The sounds were recorded on audio, but nothing showed up later on video. They were obviously disembodied.

Our teams had no sooner set themselves up in their new positions when a member radioed us (we were using walkie-talkie then for communication) that we needed to return to the main floor, near the rear of the building. Upon arriving there, one team member was engaged in a conversation with an entity none of the rest of us could see. We were standing near the doorway to a storage area while Tracy—not MY Tracey, but another team member of the same name but different spelling—was pointing down and saying, "There's a little girl sitting there, and she says she scared—can't any of you hear her?"

We assured Tracy we could neither see nor hear the girl. Then Tracy went on to describe the girl in the same manner she was described to me by Annette on my first visit to the restaurant. This was all very frustrating to Tracy, because she was obviously agitated that only she could see or hear the girl. She then went on to try to comfort the cowering spirit, until her eyes suddenly widened and she said, "She's leaving now." She said the little girl was put off by all of us staring at her and exited through the storage room door, not to return.

The rest of the evening had the requisite phenomena associated with a haunting. We heard what sounded like more footsteps as well as the slamming of a door up on the upper floor. There was also the occasional cold spot, but with a building this old, it's difficult to determine if it's a spirit wafting around nearby or just a draft.

If any building should be haunted, it would be the Bella Notte. It has been around since the late 1800s and has gone through many incarnations in its lifetime. It has housed everything from a harness shop to a furniture store to a bordello. In fact, the top floor is graced with a full-sized fireplace and still shows remnants of the small rooms where the ladies would entertain guests on a private and personal level.

It's that third floor that has made me question a long-standing opinion of mine. For years now, whenever people discover I write about haunted places, one of the things many of them do is show me odd photographs. Sometimes they are truly strange, such as faint images of figures hanging out amongst the living, but mostly they're shots of what these folks refer to as "orbs," those opaque circles that sometimes appear individually or in the company of dozens of other orbs. These folks, and many ghost hunters, insist that orbs are evidence of spirits trying to manifest themselves—proof that ghosts exist.

Since I never automatically assume a place is haunted, or that an image caught on film or tape is that of a person who has long left this mortal plane, I have always raised my eyebrows in belief that these white circles were nothing more than simply dust on the lens of the camera or moisture in the air. After all, not everything that goes bump in the night is a ghost.

On this particular night at the Bella Notte, however, my thinking was seriously challenged.

We had been on the top floor for a few minutes as a team when it happened. We were wrapping up the evening and had gone upstairs to check out the old hooker haven for a laugh or two. The late hour was making us punchy, and we were in a rather silly mood. One of our team members mentioned we should take a few shots with our digital cameras and see if we could get any images of these ladies of the evening. We started snapping away and checking our screens for results, of which there were none. We began kidding one another about how no respectable evening flower would grace the presence of such a strange group as ours when the same member who initiated our actions said, "Well, it's rude to just start taking pictures, we should ask permission first."

That whole permission thing seemed formal, stiff and silly to me, but Tina asked out loud if she could have permission to take their photos. She snapped a shot and proceeded to show us several orbs floating around the fireplace. Intrigued, Glenn offered the same courtesy and got the same results. Then two others on my team asked permission, and their screens were resplendent with these opaque circles.

We purposely took shots without asking permission and shots only after we had humbled ourselves enough to once again make the request. Every single shot taken without asking permission showed an empty room. Every shot taken when permission was requested displayed dozens of these opaque circles. It got to be a joke. After all, the hour was late, we were feeling funky, and we were actually addressing the spirits of prostitutes from a century past. Glenn, our resident skeptic and stand-up comic, referred to these images, not as orbs, but as "whore'bs," uniquely coining a new term connecting an age old profession to a spiritual presence.

I would be remiss to close this tale without sharing one more experience from the staff of the Bella Notte.

Her name is Regina (not her real name), and she had been tending bar at the restaurant for about a year.

It was a busy night last fall. I was filling drink orders for the wait staff and serving drinks at the bar, just running from bar customer to waitress pick up for a couple of hours. Everything was going smooth but I kept seeing this guy seated at the far end of the bar, away from where the staff picks up drinks for the dining guests. I'd catch him out of the corner of my eye, and I knew I hadn't served anyone there. Every time I thought I should check on him, there wouldn't be anyone sitting there. This kept up for over an hour. Then when it slowed down a little, I decided to use my peripheral vision. I had heard about the ghosts in the restaurant, and it's not that I'm not a believer, it's just that I'd never had anything strange happen to me ever.

I served a drink to a customer at the bar, then stood there and slowly paid attention to my peripheral vision out my left side. Sure enough, the guy was sitting there. I just stood real still and didn't move so I could get a more solid look at him. Just then, the man I had just served noticed what I was doing and asked if I was watching the guy at the end of the bar. I was fascinated. I asked him if he could see the man, and he said that, yes, he'd been watching him for over an hour. He said it was a man around forty, slenderly built with curly black hair. He said the man was primarily watching me serve customers, but that when he noticed someone looking his way, he'd disappear. I asked him why he didn't bring it up earlier, and he said he'd lived with ghosts all his life, and he knew if he just brought it up out of the blue, without any hint someone else had seen the guy, that I'd probably stop serving him his rum and Coke.

Regina told me that when she got home that night she couldn't sleep. She felt, in the term so many people use to define a ghostly experience, "creeped out," like he was still very near.

No good ghost story is complete without an epilogue, and I just happen to have one. It deals with a ghost tour I agreed to conduct for the Jackson Public Library's downtown branch. It's just a couple blocks from the Bella Notte and very close to several other downtown haunted places of interest.

I had finished my lecture, expecting to have about ten or fifteen people tag along with me on the tour. I had over fourteen interested participants. We passed by the Jackson Antiques Shop, the Michigan Theatre, a health food store, and a Catholic book shop, all of which are reportedly haunted. At each place I gave a little history of the haunting, having to raise my voice enough to be heard by such a large group of people with nothing better to do than follow me around as I spun my true stories of the macabre. When we approached the Bella Notte, I realized the restaurant was still open, and I couldn't stand outside their front window without disturbing their guests. I ushered everyone across the street under the guise it afforded a better angle to snap their photos.

As they snapped their shutters, I used my loudest and best monotone voice to relate stories of the haunting of the eatery. Now, you have to picture this scenario—by now it's nearly 11 p.m., and I'm on a city sidewalk with a mob of people talking loudly. That would grab just about anyone's attention. However, what I didn't realize was that we were all standing in front of a controversial topless bar that had been picketed in the past by straight laced fundamentalist folks. The bouncer had heard my voice, saw the crowd outside his front door, and approached me with fire in his eyes. Now, I've stood in the presence of frightful spirits almost all my life, but this guy scared the sniffles out of me.

This burly fella was out for blood—mine—until he saw me point at the Bella Notte across the street, and then he came to a halt. He paused to listen for minute or two to what I was saying, and the fire in his eyes dissipated. When I paused to catch a breath between sentences, this guy piped up and said, "He ain't lying folks, I've been in there and I ain't goin' back." And this is from a guy who enjoys physical confrontations with drunken, lecherous patrons.

If you get a chance to visit the Bella Notte, be a patron, not a pain. Order a drink or a meal, and relax. Ask the wait staff if they've had any strange encounters. Ask to see and speak with Annette if you wish, but don't interrupt these nice folks when they're busy. Most certainly, don't just drop in and ask if you can investigate the place. The Bella Notte has a lot of class, and you should show a little yourself.

Planning a Visit? No problem. You may well encounter a ghost or two over iced tea and a wonderful salad. Want to investigate? Call or email first. Please don't use my name. I don't know you and cannot vouch for you.

Still Haunted? Does a one-legged duck swim in circles?

Chapter 7
Cross in the Dirt

Place Visited: The South Lyon Hotel, 201 N. Lafayette, South Lyon, Michigan

Period of Haunting: Probably over the past 100 years, give or take a few.

Date of Investigation: Three separate investigations from 2007–2009.

Description of Location: The South Lyon Hotel is perhaps the most popular eatery in South Lyon, or the surrounding area for that matter. Constructed in 1867 as a hotel to house overnight travelers, it was said that when the passenger trains would stop in South Lyon, a buckboard from the hostelry would race from the hotel to the train station to get to the passengers before the local competition did. The property upon which the hotel is built—are you ready for this?—was originally a cemetery, and the city records prove this to be true. The coffins were dug up at the approval of the town council and removed to a new resting place on the other side of town. The men hired to do the job, two brothers, received $2.50 per body dug up and re-planted.

At the time of its opening, the place was known as the Commercial House. Off the beaten path, the village didn't even receive electric lights until 1923. The hotel is an imposing building, consisting of a Michigan basement (dirt floors for those of you with puzzled looks), a ground floor, and one upper floor. Both above ground floors are dining and drinking areas, as the place hasn't housed tenants for several decades now. There is an outside balcony running around two sides of the upper floor, a popular spot in summer months to enjoy some good food and drink. The "Hotel," as it is called locally, serves sandwiches and full meals, and all of their offerings are top notch. I particularly enjoy the barbecue chicken pizza, and they're praised for their ribs, mile high meat loaf and fish fries as well. As for alcoholic offerings, their whiskeys run the gamut from Jim Beam (pasteurized panther pee, in my view) to Eagle Rare (glorious tears of the Kentucky maidens). There are a multitude of beers from which to choose as well.

The South Lyon Hotel has a family atmosphere, although it didn't always carry such a respectable reputation. Credit Paul Baker, now deceased, for the wonderful transformation. Paul was a highly respected businessman and a great community activist. His death was a loss to the community, and he is still missed greatly. He took the hotel from a rather rough and tumble biker bar and gave it the class and fun for which it's well known. It was no small job. During the Depression, the hotel fell into disrepute, and it became shabby and housed transients looking for work. Fights were not uncommon, and the place stayed that way through the 1960s. The local police were frequently called to break up altercations, and many locals still recall watching patrons brawling out into the streets. A fire did considerable damage on the upper level when the place still rented rooms, and it is said that at least one man was killed in the blaze.

The hotel is known to be haunted, and the management and staff are pretty comfortable with it and have their own stories to spin. Now it's time for me to relate mine—and theirs.

Haunt Meter: * * * *

I CANNOT RECALL how I first heard about the ghosts of the South Lyon Hotel. I only know that when I did hear about it, I couldn't wait to go have lunch there. Striking up a conversation with my waitress, I asked if the staff had ever seen any spirits floating around the place. She never thought twice about it and assured me there were many of them prowling the premises. She said I needed to speak with her manager, an affable young restaurateur named Corry Bala who is also part owner of the establishment, and she even fetched him for me.

I introduced myself to Corry and knew I was going to like him even more when he offered to buy me a drink as we spoke. When he discovered I wrote about haunted places, he graciously offered me access to the hotel to conduct an investigation. Then he began to relate an experience he'd had just that past week. They closed up late on Friday night due to a high volume of business, and Corry was sequestered upstairs in his office counting the receipts and posting the invoices. He went downstairs to lock up after the last employee checked out for the night, then returned to his mundane duties.

> I closed the door to my office for safety and privacy, but also because I often hear footsteps across the old wooden floors up there. I finally finished my work and locked my office. I had a strong feeling I wasn't alone in there. I went downstairs and left the building by the rear entrance. My office has one window that looks out over the back parking lot. I had gone down the steps and into the lot when I heard a tapping sound. I looked up at my office window, and there was a man standing there staring out at me. Now, that's my office, and I knew I had been alone in it, and that I had locked the door when I left. I didn't really need any time to

wonder if someone had gotten locked inside, I just knew it was one of the ghosts. I went to my car, and when I looked back up, the man wasn't there anymore.

Corry is by no means the only person on staff to witness strange phenomena. In fact, it's rare to find an employee who hasn't had a ghostly encounter—like Rosie, a Latino woman whose husband also worked at the hotel. He worked in the kitchen, and she was the cleaning lady. Naturally, her shift began after everyone else had gone home and the place was hers alone to deal with.

Rosie enjoyed her job and was good at it. However, one night she came in to clean, as usual, and was an hour or two into her duties when she went upstairs to clean the restrooms. The upper level has one large room where group parties and overflow guests are seated. It has its own bar, and that's where many community fundraisers are held. There is also a private banquet room in the rear, with French doors leading to a private balcony. The restrooms are actually somewhat hidden behind the bar, off a small corridor, which is sort of nice if you're a private person and not prone to having people watch you enter and exit the privy.

Rosie said that she stepped into the ladies room and was immediately greeted with the presence of a tall man in strange black clothing. She knew immediately he was a ghost, and she spent the rest of the shift sitting on the front porch of the hotel waiting for her husband to show up for his shift. After that, she decided to come in to work after sunup when other employees were around. She had often heard footsteps and the occasional disembodied voice, but running into a strange man in the ladies room sealed her decision not to be alone in the place any more. Rosie is a very religious woman, and she was convinced the man was evil. Not long after her encounter, she left for a more normal place of employment.

The man in the ladies room has been seen by more than one patron and staff member. Some believe he was the man who burned up in the hotel fire decades ago, and others think he's just one of the spirits of someone who frequented the hotel when it actually was a hotel. Their thoughts are that maybe his favorite room back then was located where the ladies room is today. I'd like to think that as well. I'd hate to think they have a perverted spirit on their hands. At any rate, he still shows up from time to time but usually as a reflection in the mirror over the sink.

The hotel presents the discriminating diner with a vast array of ghostly offerings. Slamming doors, the voices of children and adults drifting through the airwaves, unusual scents, cold spots, shadowy figures, objects moving without physical help, and just about any other spectral surprises one can imagine. And these things aren't relegated to a limited area, they happen all over the place. Take, for example, the report from a young woman on the waitstaff named Nikki. She told me she has had a few run-ins with the ghosts herself, and they occur as much in the light of day as under the cover of darkness.

Nikki explained to me how, just inside the kitchen, there is a clipboard hanging on one wall. It holds sheets of paper pertinent to supplies needed to help keep the place running at top efficiency. One afternoon, when it wasn't particularly busy, she had gone into the kitchen and was looking through her lunch orders. The clipboard was on the wall behind her, and no one else was anywhere near her. She heard the clipboard snap shut just as she saw all the papers it had been holding fly across the floor. She said it seemed just like someone had opened the clipboard so the papers could spew through the air, and then let the clasp snap back into place. Naturally, with stories such as these, I couldn't wait to bring my crew and their equipment to the hotel for an attempt to have our own encounters.

It was a hot summer's weeknight when we showed up for our visit. The hotel was still open for business, so we all sat around one of the tables near the bar and sipped some soft drinks as we checked and readied our equipment. The night manager was on duty, and we were informed that we would have the run of the place all to ourselves for the entire night. That's usually against our rules, as we require at least one employee to remain on staff, so I stepped over to the bar and asked the woman serving drinks if she would like to stay with us. I received an emphatic, but polite, "No." She had seen too many ghosts while getting paid and had no intentions to stick around and see them without remuneration. When I asked her to relate some of her experiences, she visibly shivered and declined my offer.

It was nearly midnight when the last customer exited the premises. We were successful in recruiting two young women from the wait staff to stick around with us, so we filled them in on our procedures and paired them up with members of our team. Then the hunt began.

One of our teams chose the basement, accessible only by exiting the building and using an outside entry. One of them, Sarah, fears neither strange presence nor power, and simply felt drawn to that part of the building. They remained down there their entire shift, which we've always set at 45 minutes. The idea is to remain quiet and observe the surroundings while recording and taking temperature and EMF readings. The basement area is convoluted, divided up into smaller areas, some of them inaccessible except through crawl spaces, others with quite low ceilings.

They were about twenty minutes into their shift, sitting on the damp earth, when Sarah became intrigued with a small area too restrictive to stand up in. She took several pictures, then decided to check out a mound of dirt within. She discovered, partially buried in the dirt, the metal legs of an old dining table. They had been refashioned into the shape of a giant cross. Later, we were told that a physic had visited the place a few years earlier, and upon checking out the basement, she declared that there was an evil ghost down there who was keeping his family hostage. She said he was abusive to his wife and children in death, just as he had been in life. She also said that the makeshift cross had been placed there to keep him from wreaking hell upon the living who frequented the hotel. It's a nice story, but without any substantiation. Still, how do you explain the giant cross in the dirt? It was Sarah's idea to remove it and see what happened, but she relented when she realized she would get to go home while everyone at the hotel would have to put up with whatever we loosed. That wouldn't be fair, so it was left alone.

Our other team staked out the upstairs ladies room where the hapless Rosie, as well as other staff members and guests, had encountered the stern man in black. They went in, closed the doors, set up their equipment, and shut off the lights. All they got for their efforts was the experience of having been in the Black Hole of Calcutta. They said at least they lost some weight from the heat, but alas, there was no sign of any paranormal activity. Any ghost hunter worth his or her salt will tell you this type of recreation takes patience and a sense of humor.

When shift time came around, my buddy Glenn and I took up quarters at the top of a stairway between the main and upper floors. We hadn't been in position long when a small energy drink cooler sitting on the upstairs bar, not fifteen feet away, suddenly lit up. It had been dark all night, as the upstairs area hadn't been used that day, and when we walked over to check it out, it shut itself off. Now, you may say that wasn't all that unusual, that maybe something was amiss with the switch. I would have said the same thing, except that the unit wasn't even plugged in. Such an occurrence warms the heart of a ghost hunter.

We returned to our position at the top of the stairs, and after just a couple moments, we heard a door slam shut near the bottom of the stairs. We knew no one had taken a position there, so we headed down to check it out. The only door near the staircase was the door to a small storage area. It was shut tightly, with a secure latch which prevented it from opening when you pulled on the handle. Later, we were told this door often swings open and slams shut, much to the chagrin of employees walking by.

I should explain that there are two staircases leading to the upper level. They are on opposite sides of the building, and one of them is a straight shot up while the other takes a couple of turns. Glenn and I were at the straight shot staircase, while Heather and one of the waitresses were positioned at the top of the other. As shift change neared, I headed over to see how Heather was getting along. She was alone. It seems the waitress had gotten a severe case of the willies and had gone outside into the parking lot for a cigarette.

As Heather—a banker by trade and every bit as courageous as the most fearless ghost hunter—and I talked quietly, she would turn to the stairway from time to time and snap a photo. I was standing next to her when she turned, pointed her camera down the staircase, and snapped a shot. She very calmly said, "Look at this," and so I did. On her digital screen was a beautiful shot of the stairway. Only it wasn't just the stairway this time. About half way up and tight against the wooden railing was a thick funnel of white, like a miniature tornado spinning up from the floor. It appeared to be about three feet high and very narrow. It was solid and had been unavailable to the naked eye. Needless to say, I was rather excited. Heather behaved as though this was a natural occurrence and seemed

White funnel

absolutely detached. Such is the nature of a banker, but then again, isn't that what we want in a banker?

Around two o'clock in the morning we all decided to meet around a table in the upstairs dining room. We sat in the dark, chatting about our experiences thus far, and I shot a few photos of the team. Altogether there were eight of us, and we were enjoying a soft drink from the upstairs bar as we talked. At the same moment, Glenn and I shot a look at one another, then jumped up and ran to the opposite side of the dining area, near the staircase where Heather had gotten her fascinating photo. We had both heard the voice of a young child calling for its mother. It was clear as a bell, except that we were the only ones who had heard it. It didn't even show up on our recording equipment.

The website for the South Lyon Hotel has a clever motto which reads, "Day or night, there's always something happening." It's most appropriate because strange events are not restricted to the still hours of the night. Wait staff admit to strange things going on during daylight hours, and there are places in the hotel where some of them refuse to go—especially the basement.

We returned to the hotel a second time, but as happens quite often on ghost hunts, nothing at all happened. On the third visit, however, we had mass confirmation of paranormal activity.

It had been pretty much a bummer of an evening, one of those times when absolutely nothing was taking place. We were all feeling sort of disappointed, and around 3 a.m. we decided to meet in the upstairs banquet room to talk about our evening, pack up our gear, and say our good-byes. This banquet room is where staff members have often seen a black form hovering above the French doors leading out to the balcony. Two of the wait staff insist that this is the most haunted room in the hotel.

We met at the top of the stairs and—as a group — stepped into the banquet room. As we did, we all halted in our tracks as looked across the room and watched the double French doors leading out to the private balcony open. We stared as the handles twisted down, the doors both opened wide, and then once again closed and locked. It was impressive and maddening. Impressive because you don't always behold such a sight in the presence of several others who also see it happening. Maddening in that none of us had our equipment running because we were finishing up for the night.

A few months after our investigation, I was asked by manager Corry if I could swing over and meet with one of his employees who had just that day had a terrifying experience. I called a couple members of my team and met with none other than Rosie, our cleaning lady whom you met at the beginning of this story. She had returned to her old job, and once again, Rosie was sincerely afraid to be in the building and was shaking visibly.

I was informed that Rosie had come back to work for the hotel as its custodian, and was now coming in around 5 a.m. so she would only have a couple hours alone in the place before the morning crew showed up to set up the place for the day's business. After the morning crew had arrived, Rosie was on the main floor over by the bar completing some of her tasks and talking to a couple of the women on the crew. As they spoke Rosie suddenly seemed to stiffen, and she told the girls that "he" was standing right behind her again. Then she shouted out in a panic, "What do you want? Why are you doing this to me?" Then she was tossed hard up against the walk in cooler and wilted to the floor in a sobbing mess. As the girls rushed over to help her up, Rosie was heard to say, "My back—he burned my back!"

As the story was related to me, I asked Rosie if the ghost had hurt her. Her husband answered in the affirmative and asked Rosie to show us her back. Turning around, she lifted her blouse, and in red welts scratched rather deeply into her skin were letters at least four inches high. It appears that when Rosie had asked what he wanted, the ghost had answered by emblazoning across her back the word "YOU." Even more bizarre is that the word was scratched into her back backwards.

Rosie's husband asked if our group could say a prayer for his wife in an effort to make the spirit leave her alone. At this point, Rosie was shaking in fear because she said the ghost was standing nearby watching us. (I often get asked to say prayers for folks in fear of the paranormal.) She insisted we stand very close to her so he couldn't get next to her. Then we held hands, I said a prayer, and then everyone kept repeating the Lord's Prayer over and over at Rosie's request. It didn't help. Rosie suddenly screamed that he was touching her and started to collapse. At that point we carried her to the outside balcony for air, and once she recovered, we insisted she return home. Rosie then quit her job at the hotel for the second time.

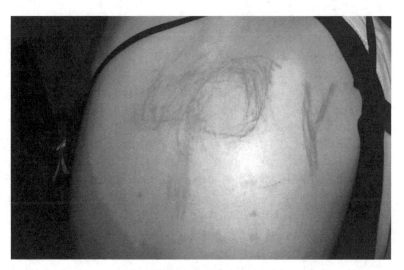

YOU scratched into back

Just who are all those ghosts wandering around the hotel? Who knows? Maybe the haunting has something to do with the cemetery below the structure, as some locals have had stories handed down to them about how the two brothers who had been paid to remove the bodies didn't actually move all the bodies. Or perhaps they are past residents of the hotel, like the man killed in the fire. Or maybe many of the spirits are just passing through on their way to who knows where, drawn to the place by the energy of other spirits.

If you check out the hotel for yourself, again, be respectful. This is a nice place and doesn't deserve rude intrusions (they have enough of their own already). Don't bother the staff during lunch and dinner hours, and be advised that weekends are extremely busy. They have a job to do at the hotel, and they do it well. They'll be glad to chat with you when things are slow.

ADDENDUM: I get a good feeling whenever I unexpectedly run into someone who adds credence to the validity of a haunted place I've visited. This happened to me with this story about the South Lyon

Hotel. Long after I had written this tale, I stopped for a burger and a brew at a place called the Copper Mug in Wixom, Michigan. It's a small, neighborhood type of tavern that's been around for years, and the food is well worth the visit if you're in the area. There's a cook out back they refer to as "the chef," and for good reason. Elongated, thick cut smoked bacon adorns the wide BLTs, and the burger and sandwich selection is top notch. But you really need to try the chili—it is enigmatic stuff, with a hint of cinnamon slipped in there somewhere. Ah, there I go again, rambling on about food. I'm told it comes with age.

The manager of the Copper Mug is an energetic blonde woman named Suze. As I often do when I'm visiting an older building, I inquire as to whether or not the walls talk when few folk are around. When I asked Suze, she indicated that, indeed, she has had brief encounters with a spirit of some sort hanging out in the basement of the bar. She told of how she was down there after closing one night, auditing the day's receipts, when she suddenly got the overwhelming sensation she wasn't alone. Pausing in her work, she began to hear faint whisperings in the voice of a man but too soft to make out the words. Suze says it has happened more than once and suspects she would notice it more often if she stuck around long enough after closing time, but by then she's ready to head home.

At any rate, Suze interrupted her spooky tale by offering me the following information about another place she had worked—the South Lyon Hotel. She told me, "Now that place is really haunted," and went on about how she had worked there as part of the wait staff.

Suze said that it was on a wintry night and that business had been rather slow, but she still had a private party to attend to upstairs. The party lasted until closing time, and after everyone had left, she began cleaning up after them and closing down the dining room they had used.

She was busily going about her tasks when she noticed a man walk out of the ladies restroom and then cross the dining room right in front of her, heading for the stairs. She thought it strange he'd been in the ladies room but had been around the bar business long enough to expect just about anything. As he passed her, she offered him a friendly "good night," but he just ignored her and kept on going toward the stairs. She described him as older, rather thin, and wearing a dark suit jacket and pants with a white shirt but no tie. His clothing seemed to her to be way out of date.

When it dawned upon her that this guy was not of the normal persuasion, she headed over to the stairway he had trod. That stairway leads directly down to the bar, and anyone using it would have to pass by the bar, where the bartender was closing up her area, and then walk across the entire length of the restaurant to get to the exit doors at the front of the building, which had been locked some twenty minutes earlier. When Suze got to the bottom of the steps, she noticed the man was conspicuously absent and asked the girls and the night manager who had let him out. They told her that no one had come down the stairs, and that the last customer had left a long time ago. They told her she must have made the acquaintance of one of the hotel's resident ghosts.

Planning a Visit? Why not? The food is reason enough. The ghosts are an added attraction.

Still Haunted? Every inch is a paranormal smorgasbord—sometimes you get a little bit of everything and sometimes just a whole lot of the main course.

Chapter 8
Hanging Out At Hank's

Place Visited: The Henry Ford, a popular historic museum and village located in Dearborn, Michigan

Period of Haunting: The ghosts having been running amok around this place for years.

Date of Investigation: Sneak visits over a period of time beginning in 2006 and still continuing. The Henry Ford is not very interested in having an independent paranormal activity team investigate their grounds and facilities.

Description of Location: The Henry Ford, consisting of Greenfield Village and the Henry Ford Museum, as well as a large IMAX theater, has been around since the beginning of the Great Depression. In fact, there are photographs of Henry Ford watching his mentor and hero, Thomas Edison, flip the first shovel full of dirt for the building of the facilities. Mr. Ford wanted to house historical ephemera and recreate the type of American village he believed typified what America was all about. Since Dearborn was always dear to him, it became the location for his efforts.

The museum is one of the finest in the nation and an opportunity for a virtual walk through history. Much of it is devoted to the automobile, as one would expect, but Henry was also fond of railroads and an impressive display of railway engines, all meeting the spotless specifications of Mr. Ford himself. These are available for public viewing; however, there's much more than motorized displays within those walls. The Henry Ford is a history lesson in constant flux. They house at least four presidential limousines, including the Lincoln Continental President Kennedy was seated in when he was shot that tragic day in Dallas. They also feature the chair President Lincoln was sitting in at Ford's Theater when John Wilkes Booth ended his life. The bloodstains are still visible on that chair.

The Henry Ford, as you most likely know, is divided into two sections, the museum and the village. The village is actually an extensive collection of homes and shops, mostly authentic, which give a snapshot of rural life and history dealing with our country. They have one of the courthouses where Lincoln practiced law, the home of the Wright Brothers of air-flight fame, Daniel Webster's home, a tavern (which is VERY haunted) brought in from rural Clinton, Michigan, and which dates to the early 1800s, and dozens of other famous and interesting places. You can take a horse-drawn tour through the village or opt to be escorted through while seated in the back of a flivver. However, the attractions are close enough to one another that it's quite possible to walk everywhere, enjoy an ice cream or lemonade, and maybe take a ride on an authentic, old time carousel.

It would take reams of writing to adequately describe all the offerings of the Henry Ford. Since you bought or borrowed this book to read about ghosts, I will head in that direction and let you buy a ticket to visit the place yourself at your convenience. You'll be glad you did, and, like scads of visitors, you just may have a ghostly encounter yourself.

Haunt Meter: * * * * *

I FIRST BECAME ACQUAINTED with the ghosts of the Henry Ford when I was asked to officiate at a wedding there. The Martha Mary Chapel, on the grounds of Greenfield Village, is a popular place for couples to tie the proverbial knot. My name is on the list of ministers available to perform such a ceremony, and I often get called to do so.

On my first visit there to perform a marriage, I arrived early through the Eagle Tavern entrance. A guard ushered me through to my destination, and I met with a wedding coordinator provided by the Henry Ford, who walked me through the procedures they use for marriage ceremonies. The Martha Mary Chapel was built by Henry Ford in honor of his mother and his mother-in-law. It's a stereotypical replica of the idyllic country church. The pews are wood, the chandeliers use candles, and the stairways leading to the basement defy anything OSHA would ever approve.

I was soaking in the atmosphere and commenting on how good a job Mr. Ford had done, and how proud he must have been, when the wedding coordinator (who wishes to keep her job, so therefore must remain anonymous) replied, "Yes, he's still proud; he's often been seen standing in the balcony." Well, that opened the floodgates of my interest in things paranormal, and I was off to the races. Soon, our conversation led to the revelation that the church, haunted though it may be, is nothing compared to other places laid out on the grounds.

Since I was refused official permission to interview employees and conduct a formal investigation, I decided to do what any intrepid ghost hunter would, I resorted to covert operations. I began to visit the place frequently, speaking with tour guides, snapping photos and running my handheld audio recorder. The employees, many of whom are assigned to a specific historic house for a full season, were a wealth of information. They truly love what they do and will share their stories openly, yet discreetly. I always identify myself and tell them I've written two books about haunted places in Michigan. My personal ethos demands that, sneaky as I may be, I must be up front about my intentions. Now... where to start?

I begin with the aforementioned Eagle Tavern. Originally a tavern offering food and bed to travelers between Detroit and Chicago along what is now US-12, the tavern was moved from its original location in the village of Clinton, was restored, and is now used for fine dining with an early American cuisine. Recipes for lunches and dinners are true to their historic setting, as are the beverages, including hard cider, raw whiskey, and good old applejack. The hosts and servers are all in period costume, and the dining is by candlelight. It is a very popular place for wedding receptions.

The Eagle Tavern is entered by stepping into a foyer, where you'll be pleasantly greeted by someone who looks just like they stepped through a time warp. You'll be regaled with stories about the place and encouraged to ask questions and take photographs. Just to the left of the foyer is the bar area, and to the right a sitting room. The dining area and kitchen are in the rear, and the upstairs area, which originally consisted of several rooms to rent, is used for administrative purposes and storage.

I was greeted in the foyer by a very enthusiastic retired fellow hosting a long beard, wire rimmed spectacles and impeccable costuming. It was a rather slow afternoon, and after a bit of conversation, I asked if the place had any spirits wandering about. My host, whom I will call Elijah—simply because he looked like an Elijah in that getup—never broke stride but instead went into verbal overdrive.

Oh, the Eagle Tavern is host to a lot of ghosts. The room you're looking at right now (the sitting room) is visited quite often by an elderly lady. She's been seen by most of the folks who work here at the Eagle and a whole lot of visitors. She obviously lived here way back in the 1800s, because that's the kind of dress she's wearing. See that rocking chair over there? She's always sitting in that chair, rocking and sewing. She's a pretty old gal with her gray hair up in a bun. Sometimes you'll see just a flash of her, and sometimes you'll get a good look. Sometimes she acts like she doesn't know you're there, and there are times she'll look up at you with a puzzled look on her face, like she's wondering what you're doing there.

One time, a family was out on the porch looking through the window into the sitting room. I was standing next to the doorway, and I could hear them talking. They had a youngster with them, and he kept saying, "Look at that lady in the chair," and they kept telling him there was no lady in there. He kept insisting she was sitting in the chair and that she was really old. A lot of folks think that because this is a restaurant they can't come inside and browse around, so I thought I'd open the door and invite them in. When they came in, the little guy ran to the sitting room and pointed at the chair. He said she had been sitting there, but that now she was gone. I just let that one go, I didn't want to stir up anything with them.

There are lots of times we'll hear footsteps and muffled voices coming from upstairs. That's where the tavern's rental rooms were, but now the management has offices up there. Anyway, we keep hearing this stuff going on up there, and it happens when we know the office is closed and no one is upstairs. The girls didn't ever want to go up and check it out, so once I went up, but I didn't see or hear anything. It still happens from time to time.

Just about everybody who works at the Henry Ford has their ghost story to spin. One of my favorites is connected to the Wright Brothers house. It's the actual home they grew up in, not a replica. Henry Ford was a big admirer of them and had it moved from Dayton, Ohio, up to the Village. It's a two story home with living room, parlor, and kitchen on the first floor, and four bedrooms upstairs. One of the bedrooms is accessible only by passing through another. Those were the two rooms used by Wilbur and Orville when they were children and young adults.

I've actually chatted with two different tour guides on separate occasions at the Wright home. Both times, after waiting for visitors to make their exit, I struck up conversations about hauntings. Both times, I struck gold. The first was with an attractive woman in her fifties who loved the home very much. I shall refer to her as Noelle. Noelle said that there are sometimes long stretches when no visitors are entering the home and she's there alone. Even though odd things happen while she's there, she says she's never been frightened, even though some guides refuse to work there.

One wet afternoon the Village was pretty slow, and I had brought along a book to fill the time. I started to hear footsteps up above me, the sound of someone walking around in the middle bedroom and then down the hallway. I listened to it for quite a while. I thought about going up there but decided that I didn't want to intrude and listening to it was very fascinating. I knew I wasn't alone. Then, after about twenty minutes of listening, I heard the footsteps heading toward the stairs and then down them. I saw the legs of a man in dark trousers and old-time shiny shoes. He came down to the landing and turned and looked at me. I recognized him from the photos of the family we keep on one of the tables in the parlor. It was Orville, clear as day. He looked at me and our eyes met, and then he turned and went back upstairs. It really wasn't frightening, at least not to me. I can't say the same for one of the cleaning ladies who used to work in this house after closing.

Noelle says she was a passing acquaintance of Clara, the cleaning lady, and that she would come in at the close of Noelle's shift. Once, says Noelle, Clara worked half a shift cleaning at another house and came into the Wright home well after dark. She was alone and started cleaning up. She was in the living room, getting ready to vacuum the rug, when movement caught her eye. She looked over at the staircase and saw the figure of a man coming down the stairs. He stopped at the bottom and looked at her, then walked through the parlor and into the kitchen. As soon as he was out of sight, she left the house and refused to ever go back in.

While speaking with Noelle, I noticed that there was a red velvet rope across the staircase, preventing access to the upper floor. I asked if they were doing renovation up there, but she confessed to me that for a while they were not allowing people upstairs because of the haunting. Intrigued, I stepped up to the landing and was immediately engulfed in an icy draft. Noelle noticed it too, and then told me that I could go upstairs if I wanted to. It was an offer I couldn't refuse, so up I went, camera in hand, and infrared thermometer at the ready.

Visually, there was nothing to meet the eye or the shutter. On the other hand, my thermometer gave perfectly normal readings until I entered the back bedroom, the less accessible one. Near the head of the bed, in the pillow area, the temperature reading dropped drastically from 77 degrees down to 56 degrees. I could extend my hand and feel the difference.

On a return visit to the Wright home, I engaged in conversation with a different tour guide, one whom I shall refer to as Erik. Erik was also about my age, in his mid-fifties (I discovered the Henry Ford loves to hire retired folks) and well versed in the history of the Wright brothers. He also admitted to hearing voices emanating from up above, but each time he checked it out, it would stop. On another occasion, Erik said he was giving his oral presentation to a couple of families. He said their backs were to the living room, and as he spoke he saw Orville cross the living room from one side to the other. He said it broke his concentration, which I believe to be an understatement of epic proportions. Other times he's smelled Italian food strongly wafting from the kitchen while alone in the building. Another time he was seated in a chair in the sitting room waiting for tourists when the bookcase doors a few feet away suddenly opened and then, after several seconds, closed again. That bookcase, he says, was in the home when the Wright brothers were growing up, and all the books behind those glass doors belonged to the family.

On yet another visit to the Village, I decided to check out other places. At the Noah Webster home (the Webster of dictionary fame) a tour guide informed me that just after opening the house for the day, she heard someone running down the upstairs hallway. She dashed up the stairs and then heard the footsteps running down the rear staircase. She called security, who went through the home, every nook and cranny, and found nothing. The back door was still locked from the inside. Security told her it was probably one of the ghosts playing tricks on her. I asked if she was scared. She told me she would have been terrified if it were a person, but since it was a ghost she was OK with it. It seems she had once lived in a haunted house and was used to their shenanigans.

That same day I met a member of my group, Sarah, and we walked over to the stone cottage, an English

Stone House

abode from centuries past. Henry Ford had been visiting
England and decided the little house would look good
on his grounds, so he bought it, had it dismantled, and
then shipped it to Michigan and had it reassembled. It's
a small cottage, two stories with stone floors. It's actually
an ancient duplex of sorts, with each side sporting one
large room and fireplace, and a private entrance to the
upper level, where the bedroom was. There is a very
short connecting doorway between the two on the main
floor, but not on the upper. Bedrooms demand more
privacy than living quarters.

Sarah and I had the run of the place for about half
an hour. We scouted out the area for official personnel,
then fired up our cameras and recorders. On that level,
we struck out. On another level, we got somewhat lucky.

A trio of visitors entered the cottage, and Sarah
and I seated ourselves on a stone ledge inside and
sat quietly. One of the visitors, a young woman in her

Stone House — Second View

twenties, seemed to know quite a bit about the cottage, so I asked if she worked there. She indicated that she had worked for the Village, but she had quit and gone back to college. The conversational door now widely open, I bluntly asked if she had ever had anything strange happen in the cottage. I hit pay dirt, and I shall refer to her as Bonnie.

> Not all the places have guides in them. At the time I worked here, I was assigned to the stone cottage. Other summer help would refuse to work there because of the stories they had heard, but it didn't scare me because I always wanted to see a ghost.

> I'd worked there about a week when the first strange thing happened. They were using the upstairs, which is off limits to guests, for storage of other artifacts from around the village. I wondered why they didn't let anyone

upstairs, either visitors or employees, and why they kept the doors to the upper level locked. Well, they were refurbishing a different house nearby, and taking stuff from that house and putting it upstairs temporarily. On one trip they left one of the doors unlocked, so I saw my chance to sneak a peek up there. I went up the stairs to the bedroom on the left, and it was really cold up there. I took out my camera, but it wouldn't work, so I figured the batteries were dead. I could see some of the stuff they had brought in stacked against one wall, but there were still items up there that belonged to the cottage itself. I was looking around when all of a sudden this black form scooted past me, really fast. I turned to look at it, and it came right at me. I screamed because I felt it run right through me, and then I was downstairs in an instant. It scared the hell out of me, but if I could, I'd go back up there again.

Bonnie wasn't the only tour guide I spoke to that day about the stone cottage. She referred me to another employee, Hillary, who had no doubt Bonnie was telling the truth. She'd been working with a curator team; they were the ones who had been taking artifacts from another place and storing them at the cottage. She said they needed to move some of the furniture in the upstairs bedroom, one of the items being a large, four poster bed, to provide the necessary space. When they moved it, they noticed one of the posts could be removed from the frame. When they removed the post, they found a cat o' nine tails made of leather and with pieces of glass attached to each tail. They figured the man of the house may have been abusive, or that someone had rather strange tastes of an amorous nature. Later that day, Hillary went upstairs alone to check on how things had been stored, and that she could hear a woman faintly crying.

The summer after these conversations, I revisited the Village. It was a hot, muggy July day, and there weren't many patrons strolling about. On days like that, they normally visit the air conditioned museum and restaurants. I had parts of the park virtually to myself.

I walked over to the Henry Ford farmhouse, where Hank had grown up. I had been there many times over the past couple years, so I knew the place very well. I entered through the front door, and looking straight down the hallway, back by the kitchen entrance, a young girl in period costume had been waiting for a customer. When she saw me, she approached and began her memorized dissertation. I told her I was just there to nose around a bit and that I already knew the story. Just then, the front door lock snapped into place, which is a latch you have to manually move from right to left. The poor teenaged girl turned pale and said, "Oh please, not again."

I pretended it was all perfectly natural and quickly engaged her in conversation about the history of the house (never prod someone about a haunting if you can see they're genuinely upset). We stood up against the velvet rope which restricted us from entering the Ford living room, and she began to tell me about life in the Ford home over a hundred years ago. There is a beautiful desk just to the right of where we were standing, with books stacked along the top. As she spoke, one of the books fell over on its side and slid across the desk. That was it. The tour was over. The poor girl screamed and ran outside.

I followed her into the yard, where she stood trembling. She told me she had informed her boss that she didn't want to work at the Ford home because every time she did something strange happened. I tried to assure her that such events were perfectly natural, but my words didn't resonate with her. She contacted security by two way radio, and they escorted her back to the main office. One of the security personnel remained behind, and I asked if this sort of thing happened very often in the Village. He looked at me in what I took to be amazement and said, "Are you kidding, this crap goes on all over this place—there are guys on my shift who won't even go into some of the houses alone."

Both the Village and the museum are fascinating places on many levels. Inside the museum there's an auditorium where they sometimes put on plays for the visitors. I was once asked to perform a wedding ceremony there, and quickly assented. When I arrived for the ceremony, quite early as is my custom, the doors were locked and I couldn't get inside. A security person noticed me standing there with my clergy robe across my shoulder and rightfully assumed my intent. She unlocked the door for me and led me to a small room off stage left where I could get ready. She then asked me if I would be all right alone in there, that she had to run an errand for her supervisor. I asked her why she thought I wouldn't be all right, and she told me there were a lot of strange things happening there.

I prodded her to recount something strange. She did. She said that one night she had heard voices inside the theater. It was late at night and after closing time, and there was no reason for anyone to be in there, so she unlocked the doors and went inside, her flashlight illuminating her way. The talking had stopped when she entered, but as she approached the stage, it started up again, the voices coming from behind her. She turned around real quick and shined her light up the center aisle, where she caught the image of none other than Henry Ford staring back at her. At that point, she screamed and ran out the side entry.

As if all these stories weren't enough, I would be remiss if I didn't include the tale of Lovett Hall. Lovett Hall is an elegant building with a huge parlor full of plush sofas and chairs. A majestic staircase twists its way up to a large ballroom. Halfway up the stairs is a giant oil painting of Mr. and Mrs. Ford, all gussied up for a white tie hoedown. Mr. Ford supervised the building of Lovett Hall himself and insisted that the upstairs ballroom floor be supported by giant springs. It was his opinion that if the floor "gave" a little while people danced, they wouldn't suffer sore joints and fatigue. That's the engineer brain for you, and Henry had a giant-sized engineer's brain.

There was no one in the parlor when I arrived, and no velvet rope strung across the staircase restricting access to the ballroom, so I headed on up. When I reached the ballroom, I was amazed at its size. I also discovered the staff was preparing for a wedding reception to be held later that night, as dozens of tables were spread with linen tablecloths and crystal glasses. As is my wont, I struck up a conversation with one of the girls, a server named Jessica.

It was an interesting and informative conversation. Jessica said that in years past, when Henry Ford was still alive, he would host major formal events in the ballroom. A lot of famous people had attended those events, and some of the best bands in the country had performed there. She informed me there was a private school on the grounds, and one of the reasons Mr. Ford had built the ballroom was to teach young men and women from the school how to dance in proper society and how to behave as proper ladies and gentlemen.

The conversation was interesting, but I wanted to hear about the ghosts. When I mentioned this, Jessica said she really didn't want to talk about it because she had to work there and those things freaked her out. However, she did go on to tell me about the night she had finished setting tables and stepped out of the ballroom to use one of the spacious restrooms nearby. When she entered, there were several women already inside, and they were dressed in fancy clothes. Her first logical thought was that they were part of a re-enactment party, but then she realized that was not logical.

They were looking into the mirrors, freshening up their makeup and hair, and they were all talking to one another. I stood there like I was frozen. When they noticed me, they stopped talking and all turned and stared at me, like I didn't belong there. The restroom didn't even look the same; it looked a lot newer even though all the fixtures weren't new ones. I remember looking at the way they were dressed, flowing heavy gowns and tiaras with feathers. I just backed out of there and took off to the kitchen. I told a co-worker what I saw, and she went back there to look for herself. When she came back, she said everything was normal. It was like I was in a time warp or something. It was even stranger because the feeling I got from them was that they knew I didn't belong there.

If you've never visited the Henry Ford, you already know it's well worth every penny of the admission fee. In fact, there's too much to see in only one day. Many people check out the village one day and the museum the next. So visit the place and take your camera along. Who knows, one of those period-dressed tour guides may not be a tour guide at all.

Planning a Visit? No problem, and by all means do so. While you're there, check out the Michigan theme restaurant inside the museum. Michigan recipes, Michigan ingredients, and all washed down with good old Michigan Vernor's or Faygo soda pop.

Still Haunted? Absolutely—both the museum and the village.

Chapter 9
Ghosts of Fairlane

Place Visited: Fairlane, the home of Henry Ford, in Dearborn, Michigan.

Period of Haunting: Ghosts have been reported gracing this estate since the death of Henry Ford in the upstairs bedroom in 1947.

Date of Investigation: There was no investigation on my part. Rather, this chapter is based on a very interesting conversation with members of the staff in the summer of 2008.

Description of Location: Fairlane is the name of the estate of Henry Ford, the founder of the Ford Motor Company. The estate encompasses 1,300 acres of prime meadows, arbors, and gardens in Dearborn, Michigan. Mr. Ford began construction on the home of his dreams in 1914, as success had brought far too much attention to his home in Detroit. The new home, built under his strict supervision, was in a location only about two miles from the place of his birth. It was named "Fair Lane" after a location in Ireland, the home of his grandfather.

The house took around two years to construct and went through many design changes in the process, all under Mr. Ford's strict and exacting specifications. At one time nearly one thousand artisans toiled year-round to complete the project. The home is built with Ohio limestone and while obviously the home of a wealthy man, is not overly expansive or ornate, as Henry was a rather modest man, not given to opulent living. He directed his architect to keep the cost to a paltry $250,000, an enormous sum in the era of the Model T, when Ford shocked the country by offering his workers an unheard of $5 a day salary. Still, the final cost climbed to nearly $3 million. That was just for the house. The interior decorations added another $175,000 to the bill, and the landscaping soaked his pockets to the tune of nearly $400,000. That's a lot of tin lizzies by anyone's estimation.

The estate includes such niceties as a man-made lake, horse barns, greenhouse, staff cottages, guest accommodations, a garden displaying thousands of roses, and other amenities too numerous to mention. Ford made certain the estate had its own powerhouse and a full staff to meet the family's needs. A few years after his death, the Ford Motor Company purchased the estate and operated it as a tourist attraction, which continues today. It is now owned and operated by the University of Michigan, which has an adjoining campus. Tours are regularly offered at a reasonable price, and you can dine in the mansion on some very nice culinary offerings.

Haunt Meter: * * *

THE NATURE OF MY PROFESSION is such that I'm often asked to perform wedding ceremonies in various locations, some classy, some historic, and some rather bizarre. This is how I came to be introduced to the haunting of the Henry Ford Estate. A couple associated with our church had a daughter who wished to be united in holy matrimony within the music room of the Fairlane. I did not want to pass up the opportunity, and quickly agreed to officiate.

I arrived quite early at the estate, introduced myself to the staff, and was ushered inside. The foyer exudes a warmth all its own, with Mr. Ford's personal library immediately to the right. I was told I could place my things within the library and make myself comfortable there, or I could roam around the mansion if I agreed not to violate the restricted areas. A good patron of history and spirits always plays by the rules, so I followed their instructions as I perused the rooms which were not off limits. Unfortunately, the upstairs, which includes the bedroom where Ford exited this physical world of ours, was off limits at that time.

Although well out of my price range, the mansion simply exudes a warmth and intimacy one would not normally expect of such a structure. The staff is very knowledgeable, which adds to the experience. Their openness made it easy to broach the subject of paranormal activity. I discovered many of them had their own stories to tell and their own opinions as to the nature of those experiences.

I begin with Kelly, one of the wait staff assigned that day to oversee the prenuptial refreshments. A cute and intelligent college student at the University of Michigan, Dearborn campus, Kelly was easy to talk to. After a bit of conversation I informed her of the books I had written and asked if she ever had any experiences of the supernatural during her tenure at the estate. Her answer was quite interesting:

> Oh yes, just about everybody who works here any length of time has a story to tell. When I took this job it wasn't long before some of the other staff members started telling me stories of the ghosts. There are some places here they refuse to go into alone, especially the basement tunnel (it seems there's a rather frightening tunnel which runs through the basement of the mansion to various other outside buildings). I wasn't convinced at first, but after so many people tell you so many stories, you start to wonder.
>
> After about six weeks here I was setting up the music room for a late night gathering

and needed to go back to the kitchen for something. The kitchen is almost at the other end of the building, and you have to pass through the living room and in front of the foyer before heading down the hallway to the kitchen. Well, I was almost through the living room when off to my left, where the stairs in the foyer lead to the second level, I caught sight of a woman coming down the steps. She was a small woman, middle aged I'd say, and wearing a maid's uniform, which is totally not like anything we wear around here. She was carrying a tray, and I just sort of stopped where I was and watched her. She was totally oblivious to me and walked right past me and down the hall toward the kitchen. I had been told about her by several staff members, that she was Clara Ford's favorite maid, and so I followed her. She went past the kitchen and into the ballroom dining area and turned left out of sight. I hurried in behind her, but she was gone and the room was empty.

It needs to be pointed out that the public dining area, often referred to as the ballroom, was originally an indoor swimming pool and was actually quite large. If this was the ghost of a maid from decades past, she would have been experiencing the dining area as still being the swimming pool. Perhaps she was taking drink requests for guests of the Fords.

This wasn't the only encounter Kelly had with the mysterious maid. Once, while cleaning up after a dinner party, she ran into her, almost literally, as she was carrying soiled tablecloths to a utility room. With arms full of linen, she was making her way down the hallway and stepped aside so she wouldn't bump into another staff member coming from the opposite direction. When she looked up, just as that staff member passed, she looked into the face of the ghostly maid. Stunned, she turned around and watched the maid, the same person she had seen once already, stride down the hall, then turn to go up the stairs.

After the wedding ceremony, we dined in the music room on some rather sumptuous offerings. It's a charming room, with fireplace, chandeliers, oil paintings, and a grand piano—roped off so guests cannot get near it—once graced by the fingers of Rachmaninoff himself. With stomach full of prime rib and head full of ghostly intent, I excused myself and headed back to the living room where Kelly introduced me to a man I shall refer to as Warren. Warren is a long-time employee of the estate and works in the field of maintenance, which gives him access to every inch of the Ford home. He's quite the interesting man, as his first tale of an encounter with a ghost shows.

I've run into the ghosts of this place for many years now. They don't bother me much, as I'm pretty psychic myself. I'm a dowser and use pendulums to speak with the spirits.

I remember being down in the tunnel one time—it runs about three hundred feet from the house to the powerhouse—and hearing footsteps. Now, I knew I was the only one who was supposed to be down there because I was the only one with access that day. I stopped and listened, and I could hear those steps clear as a bell. Then I heard what sounded like a couple of men talking. I just walked real slow toward where it was coming from, but as I got closer it all just stopped. And that's not the only time. I've seen and heard things down there a lot. Some folks claim it's Henry Ford wandering around, because that's a route he would take after supper to his secret workshop in the powerhouse. Once I caught a pretty clear look at someone standing way off down the tunnel, but I couldn't make out if it looked like him or not. There are a lot of fellows I work with who are a little nervous about being down there alone.

I've actually seen ghosts all over the place. This is a historic place and lots of activity went on here, with lots of famous people dropping by to visit the Fords. The family was pretty attached to the place, and so were a lot of the staff. They were really loyal to the Fords and the mansion. He picked out people who were very particular about doing their jobs the way he wanted them done. They were a persnickety bunch. I remember checking on some wiring upstairs, and when I walked past one of the bedrooms I saw a woman in there rubbing away at a piece of furniture, like she was polishing it. I knew right off she wasn't from our time because of how she was dressed in those old-time outfits they had to wear back then. I stood and watched her working away, and eventually she picked up a can of polish and turned to leave the room. She looked right straight at me with this surprised look and then vanished. I didn't take it hard because I've been around ghosts most of my life.

The one person you'd think you'd see around here, or the one you'd like to see, is Henry himself, but I don't know of anyone who's actually sure they saw him. Usually it's a staff member, like a maid or a cook or servant. But that's enough for most folks since they don't always do so well when they see a ghost.

It's actually pretty interesting around here. Always something new and different. I recall once hearing splashing and people whooping it up in the pool. I headed on over to check it out because the pool was filled in with concrete a long time ago. The noise stopped before I arrived. We've had a couple groups come in to check the place out for ghosts, and I guess they got a lot of voices and such. There's even a photograph of one of Henry's cars taken out in the garage, and if you look closely you can see him sitting in the rear. At least it looks like him.

The evening had worn down, and it was getting on toward midnight. Warren had mentioned he could contact spirits, and so I asked him if he would give it a try. Without hesitation he produced a string with a metal nut attached that he said he always keeps in his pocket. He called it his pendulum. I asked how it worked, and he explained that you rest your elbow on a table, and let the string hang down. You then proceed to ask the spirits around you questions that can be answered yes or no. Then, if the answer is yes, the string starts to move in a clockwise direction. If the answer is in the negative, it spins the other direction. He said the more powerful the spirit's presence, the wider the arc of the circle.

Warren then proceeded to ask if there were any spirits present who wanted to talk, and the pendulum headed off clockwise. He asked if the spirit was a woman, and it widened its arc. Then he realized I may have looked skeptical, so he asked me to put my hand on top of his to make sure he wasn't influencing the movement of the string. He didn't appear to be and continued his questioning. From the nature of his questions and the answers he received, it seemed we had contacted the female maid everyone runs into around there. He was actually disappointed because he said she's almost always making contact with him, and he'd really like to hear from the other ghosts. He figures she's the most powerful spirit there although he also reports having seen and heard from a man, who he understands to have been a butler at one time.

Warren knows that not everyone believes the way he does, and he's not offended by it. He often goes to people's homes to help them understand their haunting and make contact with the spirits wandering through their halls. He uses his pendulum and often teaches others how to do the same. In fact, he taught me. It appears to be quite simple, actually. Just let the string hang and ask questions. I haven't really tried it very often, and the only time I did use it, I got mixed results.

The haunting of Fairlane runs the gamut of paranormal phenomena. Visitors report seeing someone peeking out at them from behind upstairs curtains as they approach the house. Others run into the maid as she diligently goes about her duties. Footsteps, voices, and even the occasional piano tune are heard within the walls of this 31,000 square-foot home. At least there's lots of room for them to roam.

Planning A Visit? By all means, do so. Call ahead first so you aren't restricted by a rush of other visitors. Make time for lunch in what used to be the pool room.

Still Haunted? Did Henry Ford make cars? The help says if you meditate a bit and snap some photos, you just might capture an inexplicable image.

Chapter 10
The Whistler

Place Visited: A two-story bungalow home on 5th Avenue East in Sault Ste. Marie, in Michigan's Upper Peninsula.

Period of Haunting: This passive-aggressive ghost has been heard off and on for at least the last twenty years and is still actively entertaining the present occupants.

Date of Investigation: A two-day investigation, conducted mostly alone because the distances between the location of the home and the locations of those homes of my team are so great. My visit was during a short vacation I took in the early fall of 2008.

Description of Location: Sault Ste Marie is a city of nearly 17,000 living souls. If you want to get an impression of how sparsely populated Michigan's Upper Peninsula is, consider the fact that this is the Upper Peninsula's second largest city. It is home to the Soo Locks, built so that large ore carriers can move from lakes Superior and Huron, which have different elevations from one another. There are actually two Sault Ste Marie's, one in the United States and the other in Canada. The population of the Canadian city of the same name and location is about 75,000 people. The "Soo," as locals refer to it, is not far from Whitefish Bay in Lake Superior, where the ore carrier *Edmund Fitzgerald* sunk into the history books during a November gale. The paper mills of the Canadian side provide much of the employment for the area, although the Kewadin Indian casino does its fair share in dividing that well-earned money from the pockets of the populace. It's a cold area most of the year, and even the summers are very mild in comparison with the downstate area. The house in question will not be identified in any precise manner due to the request of the present occupants. I will also obscure their names. Suffice it to say that it sits on 5th Avenue East, between Augusta on the west and Seymour to the east.

Haunt Meter: * * *

MIKE AND JUDY are a happily married couple in their late forties, both of whom have grown up in the Soo. When they married nearly twenty-five years ago, they lived with her parents for a few years in order to save money to purchase their own home. Eventually, Mike was able to snag a pretty good job on the Canadian side of the border, and they bought the home on 5th Avenue East.

They hadn't lived there long when, invited to a party at one of their neighbor's homes, they caught wind of the fact that their house was considered to be haunted, and that the previous occupants had often spoken of the ghost who made himself known in a rather odd manner. Since mortgage payments trump fear of apparitions, they decided that if and when the activity manifested itself, they would just live with it. After all, they had invested several years of savings into their new home.

About three months after setting up housekeeping, they began to notice odd and subtle things going on. Lights they had turned off before retiring for the night would be on in the morning, and one of the kitchen windows would be cracked open a tad, which is no small thing during an Upper Peninsula winter. Sometimes, the trash bin in the kitchen would be found overturned, and quite often the throw pillows on the sofa would be, well, thrown about the living room. Compared to other hauntings, these were rather mellow events, sometimes unsettling and sometimes intriguing. One fall day a new twist was added for their enjoyment. As Judy says:

Mike called me one afternoon to say he had to pull a few more hours down at work. It was the middle of winter and the days were really short, so it was dark around four-thirty. I turned the soup down to simmer so we could eat together when he got in, and I went into the living room to read.

I had been reading about an hour with our cat, Sparky, laying on my lap. All of a sudden she raised her head up quickly and stared at the kitchen door. Then she hopped down and walked slowly all crunched down close to the floor, toward the kitchen. She just stood real still and stared for a couple of minutes then straightened up and came back up on the couch. It was a little freaky, but I figured she had just heard a mouse or something.

I started reading again, and after about a minute or two I started to hear whistling. Not real loud, but soft and kind of far away but still inside the house. It seemed to be coming from the kitchen. Sparky heard it, too. We both sat there and listened for several minutes; then it just stopped. It was scary, but at the same time it was a pretty tune I'd never heard before. It sounded old, definitely nothing modern.

Around six thirty I decided to go upstairs and put away some laundry. Sparky follows me everywhere, and she was laying on the bed while I folded the clothes. All of a sudden it was back, the same whistling and the same tune. I could tell Sparky was hearing it, too, because she was sort of standing at attention and staring out into the hallway. We listened to it for a couple minutes, then I put down the clothes I was holding and tiptoed out of the bedroom toward where I thought it was coming from. It was really weird because no matter how far I walked through the house, it always seemed to be the same distance ahead of me.

When Mike got home that night, Judy told him all about what had happened, adding that Sparky had heard it all as well. I guess cats are able to lend credence to human credibility in these situations because Mike didn't doubt her. At the same time, he was tired from working an almost double shift, and the couple went to bed, Sparky spread out in comfortable repose at their feet. Once again, it was Sparky who brought attention to her owners that something was amiss in their presence.

It was about two in the morning, and Sparky woke me up by walking across my chest. I opened my eyes to see what she was up to, and that's when I heard it again—the same whistling, the same tune, and still inside the house but sounding far away.

I knew Mike was really tired and needed his sleep, but I needed him to hear this, so I woke him up. I held my finger up to my mouth and whispered for him to be quiet and listen. He lifted his head, and after a few seconds looked at me with this really strange look on his face. Then he got up and started to search through the house. When he came back, he said he could hear it all through the house, but he couldn't get close to it. What's really strange is that all the while it was ahead of him I could still hear it up in the bedroom.

Things quieted down a bit for a few weeks. There was no more whistling and no more trash or window incidents. However, just as it always seems to be with ghosts, they come back just as soon as they think you've forgotten about them.

Mike and Judy double dated one night, taking in an early matinee with plans for dinner later in the evening. After the movie, the two couples decided upon a restaurant, and as they were headed toward their cars, Judy remembered she had forgotten to feed Sparky. Now, in my mind, a cat can wait an extra hour or two for mealtime, but Sparky was like a child to Judy, so she retrievcd her cell phone from her purse and called a neighbor lady to see if she could run over and pop open a can of Nine Lives. She said she couldn't, but that her teenaged daughter, Nicole, would be glad to.

The rest of the evening was a model of normalcy for Mike and Judy, but not for poor Nicole.

Mike and I had a nice night out with our friends. When we got home, the back door was unlocked, but we thought Nicole had probably forgotten to lock it up when she left. Then we heard the sound of someone crying, a girl's voice. We stared at each other, wondering what the heck was going on. Then we headed off toward the crying.

I followed behind Mike, and I had my cell phone out in case I had to call the police. When we passed through the living room, we looked over at the bathroom, and there was Sparky laying in front of the door. Then we heard the crying again, and it was coming from inside the bathroom. Mike shouted out something like, "Who's in there?" and then the door opened. It was Nicole, and she was really upset. I mean, her eyes were all red and her mascara had run all down her cheeks.

We calmed her down, and after a minute she told us that she had come over to feed Sparky, then felt the need to answer nature's bidding. After she had gone into the bathroom, she said she started to hear someone whistling. She knew she hadn't locked the door back up when she came in, and she was sure someone had followed her in. She said the whistling kept getting louder and closer, so she locked the bathroom door and just sat there, listening to whoever was out there. I guess she'd been in there the better part of two hours. I really felt sorry for her.

Nicole went on to tell Mike and Judy that at one time it sounded like the whistling was right outside the bathroom door. She had been too afraid to open the door and make a run for it whenever it got quiet. She said when the whistling would stop she would hear other things, like someone breaking glass and footsteps pounding on the floor up above her. Altogether, poor Nicole admitted she was inside that bathroom over two hours, petrified that whoever was in the house would find her and do who-knows-what to her.

Mike and Judy walked Nicole back home, where her mother was unaware she had been in distress. She figured Nicole had fed the cat and gone to a friend's house, because that was her original plan. Sensing a need to calm her down, Mike and Judy informed Nicole and her mother that they had also been hearing the whistling and experiencing strange events inside their home. Their disclosure achieved the desired effect. Nicole was relieved it was a ghost and not a flesh-and-blood intruder. In fact, she was fascinated and even volunteered to feed the cat again sometime.

The haunting of their abode continued off and on for another year or so before Mike and Judy decided to delve into an attempt to make sense of it all. They called in a psychic (I don't reveal names of individuals who claim to be psychic unless I'm convinced they have that gift, and then only when they offer me permission). Sasha—not her real name—came to their home one evening and spent a couple of hours asking questions, nosing about through the private quarters, and sitting for several minutes in a trance. It was her opinion that the spirit was a man from the 1800s, which is interesting because the house wasn't there way back then. She said he was a Civil War veteran who had been in terrible battles and was quite withdrawn in his former life.

Sasha went on to say that the man's name was William and he had died nearby, a sudden and unexpected death. She added that William was a frustrated spirit. He liked to live alone and didn't want anyone in the house with him. She also said he didn't like conflict, and while most ghosts who want to get rid of someone will allow themselves to be seen, William didn't want to be seen. She said the spirit in their home was "passive aggressive," that he would make noise, but he wouldn't directly confront them. I don't know the size of the bill Sasha presented for her services, but I was of the opinion it was too much by 99 percent.

The haunting of their home continued, as did the search for answers. Both Judy and Mike learned the tune their ghostly whisperer was offering but had no idea of its origins until an uncle came to visit and they rented a movie. Judy says they were munching popcorn and watching a Civil War movie when both she and Mike suddenly turned and stared wide-eyed at one another. A character in the movie was singing a song to the tune their ghost always used. Their uncle identified the song for them, explaining that it was called "Lorena," and it was a favorite of soldiers on both sides during the Civil War. Perhaps I owe Sasha an apology.

With little difficulty, Judy next contacted the former owners of the house, explained what had been happening, and asked if they had ever had strange things going on while they had lived there. The answer was in the affirmative. In fact, Judy was told that they had actually seen the spirit once. It was a man. He had passed through the kitchen one evening as they had been eating supper. He had been dressed in loose fitting cotton clothes of an era long past, and the right side of his face was disfigured.

Judy once again contacted Sasha, and this time Sasha came out of her trance to announce she had made contact with William the ghost. He informed her that he indeed had been a soldier in the Civil War. He had been shot through the face during the battle of the Wilderness in Virginia. She said he was ashamed of his looks and just wanted to be left alone. Why he was invading the sanctity of the house was still anyone's guess.

As I said earlier, I had spent the better part of two days visiting the home of Mike and Judy. I spoke with their neighbors and with young Nicole as well. I'm convinced they are telling the truth, even though I had nothing subjective, let alone tangible, for my efforts.

Planning a Visit? Don't. Mike and Judy don't wish to be disturbed and are quite content living with William and learning more about him from Sasha. When I called them a few weeks ago, they informed me that William is getting bolder now and is allowing himself to be seen on occasion. His disfigured face, according to Sasha, is such a traumatic part of his life that, even though he could manifest himself without the wound, he can't shake it, even in death.

Still Haunted: You bet it is.

Chapter 11
Messy and Mean

Place Visited: A remodeled farm home in Gratiot County, Michigan. Sorry, but this is the best I can do for you in terms of location. I had to beg for permission to write this story and was granted freedom of the pen with the caveat that no correct location or names be used.

Period of Haunting: The present occupants have lived in the home for over seven years, and the haunting has permeated the longevity of their tenure. The previous long-time owners would not speak to me about the home or their experiences within. My guess is that the haunting has been one of great length.

Date of Investigation: Spring of 2009

Description of Location: Ithaca, Michigan is the Gratiot County seat. If you look at a map of Michigan, Gratiot County is smack in the middle of the Lower Peninsula. About 43,000 people live there, and the population density is only about 75 people per square mile. This means Gratiot County has always been quite a rural place to live. Many farms date back to the early history of Michigan's settlement. It is also the location of Alma College, a fine undergraduate school with a very good reputation. The home in question is about four miles outside the limits of Ithaca on a dirt road. It is a large home, as most farmhouses are wont to be.

Haunt Meter: * * * * * *(This is not a nice ghost.)*

WHENEVER SOMEONE ASKS ME about the nature of ghosts, I try to explain that they are just people like you and me with only one difference between us: they are dead and we are not. Ghosts, in my estimation, are people who are hanging around the living for a variety of reasons. They can be attached to a place, in which case they can get somewhat upset if present residents begin a remodeling plan. They can be attached to a person, perhaps someone they have loved (or hated) intensely, or to whose energy they are attracted. Ghosts can stick around because they are afraid to move on, fearing retribution for love left unexpressed. Sometimes, they don't know they're dead and are wandering about, trying to figure out what's happened to them. Sometimes, they choose to stick around simply because they enjoyed making people miserable in life and wish to maintain that attitude in death. Such seems to be the case here.

The Browns moved into this cavernous farmhouse sometime in the early 2000s, having purchased the place from previous owners whose family had spent previous generations beneath its roof. Though quite old, the home was, and is, in remarkably good condition. To me, it resembles the type of home you'd associate with great-grandma and apple dumplings, and that's only on the outside. The inside still reveals the wide wood moldings around the windows and doors, and the ceilings are high by modern standards. Since the Browns have decorated the place in early farmhand decor, with antique furniture and baubles, it looks a bit creepy to a guy like me. After all, if I'm likely to have psychic experiences at all, they always seem to happen when I'm around antiques.

With all the activity of moving in and getting settled, it was several weeks before the Browns discovered they weren't alone in the house. Chris and Dawn (again, not their real names) had worked hard, day and night, to set up housekeeping for their three children, Natalie, Erica and Sam. The children were allowed to choose for themselves which bedroom they would like, the first time they had lived in a home large enough to afford such a luxury. Since the oldest two, Natalie and Erica, were in high school, it was deemed necessary to give each daughter the privacy young girls seem to cherish. It was the number two child, Erica, who first approached her mother with the news that something was amiss inside her second floor bedroom.

Erica is a polite and petite girl of fifteen who didn't strike me as someone who would fabricate stories about spirits. That's why her mother took it seriously when her daughter approached her shortly after the new school year had started with the story of her strange encounter.

It was late in the evening just a few days after school had begun, and I could tell Erica was troubled about something. I just figured it was nerves over making new friends and getting used to a new school, but as the evening progressed, I could tell she wanted to talk about something. Then, just before it was time to head up to bed, she said, "Mom, I think there's a ghost in my room." She said it just like that, just sort of blurted it out.

I went upstairs with the girls, kissed them good night, then stayed in Erica's room so she could talk to me in private, without her sisters hearing what she had to say. She told me that several times she had woken up in the night to see a shadow standing by her window. I asked her what it looked like, and she said it was a man. Each time she saw him, he was staring out the window, like he was looking for someone. After a couple minutes, he'd just disappear. She had the feeling that he was the cause of her waking up, because she'd never had trouble staying asleep before. I told her it was probably just a shadow from the mercury light—the windows in her room face the driveway—and not to worry about it, but if she saw it again to come and get me. The next night, she came and got me.

It was about one in the morning when Erica came into our bedroom and told me she couldn't sleep. She didn't say anything about the shadow because she didn't want her father to know anything about it. It wasn't because he would be mad or wouldn't believe her, but because she was embarrassed. We went into the kitchen and I made some instant hot chocolate for the two of us, figuring it would calm her down. She told me it was the same shadow, doing the same thing. I let her talk about it, then the subject changed to school and school activities. I figured some normal talk would settle her down and then I'd go upstairs with her so she wouldn't have to go up to bed alone. Just about the time I thought it was okay to go up, we both heard footsteps above the kitchen. Her bedroom is directly above the kitchen, and the floors at that time were hardwood with no carpeting. I told her to stay in the kitchen, that I was going upstairs to see what was going on. In hindsight, it was a mistake on my part.

I went up the stairs telling myself that one of the other girls had probably gotten up and gone into Erica's room for some reason. That's what I told myself, even though I knew I was just placating myself. The footsteps were too heavy, and it sounded like someone was wearing heavy shoes or boots. Anyway, I pushed her bedroom door open, looked around the room, and not seeing anything out of the ordinary, I went in. Nothing looked out of place at all. I walked over to the window where Erica says she always sees the shadow, but there was nothing there. Then, all of a sudden, her bedroom door swung shut. It didn't slam; it moved slowly and steadily until it was shut. And it squeaked because it's an old door, so it seemed like it was taking an eternity to close.

I stood by the window, staring at the door, when from the left hand corner of her room, over by the walk-in closet, the black figure of a man stepped forward. I could just feel the tension in the room, and I sensed he was very angry. Then he raised his arm and pointed at me, shaking his head. I could barely make out his features, but I knew it was a man. Then he lowered his arm, shook his head in disgust, and stepped back into the corner and disappeared.

Dawn told me that at that point she had to make a decision. She could make things worse by showing fear and telling her daughter what she saw, or she could keep quiet about it and offer to sleep with her in her room. She chose the latter, and the rest of the night was uneventful.

In the morning, after the girls had gone to school, Dawn said she went back up to Erica's room to check things out. Exactly what she was looking for, she didn't know. She said she went through her daughter's closet, where the ghost seemed to have emanated from, and noticed a small door leading into an attic area. Looking inside, she found some old newspapers and magazines, some dating back to the 1930s, but nothing which would indicate the presence of some sort of entity.

Dawn spent the rest of that day with her nerves on edge, waiting for something to happen and worried that nothing would happen until after the girls came home from school. Then she got the big idea to put a cross figurine on her daughter's dresser. *At this point in the story I should explain that the family is Protestant, hence the cross and not a crucifix.* She told Erica what she had done, explaining that it was her grandmother's figurine, and that it would protect her. She was hoping that the power of suggestion alone would keep her daughter from awakening in the night and seeing the shadowy figure looming over by the window.

Just before supper that night, Erica had gone up to her room. When she came down to help set the table, she asked her mother where she had placed the figurine, because it wasn't on her dresser. They both went upstairs, and it was nowhere to be found. They searched everywhere in the bedroom, even looking under the bed and in the dresser drawers, but it was gone. That's when Dawn asked her daughter not to mention anything to her sisters, and to let her know if anything strange kept happening in her bedroom.

Dawn's request was a sincerely hopeful one, but negated almost immediately by the ghost, who decided it was time to harass another daughter. This time, it was Natalie's turn to experience a nocturnal visit of a less-than-amiable nature. She was up late one October evening working on a report for a school project after everyone else had gone to bed. She was disturbed several times when, out of the corner of her eye, a shadow seemed to pass by very fleetingly. Thinking she just wasn't used to the house with all its new quirks to get used to, she passed it off and kept on working—until things heated up a bit.

Engrossed in work on her computer, she heard the bedroom door open behind her. Thinking it was odd that her mother would come up to check up on her, she turned around to speak to her, only to be met with an open door—a door she knew she had closed when she had begun her schoolwork. With a note of trepidation, she closed the door then returned to her computer desk. Not thirty seconds later her peripheral vision caught movement atop her dresser. Slanting her eyes that direction, she spied a small bottle of her perfume slowly but steadily making its way toward the edge of the dresser. Natalie stared in disbelief as it left the dresser, flew about sixteen inches off the side, and then fell to the floor.

Being the oldest child, Natalie possesses strong first-child traits. She's always in control, watches out for her siblings, and has a deep sense of responsibility. This event was therefore something out of the realm of her experience. She did what most level-headed first children do, she thought up a reasonable explanation for the unreasonable. It did not work.

Shivering a bit as the hair on her arms stood up, she attempted to get back to work on her assignment. That's when she heard what sounded like a hard fist slam itself into her closet door. Spinning around out of reflex, Natalie found herself looking into the pinched face of a man perched in front of her closet. He was tall and thin, with closely cropped hair and odd clothes from a period she couldn't identify. She described him as having form, but at the same time looking "shadowy." Frozen in the moment, the man gave forth with a smirk, then raised his right hand. He was holding what looked to her to be a hefty stone, which he then violently threw at her. She ducked away from it, landing on the floor. Looking up, the man was gone. She had not heard the stone hit anything, and later, when she looked for it, it was nowhere to be found. It were as though it disappeared into thin air as it left the specter's hand.

Afraid to leave her room because she would have to pass by where the ghostly figure had been standing, she began to stomp her foot on her bedroom floor to get the attention of her parents, sleeping below. She admits she was too afraid to call out to them. Her parents, hearing the pounding, immediately came up to her room to see what was going on. When she told her story, her father was inclined to write it off as a sort of waking dream. Natalie was supported by her mother, however, who informed her husband that Erica had also had an encounter with an apparent ghost.

After settling Natalie down, Chris and Dawn decided a family meeting was in order. The next day, after Chris came home from work, they sat around the kitchen table and invited both Erica and Natalie to share their stories. The two sisters seemed somewhat relieved that each of them had strange events in common, but the conversation was especially unsettling to Sam (Samantha), who hadn't had anything out of the ordinary take place within her realm of consciousness. She took to sleeping on the floor in her parent's bedroom for several nights, returning to her room only when it seemed the ghostly activity had abated.

> Things were relatively quiet for a few weeks, with just a couple of strange things that I alone seemed to notice. Once, when Chris was at work and the girls were in school, I came into the kitchen for something, and the milk was on the floor. I mean, the whole gallon plastic container was out of the fridge and sitting on the floor between the fridge and the kitchen table. I picked it up and felt it, and it was still really cold, so I know it couldn't have been me. I hadn't been in there for over an hour, and the milk would have been warm. Besides, I would have remembered if I had set it on the floor, which I would never do anyway. It's just funny how your mind works under those circumstances.

> The other odd thing I recall was when I was doing laundry down in the basement. I tossed the wet clothes into the dryer and pushed the button to start it, but nothing happened. I checked the settings and everything was all right there. Then I noticed the dryer wasn't plugged in. It's an old basement with electrical plugs up high on the

walls. I plugged it in, started it up, then went upstairs. About an hour later I went back down to get the clothes, and they were still wet. I looked up, and the dryer was unplugged again. By then I was getting pretty spooked, but I thought maybe the outlet was loose. It wasn't. I plugged it in again and started it up. I was halfway up the stairs when I heard it shut off. I looked over—there was no way I was going back over there—and I could see the plug was out of the wall. I went upstairs and left the clothes for later, for when Chris came home. I told him my story, and he said maybe it was time to find someone to help deal with what was going on.

Dawn called her sister, Anne, the next day. Anne was a true believer in ghosts and claimed to know someone who could help. She put Dawn in touch with Brice, a psychic healer she said had helped her with her back pain. I'm not familiar with the work of psychic healers, but I guess if they can relieve the body of a pain in the back they can relieve the home of a pain in the neck. After a couple of telephone conversations, arrangements were made for Brice to drop over one evening and check the home for any invasive species. He says he only found one, but the one he found turned out to be a doozie.

I knew instantly, as soon as I walked through the front door, there was a spirit in the house, and that he was very angry. Actually, he was more than angry; he was just a real negative energy. It was a man, and I took him to be in his middle years, although you can't really tell with spirits since they can manifest themselves at just about any age they wish.

I asked to be left free to go through the house on my own, and right away I knew he didn't want me there. Angry and negative spirits are afraid of people with psychic abilities. They know they can be expelled so they either run for cover or get nastier. This one didn't run for cover, so I knew I was probably going to have an interesting visit.

I could sense that the spirit was most dominant on the upper floor, so I began my walkthrough on the lower level. I do that to build up my will and to tune into the peripheral stuff before exposing myself to a head-on encounter. I centered myself for a few moments, then walked through the living room and dining area. I could sense negative energy there, especially in the dining room. It was like he had lived in this house once and was abusive to his family during their supper times together. I sense cowering on the part of the residual energies of his family. They weren't really there, but their energies were.

Things were quiet in the kitchen, and the downstairs bedroom surprised me by how calm it was. By then I had gotten a handle on who I was up against, so I headed upstairs. The closer I got to the top of the stairs, the more the negative energy increased. It was like walking closer and closer to a fire, things seemed to get hotter. When I went into the first bedroom just off the upstairs hallway, I could sense his energy throughout the room. I would sense him standing in the doorway watching me, but every time I turned to see him, I would just catch a glimpse of him sort of sliding away. I stayed in that room for several minutes, trying to tune in to why he hung around there. I didn't like what I sensed, and

I kept getting the mental image of a crying girl, like she was frightened of whoever he was. This girl appeared to be from the '30s or '40s by her dress and hair, and she knew I was there. I could sense her needing my help.

After I said a prayer of blessing, I went into the next bedroom, the one that's right over the parent's room downstairs. Going in there was like leaving a hot electrical field and stepping into a freezer. It was so cold that at one time I could see my breath. I knew he was in there with me but wasn't showing himself. He was really trying to intimidate me, and for a minute I thought it was going to work, but I closed my eyes and centered myself spiritually, calling on my spirit guides to protect me. Then I walked through the room, touching the walls and floor and the closet door, trying to get a clearer picture of what was going on. I knew right off this guy was possessive. The house was his, and he didn't want anyone else living there. He knew he was dead, but he was hanging on, refusing to leave and determined to make anyone he encountered miserable.

I found myself drawn to the closet, so I opened it up and looked inside. It's one of those old-time, huge walk-in closets originally made more for storage than for clothes. Right away I got the image of a girl cowering in the corner of the closet, sobbing her little heart out. I mean, she was petrified. I tried to communicate with her, but she wouldn't allow it out of fear of the man. I stood still for a couple minutes and opened my mind. I could sense that she was somehow related to the man, probably a daughter, and that he was horribly abusive to her in a sexual way. It actually started to make me feel nauseated.

I left the closet and went over to the bed and sat down. When I did, the closet door slammed shut. It didn't just close; it slammed itself shut, like I had no business being in there. Then I got the overwhelming feeling of pain, the kind of pain you get when you know someone else is being hurt. I started getting images of this man holding down the girl and violently raping her. I could hear her crying and him cursing at her. It was heartbreaking— it was so hard to see what was happening and not being able to do anything about it.

I could tell he was letting me see all this in order to scare me away. I've had spirits try to do that before. I have to admit that sometimes it worked, but this man was a coward. I mean, any man who abuses those weaker than him is not brave, just mean and cowardly. I began to address him directly, and told him he had to release the spirit of the girl and leave her alone. He got really mad and started to show me images of things I don't even want to describe. It was really tough going, but after a while I could feel him pulling away and leaving the room.

I finished my walkthrough and went back downstairs to meet with the family. I told her there was the strong spirit of a man in the house, and that he was very negative, but cowardly. He liked to scare the young girls because that's who he was abusive to when he was alive. Then I asked them if they wanted me to try to make him leave the house. Of course that's what they wanted, so I asked to be left alone upstairs.

I went to the bedroom where his presence was strongest and went into a trance, asking my spirit guides to protect me. We confronted him, and he showed himself as ugly as he could to us. He refused to speak, but my spirit guides were stronger and more centered than he was, and he had to expose himself to us. He was a nasty spirit who had been a nasty man in life. He didn't want to admit he had been abusing his daughter, but he finally did. For most spirits, this kind of admission relieves some guilt releasing them from the negativity of their lives, but this guy had no intention of leaving. He remained firm that the house was his and that he would never leave it. He wanted his "boarders" out. With the help of my spirit guides, we surrounded him with a veil of peace so he wouldn't be able to harm anyone.

After Brice and his spirit guides made their departure, things seemed to settle down in the old homestead. The girls reported no nocturnal visitations, and no paranormal interludes interrupted the new-found normalcy of their lives. For a while.

A couple months had passed since Brice's visit when the nasty old man with short eyes once again made a rather theatrical comeback. It began as daughter Erica was soaking in a tub as a prelude to a good night's sleep. It seems the bathroom door began to rattle and shake, and then it sounded like someone starting banging on it with their fists. At first, Erica thought it was one of her siblings playing a joke on her because when she called out for whoever it was to knock it off, there was an immediate halt. Then, as she lay back in the tub making plans on how to get back at whichever sibling had so rudely interrupted her watery repose, items on the vanity started to, as Erica puts it, "tremble." Her hairbrush, toothpaste tube, and makeup began to shake the way they would during a mild earthquake. Then things transcended the realm of the mild. The medicine cabinet mirrored door swung open and began to swing back and forth. Each time it passed a certain point, she could catch a glimpse of the foul man's face reflected back toward her. It seems Brice's spirit guides must have packed up and headed for holier ground, setting this guy free to once again produce his negative shenanigans.

My conversations with the Browns, which have been numerous, have indicated the necessity of staying in their home. The dismal Michigan economy has dampened their income potential rather severely, and they haven't the means to purchase a different home. They are staying put and putting up with a ghost who seems to adamantly refuse to go away. In short, the haunting continues.

Planning a Visit? Sorry, it's not possible. They don't want publicity and the only way you can get me to talk is to tie me to a chair and make me watch country music videos.

Still Haunted? Absolutely. The Browns are consulting with new mediums in an effort to calm the place down. So far, no luck, but who knows?

Chapter 12
The "King," the Books, and the Spirits

Place Visited: The John King Bookstore, 901 West Lafayette, Detroit.

Period of Haunting: Recent. In fact, the ghosts may still be wandering amongst the stacks—and they have plenty of stacks to haunt.

Date of Investigation: This wasn't an investigation but information I gleaned as a customer. I had picked up a couple volumes and was delighted to purchase some old autographed photos from the glory days of Hollywood. I was there in May 2010. I apologize for the brevity of this story, but I didn't have time for any sort of investigation if I wanted to meet my self-imposed deadline for finishing this manuscript.

Description of Location: The John King Bookstore is where a bibliophile longs to have his ashes scattered upon his demise. This is one of the largest used book emporiums in the nation. It consists of two buildings, the first four floors high and packed with rare and used books. The second building is directly behind the main building, but just as imposing, and it hosts the ultra-rare books and documents that actually made my hands shake and my mouth water. This second building houses somewhere near 30,000 tomes, and it is by far the smaller of the two. Mr. King, who began the business as a student in high school, lives for books, is expert in their worth, and is a fascinating person to encounter. He's always there, quite literally, except when off on a buying expedition.

The buildings are old and spacious, yet clean and packed to the rafters with reading material and collectibles. The books are well organized, and the staff, who all love their work, know exactly where to look for whatever volume interests you. Parking is free, and it is very accessible off the major freeways. You cannot say you love books without first having made the pilgrimage to Mr. King's edifice of literary delights. Simply get on the internet and type in the name. You'll be given precise directions to either of two of their downtown Detroit locations.

Haunt Meter: * *

I HAD WANTED TO VISIT the John King Bookstore for years and really can't tell you why I waited so long before going. From the moment I walked in, I felt as though I could sell my clothes because I had entered heaven. This was no antiseptic, blow-dried and stylishly coiffed upscale clone with overstuffed leather chairs and a chic coffee bar. This place looked, smelled, and felt like a bookstore should look, smell, and feel. Coffee comes from an old pot kept behind the checkout counter and is drunk from Styrofoam cups. The chairs are leftovers from old schools and libraries, and scrape loudly across the floor as you belly up to one of the scarce desks laden with stacks of paper. Old photos and documents stare down at you from behind their frames as you peruse your discoveries. I knew I was on holy ground.

During the course of my visit, I struck up a conversation with Mr. King. An unpretentious man, he was dressed casually and sported a long, graying ponytail. His trim physical condition and appearance would lead you to believe he is much younger than his actual birth certificate would indicate. At any rate, the conversation led to my admission that I had written a couple of books about haunted places, and that led to a sly smile and his admission that some have indicated to him that his place of business is home to a spirit or two although he was not really a believer in such things.

It seems that more than one customer, and one or two members of the staff, have had ghostly encounters within the main building. The activity seems to restrict itself to the third and fourth floors of the main retail building. It seems the lights often turn themselves on and off when no physical hands are present. Sometimes, upon opening up for the day, lights that were shut off the night before are found to be burning brightly. There seems to be a couple of ghosts wandering around amongst the stacks; a woman on the third floor and a man on the fourth floor.

The woman on the third floor may be that of a regular customer who used to buy and sell books to Mr. King. He said she was not the most pleasant of people, and when she died, he was approached to buy out her collection of books, which he had done. After that purchase, patrons and paid staff would sometimes catch a glimpse of her shadowy form sliding among the aisles. She hasn't harmed anyone or disturbed any of the merchandise; she just seems to flit around every once in a while. She also seems to have made a visit to Mr. King's inner sanctum—his living quarters.

Shortly after her death, Mr. King purchased her personal collection of books, as I have indicated. Having retired for the night, he was awakened by sounds unlike any he was used to hearing inside his home. Looking up, he saw the dark figure of a woman entering his bedroom and approaching his bed. She paused for a few moments and then filtered away. He was sure it was her because they were well acquainted before her demise. What's fascinating about this encounter is that Mr. King is certain this was a paranormal experience; yet he continues to claim he doesn't believe in such things.

As for the man said to haunt the uppermost floor, very little information is known about him or his appearances. Every once in a while someone will say they saw a man standing in one of the aisles who looks as though he belongs to another period. When they turn their heads to take another look, he is gone.

Planning a Visit? By all means, do so. Businesses like this are few and far between. Who knows, you may find that special book or share a table with one of the ghosts.

Still Haunted? I don't know why it wouldn't be. It meets all the prerequisites and more. It's a set of old, historic buildings, and it's full of the prized possessions of the long dead. There are a lot of books in there that a lot of people were attached to in life and may still be clinging to in death.

Chapter 13
Hissing Hag

Place Visited: A single family dwelling located on W. Cottage Street in Shepherd, Michigan.

Period of Haunting: According to the family members, the place was haunted when they moved in several years ago, and the haunting continues.

Date of Investigation: Early summer, 2009.

Description of Location: Shepherd, Michigan is located about in the center of our lower peninsula, along the US-127 corridor in Isabella County. The home in question is owned by Mike and Sue Harley (not their real names) and their children. This is a small community, so along with not using real names, I'm not even going to indicate how many children are in the family or their ages. Shepherd is a well maintained spot on the Michigan map and seems much more like a village than a city. A community of about 1,500 living souls, it is home to two annual events: the Maple Syrup Festival and the Salt River Bluegrass Festival. Try to opt out of lunching at one of the chains spots along the highway and instead traverse the extra few blocks to the downtown area and select one of the eateries owned by the locals. Fast food in a laid back community just doesn't fit.

Haunt Meter: * * * * *(This place is pretty interesting)*

MY FIRST CONTACT WITH THIS HAUNTING came to me much the same way most other hauntings get my attention—through my publisher. I have a firm rule that I won't look for haunted places, but let the inhabitants of haunted places contact me. I make exceptions in some cases but not often. People read my books or hear about my exploits, then pen a note to or email my publisher. Those contacts are then forwarded to me. Some of the tales they relate intrigue me, and I they feel deserve a closer look. Many others cause me to shake my head in worrisome concern about the sanity of a good percentage of our populace. Those latter contacts are either introduced to the jaws of death (my shredder), or take up residence within my "delete" file.

The letter I received from the Harleys was one which intrigued me. Although, by their own admission, it wasn't well written, it was obvious these folks didn't simply want to get their names in a book, and they really wanted to tell their stories to someone who wouldn't judge them insane. I began, as I am wont to do, with an email requesting further information. Having received that, I continued communication with a phone call. Convinced they were on the level, I arranged a visit. I'm glad I did.

The Harley home is a comfortable one, tidy on the outside and neat as a pin on the inside. There are children in the family, but the nature of this haunting seems to be connected with Sue, so they have asked that I not mention the children's names or ages. Judging from the neatness of their rooms, these children are quite tidy compared to other kids.

Sue is an attractive woman, who obviously cares about her appearance—both physical and psychological. One of the first things out of her mouth was a question as to whether or not I would judge her insane based upon our in-person conversation. I assured her she seemed as healthy as anyone could expect considering she was living with a ghost that seemed attached to her and her alone.

Her first inkling that something wasn't right came quite soon after the family took possession of the home. One day the first week when Sue was alone in the house after Mike had gone to work and the kids were off to class, the eerie incidents started taking place. For instance, having spent the first couple hours of the morning unpacking clothes and hanging them in the closet in her bedroom, she headed off to the kitchen to pour a cup of coffee. She returned to the bedroom to finish the task at hand only to find all the clothes she had hung in the closet now resting comfortably in piles across the bed. To quote Sue, who strikes me as a master of understatement, "That unsettled me a bit."

Having replaced the clothing in the closet, Sue said she sat in the bedroom for a while, sipping her coffee and puzzling about what had just taken place. She says she wanted to pass it off as only having thought she had hung up the clothes, but she knew better. Even in the face of that strange morsel of paranormal pie, Sue felt comfortable with the feel of the house and simply continued her chores of settling in.

It wasn't long before something in the house decided to bless Sue with another in-your-face wake-up call. It was a Saturday morning, and she had decided to treat herself to sleeping in. The kids had the same idea, and Mike had left before sunup to pull an extra shift down at work.

I'd been working hard all week, getting everyone moved in to their rooms and setting up the kitchen, and I was dog tired. I had seen Mike off to work and had gone back to bed. I remember how good it felt to snuggle in and fall back to sleep. I don't know exactly how long I'd slept, but I was awakened by the sound of the bedroom blinds suddenly opening up, and the sunlight blazing into my eyes. At first I was steamed, because I thought one of the kids had come in and decided it was time for me to get up. When I opened my eyes, there was no one in the room. I just lay there for several minutes, trying to figure out how those damned blinds could have opened up. It wasn't like they had been open all the time and the sun gradually woke me up, it was a sudden, blinding light from the blinds all opening at once.

I looked at the bedside clock, and it was well after nine, so I went ahead and got up. I fixed breakfast then took a shower. The kids were still in bed, and I went back to my room to get dressed. When I stepped into the room, it was dark again. The blinds were shut. They're the type that open and close by turning a rod, and I never turned that rod. That's when I started to tell myself the truth, that something wasn't kosher in my bedroom. I remember thinking how glad I was that this was happening in my room and not one of the kids' rooms. I guess that's the mother in me.

Sue was beginning to think her family was sharing their home with an uninvited guest, and she hoped that the activity was limited to her bedroom. She didn't want the kids to know what was going on or to have them run into strange happenings in their new house. She got half her wish, as the haunting avoided contact with the children but began to extend its creepy fingers just about everywhere Sue went.

No two hauntings are exactly alike. Sometimes it's houses which are haunted, and sometimes it's people. Since Sue had never experienced anything out of the ordinary before, it's somewhat safe to say the house is haunted. However, since she is the only one in the family to experience the ghost, it would appear the spirit is attached to her for some reason. This leads to a couple questions. Did the ghost always reside in the home and is simply discriminating in its choice of whom to haunt? If the ghost has always been there, had it been waiting for someone sensitive with whom to make contact? Who knows? And instead of waxing philosophical, let's get further into the story.

Odd things continued to happen to Sue over the next several months. As they occurred, she couldn't discern whether they were playful or sinister. Mostly they were little things: the medicine cabinet door opening and all the items from the shelves lying in the sink, the dining room chairs suddenly found lined up against the wall. These mysterious events only happened to her. Since she had heard of nothing strange coming from the rest of the family, she remained silent about it all, not even mentioning it to Mike. That is, until the late night visitation while watching television.

> I had settled in for a movie on DVD. The kids were in bed, and Mike had turned in early because he'd put in a long day. This was supposed to be my time; I've always enjoyed watching movies late because there would be no interruptions. Besides, no one else in the family appreciates my kind of movies.

> I was being indulgent and had fixed myself a bowl of black cherry ice cream, a glass of milk, and a stack of cookies. I was about an hour into the movie when the power went out and everything shut off. This wasn't unusual; it seems we lose power quite a bit in this area. Anyway, the power was only out for a few seconds, and since I'd been watching in the dark, I knew it had come back on because the lights on the DVD were back on. I got up to turn on the television, and when I turned back around, I got the shock of my life. There was this woman sitting on the couch, right next to where I had been sitting. She was really old looking and had what looked like

open sores on her face. She was small, her feet didn't touch the floor, and her face was shrunken in. I just stood there staring at her for a few seconds. Then she turned her head toward me and hissed at me. I could actually smell the stink of her breath. Then, as quick as it happened, she was gone. That's when I totally freaked out and started thinking all kinds of things—not the least being had she been sitting next to me in the dark before the power went out? I was so scared I couldn't move. I just started shouting out for Mike.

It was that night Sue finally disclosed to her husband all the strange things that had been happening over the past several months. According to Sue, the two of them sat up most of the night, drinking coffee while she gave a full narrative of the weird events. Mike told her he trusted her enough to believe her but wondered why no one else had heard or seen anything. If he harbored any secret doubts about what his wife had revealed to him, they were put to rest not long after their conversation.

The kids were in bed one evening, and Sue had just purchased a jewelry armoire that needed to be assembled. Mike spent about fifteen minutes unpacking it and putting it together, and had placed it in the spot in the bedroom his wife had selected. She then spent an hour sorting her jewelry and putting it to rest in individual drawers and on side hangers.

Having finished arranging all her jewelry in her new piece of furniture, she dragged Mike into the bedroom to examine her handiwork. Then, they headed off into the kitchen for pie and coffee. Having finished their late snack, they headed off to bed, only to be stopped in their tracks midway through the living room. There, in plain sight in the bedroom doorway, stood the new jewelry armoire. Mike was visibly shaken, but Sue says she felt a tinge of relief. After all, she now had visible proof that something was amiss in their new home.

Mike did what most men do at a time like this. He looked for a way to explain it all away. He asked Sue if she had sneaked into the bedroom and moved it as a joke, which he knew was not true because he knew she hadn't left the kitchen. He examined the carpeting to see if the armoire had been dragged across the floor. It hadn't been. It was as though someone had carefully lifted it and then placed it in the doorway. Upon inspection, not a single piece of jewelry was missing or was out of place.

The incident put Mike on nervous alert, constantly waiting for something to happen in his presence while at the same time not wanting anything to happen. He needn't have worried as nothing odd has presented itself since that singular experience. That's not the case, however, with Sue. Her adventures continued.

It seems to slow down and then pick up again. After the jewelry incident, as we call it, nothing happened for a couple of months. Then one day I was putting groceries away when I heard a woman's voice say, "Not in there." It was just like someone was standing in the kitchen with me, the voice was that close. I stood real still for a minute, then started finishing up. That's when I heard it again, really clear, "Not in there." It was like the voice of someone who was disgusted.

I sat down and started to ask questions, like, "Who are you?" and "Why are you here?" that sort of thing, but I didn't get any answers.

At this point, Sue became a bit angry. Anger seems to be one of the stages folks go through when they have a ghost upsetting their domesticity. She went to her closet, retrieved a mini recorder, and returned to the kitchen.

Then she wrote out a set of questions for her angry spirit, turned the recorder on, and began asking away.

Listening to the recorder afterward, she found she received no answers to any of her questions. She did, however, pick up a woman's voice saying what sounded like, "Leave me alone." To Sue, the voice sounded like that of an older woman, but she admits her judgment may have been clouded by the remembrance of the old woman she had encountered back on movie night.

Now determined to take control of what was happening, Sue began her communication with me. After several phone conversations and a couple of visits, I convinced her that whoever was in her home was not some evil spirit from the bowels of perdition, but simply a human being. For some reason the ghost of this person had chosen to hang around after death. I made that assumption based upon all the things Sue had related to me over several conversations. I advised that she confront the person, and tell her to either leave the home or at least leave the family, and in particular her, alone.

Sue decided that the next time she felt the presence of this woman she would do as I suggested. One morning, when the lights began to dim and she found the contents of her silverware drawer spread across the kitchen floor, she took advantage of the situation. She called in a friend (that was good), and they broke out a Ouija board (that is never good). They claim they contacted the spirit in the house, and it identified itself as Anna. From the questions they asked, they claimed Anna had lived in the home for years and still considered it to be hers. They also said Anna indicated she was looking for her daughter. At any rate, after the ill-advised Ouija session, the two friends held hands, said a prayer, and then instructed the woman to leave her alone, that they didn't know where her daughter was, and that she should look for a bright light, that her daughter may be in that light.

Sue claims that the Ouija board and the prayers did the trick. I tend to believe that the confrontation could have had the same results without the board. At any rate, it's been nearly a year and nothing odd had taken place. No midnight hissing woman. No moving furniture. No voices amongst the groceries.

Late addition! While writing this narrative, I received a call from Sue. It seems the ghost may be back. She said that earlier that week, while taking a bath, she was lying back soaking in the suds when she heard what sounded like someone smacking the water. She said she opened her eyes to behold the water splashing at her feet, as though an unseen hand crashing down on it. It continued, she says, for over a minute and then stopped. Same ghost? Who knows.

Planning a Visit? Sorry, it's not possible. They don't want visitors and I don't break confidentiality.

Still Haunted? Sue was certain the haunting was over, but it seems she's not in full control of the situation. It sounds to me like the old hissing hag is back at it.

Chapter 14
The Historic Fort Wayne

Place Visited: As the title indicates, this place is officially known as the Historic Fort Wayne. No, we're not referring to Fort Wayne, Indiana. This is a military installation dating way back to the year 1843 when the first shovel load of dirt was turned upon the green grasses near the Detroit River for the construction of a defensive edifice. Construction continued from that time until its conclusion in 1851.

Period of Haunting: The paranormal activity dates back to at least 1900 and most likely predates that. Accounts of ghostly figures spiriting through the barracks, crossing the commons, and traversing the old halls of several buildings seem to have been handed down from one generation to the next. There's even a book about the fort, and inside is a photograph of a mystery soldier—someone who wasn't in the viewfinder when the photograph was snapped. What's interesting is that this photo was taken at least one hundred years ago.

Date of Investigation: Our investigation began in 2010, carried on with visits in 2011, and good Lord willing, will go on for many years to come. Our team made several visits to the gracious old fort during that period of time, and even when we didn't witness something paranormal, we always cherished with a sense of awe the history bulging at the seams of every structure on the grounds.

Description of Location: Nestled against the western shoreline of the Detroit River, the grounds cover some ninety-six acres. Its genesis came as the result of a war most of us have never heard of—the Patriot War of the late 1830s when the United States was fearful of a British invasion from the Canadian side of the river. Tensions had not yet simmered down since the colonists revolt in 1776, and those hot passions were further inflamed by the War of 1812. Border disputes after the Treaty of Ghent in 1815 inflamed sentiments once again. The British suspected we had designs on Canada, and the fledgling United States wanted Britain to give up control of part of North America then known as the Oregon Territory. At any rate, Congress decided to protect our young nation's western borders—Michigan, Ohio and Indiana—by constructing a series of forts out on the frontier. Fort Wayne was, of course, seen to be strategic, as it would sit on an advantageous bend in the Detroit River and could watch over suspect ships passing across the waters.

The fort was built in a star-shaped configuration, which basically means the fort jutted out in points around its perimeter, giving defenders ample views of the terrain and of any invading force. Entry into the fort was cleverly designed. The main gate sits today at the bottom of a small rise. Any force attacking that entry would find themselves caught between a grassy mound on their left, the high walls of the fort, replete with gunnery "windows" on their right, and a frightful set of cannon to their front. Such an approach would not be warfare, it would be suicide.

To this day to enter the fort one must traverse the original approach, pass through huge reinforced wooden doors, and then through a brick tunnel extending dozens of yards where it finally opens up into the fort proper. Inside the fort there were, at one time, several buildings, everything from latrines to barracks to officer quarters to name just a few. The barracks, a four story edifice where much of the ghostly activity seems to find its genesis, is the only remaining building inside the fort today. However, those strategic "star points" which I addressed earlier are still accessible, and one can wander through the winding corridors within the perimeter of the fort where defensive cannon were once placed and visit the gunpowder storage areas conveniently located underground to prevent any explosion from damaging the fort walls. These locations are wonderfully haunted as well, with many an unsuspecting visitor suddenly looking up into the face of someone who had lived in the fort decades, and even generations, past.

It is sadly surprising how many people still don't know that the Historic Fort Wayne exists in Detroit. They are further surprised when they learn that there were missiles with nuclear capability located there until around 1970. The government kept that information conveniently quiet. I have been aware of the fort's existence most of my life, as that is where I reported for my draft physical during the Vietnam War. Back in 2010, when I paid my first visit to the fort for a ghost hunt, I was not particularly grieved that the building in which that physical was conducted had been razed for a parking lot. After all, it had been a less-than pleasant experience for me back then.

Outside the fort, covering dozens of acres of land, are many of the buildings and homes that once housed military personnel and civilians alike. A great deal of training was carried out at the fort during the Mexican and Civil Wars, and Ulysses S. Grant was once stationed there, long before he became a lieutenant general in that brother-against-brother fiasco and then our president. In a storage room on the main floor of the barracks, there is a long section of a tree with at least three Confederate cannon balls embedded inside. It's chilling to imagine hundreds of those giant projectiles raining down upon infantry soldiers carrying single shot muskets. The fort was active throughout the Spanish American War,

World War I, World War II, Korea, and Vietnam. During World War 2, the entire grounds were a city unto itself and an important supply depot for our forces overseas. It also housed prisoners of war, mostly from Italy, and many of whom enjoyed the America they saw enough to stay once the war ended.

Fort Wayne, named for the famous general of the Revolutionary War, "Mad" Anthony Wayne, virtually reeks with history. It is, in fact, a historical gem. No longer owned by the federal government (although the Army Corps of Engineers still maintains residency in a building or two down by the river), the City of Detroit now reigns over its walls. With money being short, it depends heavily upon donations to the fort. This is where my friends the Metro Paranormal Society enter the picture.

With a passion for history, and in particular the history of Fort Wayne, the Metro Paranormal Society has been given permission to raise monies to help preserve and restore the old fort. They are involved in many special events throughout the year, everything from military re-enactments to boy scout outings to well-orchestrated ghost tours, at which they are quite adept. It can easily be said they are as much interested in restoration and preservation of the site as they are of the paranormal activity that permeates the place.

It was through my contact with the Metro Paranormal Society that I first became acquainted with the ghosts of the fort. They graciously invited me to bring my group of amateur ghost hunters to the fort for a tour and a ghost hunt of our own. While I'm always skeptical of ghost hunting societies and have placed little trust in most of them I've met throughout the years, this outfit proved to be the professional exception. They have invested thousands of dollars in their equipment and are darned particular about who they will admit into their organization. They are refreshing in that they never go into a purportedly haunted place without an open mind and a scientific approach. Whenever they experience something that may seem extraordinary, they try diligently to find a normal reason for its occurrence. They follow a rigid pattern of documentation and spend countless hours beneath headphones and in front of monitors reviewing audio and video. For these reasons and more, I trust this group implicitly. If you've got a ghost or two floating within or around your home or business, these are the guys to call.

One of the founding members of Metro Paranormal is an enthusiastic fellow named Chris. Chris has a passion for paranormal research and is fascinated with the fort. He spends more than just a few of his free weekends cutting grass, painting walls, and tending to whatever other tender loving care the edifice needs. He's had his share of encounters with the spirits of the fort throughout the years, as have all the members of his group. What I particularly liked about Chris and his gang was how, when our group visited, they didn't tell us their stories or try to influence our minds. They let us roam around the grounds and through the buildings to discover our own treats within. Only after our investigations did they fill us in on a few of their experiences and encounters, and they have some remarkable photographs and intriguing audio.

Wow, am I really rambling this much in giving a description of the place? Well, with the internet maps available to you, all I need to say is if you're familiar with Livernois Avenue, just follow it east until it dead ends at the front gate of the fort's compound. Upon entering, you must check in with the guard at the gate. They won't let just anyone in for a private ghost hunt. Ghost tours are regularly scheduled only through Metro Paranormal. Now, on to our story.

Haunt Meter * * * * *(lots of ghosts—lots of scares—no real malevolence)*

IT WAS AN ABSOLUTELY beautiful summer's evening when my gang and I arrived for the first of many visits to the Historic Fort Wayne. We checked in at the guard shack and were directed to the visitors center, where the pros of Metro Paranormal awaited us. After helping us unload our equipment, which must have brought a few smiles to their faces when compared to the heavy duty, high tech stuff they drag along with them, they took us inside the visitor center so we could get to know one another. That time together was followed by the spelling out of some rules for us to follow concerning how to treat the fort with respect and what places on the compound we could enter and which were off limits. Then they offered us a grand tour, replete with historical information that was fascinating and helpful. Afterward, we returned to the visitor center to grab our equipment and get started, confident in knowing they were going to be monitoring our movements and checking up on us regularly.

We passed through the sally port—the secure entryway I described in the opening paragraphs of this chapter—and into the tunnel leading into the fort proper. That tunnel is brick lined, and scratched into the walls are names of soldiers and the dates they served their country inside those walls. There were four of us, and we all decided we were feeling drawn to the barracks, that imposing structure where so much history bedded down long ago. The two women headed to the third floor while we two men decided to set up a watch on the second floor. Each floor, by the way, is composed of a myriad of rooms and corridors. There is no straight view from one end of the barracks to the other on any floor. That's because, although it is one structure, it was built to comprise five separate sections. Only later in its history were the walls pierced to allow access from one end of the barracks to the other.

After a few hours stationed within the barracks, our two teams of two went our separate ways once

Fort Wayne Barracks - perhaps the
most haunted place in the fort

again, this time into the bowels of the fort's perimeter
walls. Lined with brick and recessing deeply, they twist
and turn and expand into several small open areas.
Some of these housed cannons in the past, and the only
"windows" within were really not windows at all, but gun
ports. At the end of each recess would be the powder
room, where the extra ammunition would have been
kept. My buddy Glenn and I set up our video equipment
and ran our audio recorders as we sat quietly within
those walls trying to get used to the darkness of being
inside an area which, if it weren't haunted, sure as
shootin' ought to be (and it is).

We left early the next morning tiredly exhilarated.
We found nothing on video or audio and hadn't
experienced any overt paranormal events, but we were
convinced that with patience and a few return trips we
would eventually encounter something totally out of
the ordinary. Chris and the gang had spent the night

watching out for us and bid us a fond farewell, letting us know they would be in contact with us for a return visit really soon.

That next visit took place a scant month later and consisted of the four of us once again—Glenn, Claudia, Sarah, and myself (there are more of us associated with the group, but not everyone has a schedule amenable to particular opportunities). The girls returned to the barracks, equipped this time with blankets, beach chairs, and a few refreshments. We two boys headed outside the fort proper to one of the outbuildings, the old jailhouse. We snapped all kinds of photos, ran hours of video and audio, and made an effort to get comfortable with our surroundings. Every creak and moan of the building raced our hearts and pulsed adrenalin through our veins, but we knew that creaks and moans are, most of the time, just creaks and moans.

Around 2 a.m., we all decided to take a break and returned to the visitor center, which, as I have said, is where the Metro Paranormal gang hangs out all night whenever we're visiting. We chatted with our hosts, helped ourselves to some energy drinks, and then headed back for more, this time switching partners. Glenn tagged up with Claudia, and I headed off with Sarah.

The four of us again took up residence inside the barracks, which has several entrances in the front. Glenn and Claudia remained on the ground floor toward the middle this time, where a great many people have reported encounters with spirits.

Side note: The Fort has been host for years to Boy Scout outings on the grounds of the compound. Once, in inclement weather, the scout leaders asked if the boys—dozens of them—could take their sleeping bags into the barracks, since lightning was streaming through the sky. Given permission, they snuggled in for the night. In the morning, when the Metro Paranormal gang went to see how they were doing, they were no longer inside. They had gone back out, where many of them had taken up refuge in cars and trucks. It seems too many of the boys, and a couple of the adults, had encountered images and sounds for which no merit badges are awarded.

Sarah and I trod on up to the second floor, setting up camp at the far west end of the barracks. We set up our beach chairs within a large room boasting a mural on the end wall depicting soldiers being attacked by Indians. We aimed our cameras at the doorway leading out into a long hallway which entered into another large room. Off the hallway on the right-hand side there is a stairway leading down to the ground floor and up to the third and fourth levels. We then placed our digital audio recorders just outside our doorway. Our position left us about twelve feet from where the recorders lay. Then we played the quiet, patient waiting game which is necessary in any ghost hunt.

At precisely 3:30 a.m. by my lime green glow-in-the-dark Seiko, we heard the footsteps of several people approaching us from the darkened hallway. In this particular situation, we kept quiet and still, and naturally assumed it to be members of our team checking up with us, even though we knew they were to remain where they were for another half hour. As it turned out, it wasn't Glenn and Claudia. Not by a long shot. The footsteps became louder as they neared our position, and we could easily tell there were more than two sets of them scuffing across the floorboards. Then we heard the muffled voices of several men, all speaking at once and in rising tones, until one voice let out the command to "secure the door," that "they are approaching," and another voice veritably boomed out the response, "closing the door" in the respectful tone a soldier would use when replying to a direct order. Then we heard the door to the stairway slam shut, which was interesting because from where we were sitting we could easily see that door and it was already firmly closed.

Barracks View Two — The far right window is
where the Bogle members encountered spirits

Sarah and I sprung up from our position and raced to the doorway only to find no one there. Not two minutes later, Glenn and Claudia came up the stairway, and members of the Metro Paranormal team approached from another area of the building.

It was obvious to Sarah and I that the ghosts of some soldiers had seen my team members and hosts approaching from below and had responded appropriately and protectively. I have since kept these audio recordings on several different formats and play them regularly to remind me there is more to this existence of ours than meets the eye. I cannot tell you how pumped up one can get after an experience such as this.

The Historic Fort Wayne is full of ghostly activity, as are the grounds outside the walls. Chris, one of our hosts, tells of how he and other members of their group were engaged one afternoon cleaning up within the

Room within the barracks where voices
are heard and spirits are seen

barracks after a day of conducting tours. They happened
to be on the second floor, west end of the building, the
same location where we encountered the footsteps and
the voices. They all suddenly heard footfalls treading
across the wooden floor and moving toward them. The
footsteps picked up speed until they were in a full out
running mode, loud and angry. Feeling as though he
was going to be run over, Chris jumped to one side, but
not before he felt a rush of energy pass through and past
him. He says it was one of the most vivid encounters
he's ever had within the barracks, and one that several
others witnessed.

In another instance, Chris told of how one of his
members was headed across the commons. She was
going from the barracks to the sally port on the way to
the visitor center. It was well after midnight, and the
lights of both Detroit and Windsor, Canada, backlit the
fortress walls to the north and the east. In the northeast

corner of the fort, there is a small rise and a path leading up to the flagpole. She stood mesmerized out on the lawn as a soldier traversed the perimeter of one wall and then move up the rise to the flagpole, where he stood for several minutes before melting away into the mist rising off the river. From what I understand, she is not the only person to have witnessed this lone soldier walking his rounds during guard duty.

Perhaps the most intriguing incident related to me was the story of an encounter with the soldier inside one of the recessed rooms of the fort. The Metro Paranormal folks were engaged in cleaning up the place, and it was broad daylight. (The ghosts here don't give a hoot what time of day it is. When they want to show up, they'll do so on their own terms.) They have a habit of taking photos as they move through the fort, and they were snapping away as they headed toward one of the cannon sites. One photo clearly shows a man standing off to the side, although no one was there and he wasn't seen by human eyes. Using their contacts with professionals, the photo was analyzed and determined to be authentic. Furthermore, it appears the man is wearing a uniform possibly dating back to the Civil War.

I had hoped to include the photo in this chapter, but ownership of the picture is disputed by a former member, and I didn't wish to get involved in any possible legal ramifications.

It's not only my group or the Metro folks who have run into spirits at the fort. As I said earlier, ghost tours are regularly conducted, and there have been many times when guests have reported ghostly figures showing up among them. Anomalies seem to appear on the photos of many guests, and there are those who have been sufficiently frightened as to resolve not to return. One such person I shall call Tyrone.

Tyrone was not a guest visitor but a security guard at the fort for a couple of years. His shift was the midnight shift, the one this author would enjoy the most, but which Tyrone held in utter disdain. Although only working there until he could earn enough money to get through his college courses, he couldn't wait to graduate so he could bid the old bastion of defense farewell.

During one of my visits, I spent some time with Tyrone. That midnight shift can be rather boring just driving around the compound checking out the abandoned houses, the administration buildings, and the interior of the star fort itself. During our time together, he made it clear he didn't wish to hear my stories. He feared it would color his approach to how he conducted his job. But he had some stories of his own.

Tyrone explained how, one lonely night in mid-summer, he radioed to a co-worker that he was taking his break, which meant he would be eating his lunch around 3 a.m. in the visitor center just outside the sally port entry to the star fort. He settled in, unwrapped his sandwich, and was munching away when he said he saw a soldier walk past the window which looks out at the fort proper. He stood up to go to the door and see if the man needed anything when he remembered there were no soldiers stationed at the fort. Furthermore, he realized it wasn't physically possible to see anyone, soldier or civilian, from the waist up through those windows, as ground level was well below the window and would have made it impossible. He said he determined then and there to either no longer take his break in that building or to do so only when in the company of another employee.

Another time, while making his rounds in a blanket of darkness, he spotted a light inside one of the officer homes out on the compound. Using his keys, he entered the building, switched off the light, and headed back out to his security car. About the time he fired up the engine, he noticed the light was back on. He said he wasn't sure he wanted to go back in there, but he grabbed his flashlight and slowly crept toward the

Fort Wayne Gymnasium where voices and
ghostly basketball games take place

empty house, certain something strange was going on.
Just as he got to the front porch, the light went out, and
as he shined his flashlight into the house, he caught
the image of a man passing through an interior room.
At that point, he decided he was *not* going inside to
check things out and continued his rounds. It had been
snowing, and he could find no tracks leading toward or
away from the house.

The last tale Tyrone spun concerned that visitor
center once again. He had gone there to eat his lunch—
this time in the company of a fellow employee—and they
both retrieved their food from the refrigerator in the
kitchen of the center when his buddy decided he needed
to use the restroom. Tyrone said that his friend hadn't
been gone for a minute when he began to hear shouting
coming from the gymnasium. (The visitor center and
gymnasium share the same building.) He said it sounded

like a basketball game was going on, but he was certain there was no one else in the compound. When his friend returned, he asked him if he had heard the voices and was surprised to receive a negative response, especially in light of the fact that the restrooms were closer to the gymnasium than the visitor center area.

That gymnasium area is one of the haunted hot spots of the fort. More than one person has stood at the entryway of the gym and listened to men talking across the floor and over by the doors leading down to the basement. A couple of people claim to have actually seen men standing over in that same corner of the gym talking to one another. If that isn't enough, several people have told of encountering ghostly images and voices inside the men's room just off the gym. They also tell of being alone in the building and listening to toilets flush or hearing the water running in the sinks.

On our most recent visit to the Historic Fort Wayne, I brought along several members of my team. We followed our rules of staying in teams of two and stationing ourselves in particular areas for a pre-designated period of time. We had a team in the visitor center gymnasium, a team in the old jail, two teams inside the barracks building, and one team tucked deep within the recesses of the gunpowder room, which gives a new definition to darkness and loneliness, even when someone is with you.

At about 2 a.m., I had to answer the call of nature. At the time, I was on the second floor of the antiquated barracks building, and the restroom I needed was outside the fort and inside the visitor center. It's absolutely amazing how the need to relieve oneself overcomes the fear of traversing across the grounds of a haunted fort all alone and under the cover of darkness.

I walked out of the barracks and began my trek across the open grounds of the fort proper when I realized I had forgotten about a nice, modern restroom on the ground floor of the barracks. In fact, I had

Sally Port entrance

passed within a few feet of it while exiting the building. I spun around and returned to the building only to find myself locked out. At least two entry doors to the barracks had been kept unlocked for our group that night, and this had been one of them. We had been in and out of those doors all night, but I couldn't get the door opened, so I headed down to the next door, only to find it locked as well. The same was true of every entry door to the barracks.

By now, my bladder took over control of my countenance, and I decided to head on over to the visitor center, realizing I would have to pass through the long, dark tunnel to reach the sally port entrance. I took my LED flashlight from my vest pocket (we ghost hunters often wear official jackets and such with all sorts of pockets for all sorts of gadgets—it makes us feel superior to the ghosts), switched it on, and walked across the commons.

I entered the tunnel, flashlight brightly illuminating my way, and was about halfway through when my flashlight inexplicably went out. I froze in place, then flipped the switch on and off in an effort to get it to light my way once again, but to no avail. I was immersed in total blackness. I then retreated back toward the mouth of the tunnel until I was once again inside the fort commons. That's when my flashlight came back on all by itself. What did I do then? I told myself the flashlight, which had never given me a moment of trial and tribulation, must have a defect, so I practiced turning it off and on, and then shaking it vigorously to see if that could affect its performance. It worked perfectly.

I headed back to the lonely and foreboding tunnel, my way brightly alive under the light I held in my hand, and as I approached the half way distance, the light once again went out. This time, logic gave way to thoughts of a more paranormal nature, and I turned and made a hasty exit back into the fort, bladder sloshing around like the nearby Detroit River. So, I sneaked across the commons and over to the side of the barracks building where, many moons ago, there was once a latrine. That became the most appropriate place I could justify sating my bladder's demand to be dealt with.

Having found my relief, I walked back to the far west entry door of the barracks, wishing to rejoin my partner on the second floor. But how was I to get back in? After a moment's thought, I decided to pound on the door with a heavy fist and hope that I could be heard all the way up on the second floor. As my fist came down for the first time against the wooden door, it simply and easily swung open.

The Historic Fort Wayne is a ghost hunter's dream come true. The paranormal activity simply abounds there, but that's because the history of the place is so rich and important. It is a place which cries out to be restored and lovingly cared for. It is a sacred place for many who passed through its grounds over the last

Fort Wayne - Sally Port Tunnel - where
my flashlight refused to work

almost two centuries. It is a place where history comes alive, both figuratively and literally. To stand on the grounds and pass through its buildings is to stand in absolute awe of the place.

Planning a Visit? Please do. Go to the website for the Historic Fort Wayne and check out the activities taking place—re-enactments, history lectures, presentations, and even ghost tours. Then make a determination to support the site with your return visits and your monetary gifts. This place must be preserved, and in these difficult economic times, it is too often neglected by the big money folks.

Still Haunted? Absolutely. And if you wish to know more about the ghostly activities, go to the website of the Metro Paranormal folks. If you have a haunting taking place in your home or business, these are the

Inside perimeter walls of Fort Wayne

most trusted and professional team of paranormal investigators I have ever encountered. They will travel the state, and sometimes beyond, to help people understand what may or may not be taking place in their midst. They are low key, high tech, and very respectful.

Chapter 15
Salvation Army Spooks

Place Visited: The old, and now closed and vacant, Salvation Army building in downtown Detroit.

Period of Haunting: Unknown

Date of Investigation: No real investigation has taken place by anyone on our team. However, one member of our team visited this defunct Salvation Army building as part of a college course in architecture, and this brief tale recounts her rather frightening experience within. Her visit was in late winter of 2010.

Description of Location: The vacant and rather large building that once housed the Salvation Army and its services in downtown Detroit. The empty edifice (except for the many homeless who still find their way in for shelter against the elements) is three stories high and is located across from the MGM Grand Casino on 3rd Street. It's a rather rundown structure, both outside and inside, and rather cavernous in places. It sports a large kitchen, an auditorium with stage, rooms that once served the homeless and destitute, as well as many administrative offices. Although the nearby casino is lavish, this is not the nicest area one should wander into alone, and such activity is not encouraged.

Haunt Meter: * * *(My colleague was sincerely frightened, but she does scare easily)*

CHRISTINA (her real name, even though some of my team members request to not be identified) has recently finished her academic training as an architect. While in school at Wayne State University, one of her assignments was to visit the old, and rather historic, Salvation Army building. Detroit, for all its shortcomings and negative reputation, is home to many historic buildings, and it's a shame to let them slip into disrepair.

The day was cold, as this was Christina's winter semester, and she was in the company of several other classmates. Arrangements had been made for them to tour the building where they were to make observations about the design of the structure and do a report on their findings. Naturally, they all took along their digital cameras to record reference points. Since the story is brief, I'll let Christina tell it:

We car-pooled from the university over to the building, which isn't really in the best side of town. It was cold outside, but not real bad, one of those days when a winter coat could be too warm but a light jacket wouldn't be warm enough. Our instructor met us there; we gathered up our notebooks and cameras and followed him inside. We were told not to split up because they didn't want anyone getting hurt and they couldn't be sure if some homeless people were hiding out in the building.

The entrance is really pretty cool. It's wide, and there's a message carved into an inside overhang with a scripture passage. The first thing we did was go down into the gymnasium where the stage is. In the old days when this served the community, they would hold plays, feed the hungry, and conduct worship services there. I was the first one down and into the gym, and I started taking some photos of it. I'd take a shot, look at it, then take another. I repeated the process for several shots; then all of a sudden on one

Detroit Salvation Army - white ghostly spirit

shot there was this huge misty figure floating in front of the stage. Nobody was smoking, and it wasn't cold enough in there to see your breath, but there it was, plain as day. Since I wasn't expecting it, I really got freaked out. I showed it to one of my girlfriends, announced I had taken enough pictures and got out of there real quick. I mean, it's shaped like a person who's trying to take form.

I showed the picture to a couple more people in the class, and they were as freaked out as I was. One guy thought it was cool and went down a second time, all by himself, to try to see if he could catch it on his camera, but it didn't work out for him. I had decided to hang out a little closer with a couple friends and make sure I wasn't the first one into any more rooms.

We did the whole tour of the place, and it was pretty impressive. You hate to see a nice facility not being used. Anyway, we had gone from room to room, taking notes and taking photos. Nothing else strange seemed to happen until we started to go into a couple of the old offices. Our instructor told us that these were the spots where the homeless and transients would hang out whenever they broke into the place, so it was kind of freaky. Well, at a couple of these old offices we noticed a thick line of some white, grainy powder on the floor, running from one side of the doorway to the other. At first we didn't know what it was, but just outside one of the doors there was a container of Morton's salt, and that's what it was. At the time, I thought it was a pretty nutty thing for someone to do, but I really didn't give it much thought. We just finished up our tour and went back to class.

If Christina was freaked out by the image she caught on her digital camera, and which is provided herein for you to enjoy, she was freaked a little further when she was informed by another member of our group that salt across the doorway of a room was meant to keep out evil spirits. Evidently, those homeless folks were encountering a little more than they had expected during their hunt for shelter from the cold and the elements.

I tried to make contact with the Salvation Army folks in the area hoping to arrange an investigation of the place. I was advised against it, as they said they didn't wish to be held legally responsible should anyone get hurt. Besides that, they told me it just wasn't a safe place visit at night. I should have realized that for myself before bothering them with such a silly request.

Salt across the doorway

Planning a Visit? Don't bother even considering it. It's not safe, and you would be trespassing.

Still Haunted? Well, people don't spread salt across doorways for the fun of it.

Chapter 16
Who's That Peeking Around the Corner?

Place Visited: A two story, wood frame house nestled amongst others of like kind, within the village of Mancelona. The owners have asked for anonymity, and that must be honored. There are plenty of other places within this tome for you, my dear reader, to check out for yourself. After all, if your home were haunted, would you want everyone and their pet ravens tap, tap, tapping on your windowpane?

Period of Haunting: According to the family hierarchy, it's been going on for at least a couple of decades. They suspect it predates their ownership as well.

Date of Investigation: Late spring of 2010.

Description of Location: Mancelona is by all means a typical "northern" Michigan town. Why do I put the word northern within quotation marks? To the bulk of Michigan's population, which resides in the southern part of the state, that area looks and feels like "up north." For those of us who have spent a few years living in the Upper Peninsula, we know you have to cross a pretty substantial bridge before you are truly "up north," which would make Mancelona a town in "mid" Michigan, but I digress.

The state organized the township of Mancelona in 1871. Among the first settlers was a farmer who was, as all fathers ought to be, dedicated to his beautiful young daughter he had named Mancelona. Now, that's not a name you hear very often, but there really was a Mancelona; her last name was Andress, and from her photograph as a young woman she must have turned a lot of farmer's heads in her day.

Mancelona—the village and township—became an important stop for the old Grand Rapids and Indiana Railroad in its day. One of the early claims to fame for the village was its pickle factory. The village thrived for a while in its early existence, then suffered for several years as a couple of its main job providers—lumbering and metal working—petered out. Today, it's a very pleasant little place to live, and there's a lot about the place to appeal to vacationers. In fact, the outdoors is a big draw for the community. The Chamber of Commerce has a website showing several photos of hearty outdoorsmen all dressed in bright orange and bent down on one knee holding up the lifeless head of a nice sized buck. Why? The community's big event of the year is the "buck pole," wherein hunters from all over the state compete to see who gunned down the biggest buck. During more mild weather there's the Bass Festival, complete with parade and other fishy activities.

There are nearly 1,500 living souls within the village, and most likely any number of disembodied entities floating around as well. If you're interested in visiting the place, make sure your visit includes a stop at Shirley's Restaurant for breakfast. That's my favorite restaurant meal of the day, and I wasn't disappointed. Be advised that I can't be responsible for how you enjoy your lunch or supper since I was out of town by then.

Haunt Meter * * * ½

CASEY YOUNGSON (don't bother doing a search of her name, I made it up) resided in the home in the 1970s when she was a young mother. Two of her children were born while she lived there, and she experienced the pain of divorce. For a while she ended up trying to support her kids as a single parent.

Casey had contacted me a few years back after reading my first book about haunted places in Michigan. After having chatted with her after one of my lectures, she convinced me of her sanity, provided me with references to support her stories, and even offered to put me in touch with the current residents of the house. (I almost never make an initial contact when I hear about a haunted place and find ways for the residents to contact me instead.)

Casey indicated that nothing really happened in the home after she had first moved in. It wasn't until the birth of her second child that she began to notice strange incidents. They didn't start out slowly but with a veritable bang. It seems she had been frustrated most of the day because her newborn had been, in the ancient parlance of the old folks, "colicky" most of the day. Having finally coaxed her to sleep, she set the child down in her crib and retreated to the kitchen for a cup of much needed coffee.

Just as she had gotten into the enjoyment of her brew, a cold chill wrapped around her for a few seconds although it was a rather balmy summer's eve. Casey didn't think much of it and passed it off as being worn out from the stress of the day. Then, just a few seconds later, she heard a loud crash as though someone had tipped over a huge piece of furniture in the baby's room. She ran out of the kitchen, through the living room, and into the baby's room only to find everything in perfect order and her daughter sleeping peacefully. She had been certain the noise had come from her room, but just in case, she visited all the other rooms in the house, and they were fine as well. Then she exited the house to see if something had fallen on the roof and to look for any construction going on down the street that could explain what she had heard. Again, everything checked out as being normal.

Puzzled, Casey went back inside feeling somewhat relieved. Being a good mother, she went directly to her daughter's room to check on her once again. She stood in the doorway stunned. There in front of her, lying face down on the carpet, was the baby's dresser. Scattered across the floor were all the baby items that had been placed atop it—diapers, creams and ointments and other things necessary to caring for a newborn. Still, the child slept blissfully on.

Author's thought—could this have somehow been a reverse phenomenon, with the sound of the crash preceding the falling of the dresser? But that wouldn't explain the still sleeping child.

To say the least, Casey found the entire incident much more than simply a little unsettling. Thinking no one would buy her story, and trying desperately to convince herself she must be suffering from some sort of post-partum influence, she managed to tuck the weirdness away within the recesses of her mind. Sometimes a little denial can be a protective friend.

A couple of weeks later, Casey was engaged in housework after having sent her oldest daughter off to kindergarten. She put her youngest daughter down for a nap and started cleaning. Having finished up the living room, she decided to tidy up the kitchen. In a telephone conversation, Casey filled me in on her encounter.

I went into the kitchen to do the dishes, and the phone rang. I answered it, and no one was there. Just as I hung it up, there was another one of those loud crashes—only this time coming from the basement. I ran over to the stairs and turned to go down when I saw, just for a quick second or two, a man standing in the darkness at the bottom of the stairs looking up at me. I could only see half of him because it looked like he was peeking around the side of the open stairway. He was an older man, and he looked skinny. That's all I can remember about him, because he

suddenly seemed to slide off to the side and
was gone. There was no way in holy hell I
was going down there. I ran to the phone and
dialed 911, and then went to the baby's room,
grabbed her out of her crib, and went outside
to wait for the police. They checked the house
inside and out and found absolutely nothing.
There wasn't a trace of this guy anywhere. I'm
sure they would have thought I was crazy if
they hadn't found our chest freezer tipped
over on its side. We had recently bought half
a steer, and they knew there was no way I
could have tipped it over by myself. They were
nice enough to help me set it back up and
even checked back with me later that evening
to see if everything was all right.

The next year and a half was stressful for Casey,
as she and her husband went through a rather testy
divorce. Little things would happen now and then, such
as a piece of furniture being moved out of place or a
door slamming shut. Other than things of that nature
her emotions were spent from the stress of the breakup
of her marriage. As a result of the divorce decree, she
got the house and custody of the children. Then she
began building a new life for herself and her daughters.

About the time her youngest daughter entered
her terrible twos, Casey says the strange activities
escalated. For instance, there was what she calls "the
babysitter incident." It seems Casey's friends convinced
her to get out of the house and blow off a little steam.
They knew a college student who they had often used as
a babysitter for their children. She was engaged for the
evening to watch over Casey's little ones while Casey
and her friends went out for dinner and drinks.

The young women were having a good time, and
Casey was able to start relaxing a little. They finished
their meal and drove over to the tavern for what they

intended to be an extended nightcap. No sooner had they entered the bar when the server on duty, who knew them all, told Casey she had to call home; her babysitter sounded upset and wanted to talk to her.

Casey used the phone behind the bar and got her babysitter on the line. The first thing Casey asked about was, of course, her children. Having been assured they were just fine, she was then filled in on the situation. The little one had been put to bed, and the sitter had been coloring with the oldest child when she heard a loud crash that sounded like it came from the basement. Feeling responsible, she had gone into the basement to inspect but had found everything down there in order. When she came back up and returned to the living room where they had been coloring, she noticed the huge mirror that had been on the wall behind the sofa was now sitting atop the sofa. When she asked the little girl what had happened, she very nonchalantly said, "Oh, the man did that."

Casey decided to forego the margaritas and return home. She inspected the wall, and nothing was amiss. The hangers were still securely attached to the wall, and there were no scratches on the drywall from it having fallen. It had to be raised up off the hangers, moved several inches over the top of the sofa, and set carefully down to have been in that location. It didn't help matters when her daughter once again said, "The man did that."

Casey paid the sitter for her time, even though she had volunteered to remain on the job and had encouraged her to go back out with her friends and enjoy her evening. It seems she had become intrigued by the idea of a ghost wafting around the place and was interested in making his or her acquaintance. Nonetheless, Casey stayed home, more than a little concerned that her daughter had mentioned an unseen man.

The next day was a quiet Sunday, and Casey decided to bake some cookies and have a little chat with

her daughter about the man she had seen. Since she
had been so matter-of-fact about him, Casey asked if
she had ever seen him before and she answered "lots
of times." Gently prodded a little further, she told her
mother that he had always been there, and usually just
stood around and watched. Intrigued, Casey asked her
little one what else the man does, and she said that
lots of times he stands behind her—meaning behind
her mother—and watches her. Other times he gets mad
and knocks things over. She asked her daughter if she's
ever afraid of him, and she gave a convincing "no" as
her answer. She said he's nice, and when she goes to
bed, he comes in and says good night to her.

It's at this point in our story where I want to pause
to make an observation. It seems that our little ones
are prone to experiencing the paranormal as though it
is perfectly normal. I've often postulated that perhaps
their innocent minds are wide open (as our adult minds
had once been), and have not yet been polluted with all
the admonishments we impose upon them. How often
have we heard our children speak of—or to—a playmate
that we deem to be invisible? Don't we just assume it's
all made up? And when they speak to us of ghosts, we
jump right into their malleable minds and convince
them that there's no such thing. Pretty soon, we've shut
down their conduit to the "other side" altogether, or at
least pulled down the shade quite a bit.

Not long after the cookie conversation, Casey
decided to find new digs. She listed the home with a
realtor, who rented it out for her while it was up for
sale. Casey and her children moved to an apartment
in another part of the village. After a few months, the
home sold, and Casey was breathing easier for having
vacated her previous premises—for a while.

Several years passed, and Casey's girls grew
up, as children are wont to do. Casey remarried and
settled in to her new husband's home. She never gave
much thought to the old haunted abode until she had

a conversation with a cousin at a family reunion and learned that her cousin, a man I shall refer to as Leon, indicated that he had bought a house in the village of Mancelona and had gotten what he called "a killer deal" on the place. It turned out to be the same house she had deserted years earlier.

Casey kept her mouth shut about the haunting, told Leon she had once lived there, and wished him all the happiness he could handle. Then she neatly tucked away all her memories of the place and returned to her normal life—but not for long.

A few months after her conversation with Leon at the family reunion, she received a text message from him asking if she could meet him at a local restaurant for coffee. She thought it odd that he had contacted her in such a manner instead of making a phone call, but she sent a text back setting up the time.

At first they chatted about the extended family and exchanged the usual pleasantries. Then Leon got right down to business. He wanted to know if Casey had ever experienced anything strange in the house when she had lived there. She knew there was no reason to be coy about it, so she confessed that, yes, there had been some hairy things going on during her tenure. It was a kind thing to admit to, because it gave Leon a chance to relate his experiences with a sense of ease he was afraid he wouldn't otherwise have had.

As the coffee cups were filled and refilled, Leon related how, not long after he had moved into the home, he and his wife had gone to bed one night. They were both worn out, as they each had full time jobs and had just finished the added tasks associated with moving into a new home. His wife, Lannie, had, as usual, fallen asleep almost immediately. Being of a different genetic makeup, Leon had lain awake for nearly half an hour, waiting for the craggy fingers of exhaustion to pull him into restful unconsciousness.

As he was finally drifting off, he said his drooping eyelids flew upward when he noticed movement at the bedroom door. There, standing full in the doorway, was the black form of a man. Leon's reaction? He told his cousin he grabbed the water glass off the bedside table and threw it. He was astonished that it should have been a direct hit but instead went straight through the guy and into the living room, the breaking glass and quick movement awakening his wife and causing the interloper to simply disappear. His wife's reaction was to assure Leon that he had probably been asleep and had been reacting to a dream. He agreed with her but only because he didn't want to frighten her.

Having an attentive listener who could relate to his experiences, Leon continued his tales of ghostly intrigue. He informed Casey it was not long after that experience that he had been alone in the house while Lannie was out grocery shopping. He had promised to hang family photos while she was gone, and had been sorting through them when he found a large photo of his mother in law. He thought it would be nice if he put it in an obvious place where his wife would be pleased and his mother in law may be inclined to offer him some much needed brownie points.

Leon hung the photo on the longest wall of the living room then returned to his task of hanging the others. He said he wasn't a minute into the job when the photo of his mother in law lifted up off the wall and passed several feet through the air, finally coming to rest on a chair with no damage whatsoever. He quietly indicated to his cousin that it was the strangest moment in his entire life—up to that point.

As he spoke, Leon also went on about the time his wife was in the bedroom getting dressed to go out to dinner with him when they heard a raging crash down in the basement. Leon told of how he went down to see what was up, and nothing was amiss. He then returned to the bedroom and announced that nothing was out of place, and they made ready to head out to dinner. They headed toward the back door, which meant they had to pass by the basement stairs. His loving wife said something like, "I thought you said nothing happened down there," and when he looked down the stairs, an old wooden bookcase they used for storing odds and ends was lying at the bottom of the stairs, the contents of the shelves spewed all over the floor.

That's when he decided he needed to confess the things he had been experiencing. It made interesting dinner conversation.

Leon is a middle-aged man with more than enough tough life experiences behind him. He wasn't about to let a wayward spirit get the upper hand within his own home. The first thing he decided to do was to show no fear. For instance, once he was down in the basement putting a new screen on his storm door as spring was approaching. It was late in the evening, since this was a project he had saved for after work. He was well into his task when he says he got the creepy feeling he was being watched. Without turning his head, he glanced over to the side and could make out the figure of a man standing about fifteen feet away, watching him. "I just kept on working as normal," says Leon, "and kept glancing over at him."

The dark, thin man stood there several minutes until Leon said he had put up with enough and turned around to face him eyeball to eyeball. He said the man stared at him a few seconds then turned to go up the stairs and simply melted away.

Leon is a brave man, and while Leon's wife is usually brave, she knows how to scream when she runs smack up against the unexpected. That's what happened one night when she was getting ready for bed. She had taken her shower, wrapped herself in a towel, and then stood at the sink in front of the mirror to blow dry her hair. Those tasks accomplished, she swung open the bathroom door and came nose length away from the man of skin and bones. "I know I screamed," she says, "but I really don't even remember doing it, I was that shocked." Her piercing voice brought Leon running to the rescue only to find his wife standing in the bathroom doorway with the towel at her feet and shaking all over. She then instructed her husband to turn on just about every light in the house, and they sat in the living room drinking beer until she had the courage to finally go to bed.

Lannie had gotten a good look at the guy. She described him as about two inches taller than herself, which would make him about 5' 9", and that his face was thin to the point of looking emaciated. His eyes were dark, and there was white stubble on his cheeks and chin. She must have made an impression upon him, because he showed up again at a most inopportune moment.

Once again it happened in the bathroom. I don't know what this guy's attachment is to the bathroom, but that's where I've run into him up close and too damned personal both times I saw him. This time I was taking a bath. It was a Sunday night, and Leon and I had worked all weekend out in the yard and were worn out. I decided to soak myself in a warm tub and lit some candles and put on some music.

I remember I was lying back in the warm water with a wet washcloth over my eyes, just chilling out, and I was very relaxed. The room was humid because I like to soak in hot water, but in an instant it got icy cold. It was so cold it actually shocked me, and I pulled the washcloth off my face. Well, there he was, standing by the sink looking down at me. It wasn't that he was simply standing there oblivious to me; he was looking right at me. This time I went hysterical, screaming at him and splashing water around. He actually backed up a step away from me, and then faded away. That was it, I decided it was time we got the hell out of that house.

Women can be very persuasive at times, and for Lannie, this was one of those times. She made Leon take her to her mother's house and informed him that either the ghost had to go or they were going to sell the place. Since they had a lot invested in the place, Leon did a bit of internet researching, and contacted a professional psychic from Traverse City.

The psychic (I'm not giving his name, since I don't know the guy and can't vouch for him) first interviewed both Leon and Lannie at a local restaurant and then asked to visit the house. At first Lannie was afraid to go along for the psychic investigation but eventually relented and tagged along, staying close to her husband the whole time for fear of what the psychic might conjure up.

After doing a walkthrough of the home and pausing in two places to meditate, the bathroom and the basement, he sat the couple down and filled them in on what he had tapped into. To their surprise, the skinny old ghost had never lived in the house but was drawn to the place years past by the energy of a little girl who had lived there. Once in the house, he felt he could contact the little girl, which he had done on many occasions. That family had moved away, but the man had stayed, feeling as though it was now a safe place for him to be. He longed to make contact with the occupants, and the psychic said he had many times made the attempt. When he couldn't get their attention, he would move things, and if that didn't work, he would knock things over.

The psychic went on to say that the old man was harmless and never meant to frighten anyone. That's a hard line to buy when you're a woman taking a bath and he comes calling on you, but it's the psychic's story and he's obviously sticking to it. He further said that the old boy had been married for years, and it had been a very unhappy union. He had been dominated by his wife, who could be overbearing and often mistreated him. She had at one time told him that in the next life she never wanted to see him again. She had died first, then he had his ticket punched for the long ride to Paducahville, and took her at her word. He didn't want to be where she was. Hence, he had taken up residence where he hoped he could find some sort of human companionship.

I don't know about you, dear reader, but that story sounds like a bunch of bunk meant to bilk Leon and Lannie out of a few dollars. However, they said their psychic performed some sort of candle ritual, went into a trance, and later informed them that he had convinced the gaunt apparition to float away to another abode. It must have worked to some extent, because in the last year or so he hasn't been seen, and only once in a blue moon do they sense he's around. Maybe he's just laying low for a while, not wanting to cross paths with that psychic fellow again.

Planning a Visit? You can't, you don't know where it is, and my lips are sealed.

Still Haunted? Yes, both Lannie and Leon insist the old goat is still flitting around the place, and once in a while will bang on something or move an object or two.

Chapter 17
An Old Fashioned Haunting

Place Visited: A two story frame farmhouse somewhere near the Village of Caledonia.

Period of Haunting: There's really no way to tell, but it seems to date back at least to the 1930s and probably well before that. There's no ending date to the haunting, as it continues on and on, up front and personal.

Description of Location: Caledonia is a small village of about 1,100 people within Kent County and not far from Grand Rapids, where a lot of folk in the area find employment. It was settled in the earlier half of the nineteenth century, when newly established settlements attracted both tavern keeper and preacher. Often it was a race to see who got there first. If the tavern keeper was first, then a tavern was constructed and a tone set for the community. If the preacher preceded him, then a church was built and the tavern keeper was discouraged from setting up shop. In this instance, it appears the tavern keeper won, but in the long run it seems religion came out on top. The area is peppered with places of worship ranging from Catholic edifices to Pentecostal churches, and just about everything in between. After all, this area is the Bible Belt of Michigan.

This portion of Kent County is quite picturesque; the landscape covered with farmland. The community of Caledonia sports an old fashioned attitude toward community life. In the summer they have an event they call "Western Days" which last for the better part of a week, and in the autumn they entertain folks with a Harvest Festival. It doesn't get much folksier than that.

Haunt Meter: * * * * * *(This is one hell of a haunted house.)*

Be advised I shall refer to the couple who, up until very recently, lived in this house as Sid and Mae. They have children, and all members of the family were quite aware of the ghosts sharing their residence. Both Sid and Mae are highly educated people and are professionals in their respective fields. For this reason, and for the protection of their children from folks who can be derisive or downright nosy, names have been changed, and the address not given.

SID AND MAE PURCHASED the home several years back, as they were impressed with the structure itself as well as its very rural location. It wasn't long after they had moved in before Mae and the kids began to notice strange things taking place. At first it was the usual cornucopia of paranormal phenomena—doors that had been locked were found opened, lights would mysteriously go on and off all by themselves, and footsteps could be heard from time to time shuffling across the upstairs floor. These are all occurrences that are easy to dismiss by chalking things up to normal possibilities, and that's what they did at first. Very soon, however, the activity escalated well beyond anything normal.

The first "in your face" moment was experienced by Mae one fall day when her children were in school. It was mid-morning, and she was busy in the kitchen with her chores when she noticed a man standing outside her kitchen window between the driveway and the house. He was just standing there, staring through the kitchen window at her. Since Mae didn't see a car in the drive, she figured it must be a neighbor who walked down to the house for one reason or another, so she stepped over to the side door of the house to see what he wanted. When she opened the door, there was no one about. Mae then went outside and walked the length of the driveway and down to the road, looking in all directions for the man, but he had simply slipped away. She described him as being in his mid-sixties, very stocky, and wearing a John Deere baseball cap and light blue coveralls. Although she thought it was a bit strange, she didn't give it a lot of thought and went back inside to finish her work in the kitchen.

About two weeks later, Mae was passing through the kitchen one morning when she caught sight of the man once again standing outside her kitchen window looking in. This time she went over to the window and started to raise it up, to ask him what he wanted. Before she could do so, he simply vanished. She then realized that in order for him to have been able to look into the window, he had to be either nine feet tall or floating a few feet above the ground. That was the first icy chill Mae experienced in her new home. It wouldn't be the last.

Not much time passed before Mae had another nape of the neck encounter. She was sitting on the sofa in her living room, reading a magazine, when she caught a reflection of movement in the glass of the curio cabinet opposite her. It was the figure of a man walking down the stairway behind her. Turning her head, she caught the full figure of a young man about thirty years old and dressed in a mechanic's jumpsuit coming down the stairs, heading toward the side door of the house, and exiting. Although she certainly noticed him, it seemed he was oblivious to her.

That wouldn't be the only time this apparition was viewed by household members. Eventually Mae and all of the kids would become acquainted with this ethereal working stiff. He would appear very regularly to all of them. Each time he looked the same, and each time he did the same thing, as though he was headed off to work somewhere. They dubbed him the "mechanic," and it wasn't unusual for one of the kids to tell their mother they had just seen the "mechanic" again.

As if this weren't enough, the strange incidents increased in frequency and tenor, and more spirits began to make themselves known. For instance, there was the time when Sid and Mae's oldest boy was down in the basement, playing with his electric slot car set, of which he was very particular. Near where he was playing, there's a storage area, which is next to the furnace room. Stacked up against a wall in that area was a set of drums no longer in use. Suddenly, he began to hear one of the drumheads being tapped by an unseen hand. Since they were his drums, he knew from the sound which one was being used, and it happened to be the one in the middle of the stack, where no human hand could rat-a-tat-tat on it. Playtime came to an abrupt end as he headed upstairs to tell his mother what was going on. When they came back down together, the drumming had stopped, but his slot cars, which were on the track when he left the basement, were now sitting on a shelf across the room.

The spooky nature of the haunting wasn't confined to the inside of the house. More than once family members would spot a young man, probably in his late teens and dressed in farm clothing, standing in the corner of the yard, or crossing the street from the cornfield and heading toward the house. He would be seen for a few seconds, and then he would be gone from sight. More than once, he was spotted by two family members at the same time, which adds credence to those events, and at least once he was run over by the family car. Yeah, run over. It seems they were all stuffed inside the family SUV and returning from a school event. As they approached their home, their youngest son, perched in the back of the car, saw a young man walk out of the cornfield and into the middle of the road. In horror he realized his dad didn't see him and wasn't slowing down. Then the family vehicle seemed to strike the figure in the road, and the boy spun around to look behind him, certain he would see a twisted corpse lying on the pavement, but there was no one there. Furthermore, no one else showed any indication they had even seen the young man. This incident would be repeated from time to time, so obviously ghosts are immune from hit and run automobile accidents.

Since our tale has taken us outside, let's talk about the barn that sits across the way from the house. When I was a kid, a barn was a great place to play—swinging from ropes into stacks of hay and other assorted adventures. For the children in this family, it was a place to be avoided. Originally, one of Sid and Mae's boys saw the same possibilities for fun most kids see when they perceive a barn in their future. He was drawn to the barn as a fun place but was skittish about going inside because of the elderly man he would see standing off behind one of the barn walls watching him. The repeated encounter would give the boy a cold case of the creepy-crawlies, and soon he headed off to other adventures in other places. Even the family dog, devotedly tagging along wherever the kids went, refused to go inside that barn.

Back in the house, the haunting seemed to shift into overdrive. Each child in the family had their own bedroom, with the youngest boy bedding down in what had once been a storage room but was now a small bedroom. The footboard of his bed nearly reached to the entry of his closet, so he had left the doors off for easier access to things he would need. One night he looked over toward the foot of his bed, and there stood two disembodied souls standing just inside the closet and watching him. He knew they didn't belong there. In his words they were "not real" and were ghosts. One was a young man, and it was he who continued to show up from time to time, always standing in the closet and watching him as though puzzled about why the youngster was bedded down in there. A bit of fact gathering indicated that before the home was remodeled there had been a doorway where the closet

Spirit Mist on Stairs
Caledonia Farmhouse

now exists. Perhaps the youthful ghost was puzzled by why someone would sleep in a closet.

Not to be outdone by the other spirits in the house, another ghost began to make his presence known in a most unwelcome manner. This guy turned out to be more than simply a bit curious. He was most unpleasant and rather interactive with Sid and Mae's daughter.

The pleasant young girl, then about eleven or twelve years of age, had gone to bed one evening, shut off the light, and snuggled beneath her comforter. As her bed faced the doorway looking out into the upstairs foyer, she had a view of all the activity that took place up there. On this particular evening, she was curious about the man who came up the stairs, crossed through the foyer past the bedrooms of her brothers, and stood in her doorway looking in at her. He was an older fellow, large and a bit craggy looking, dressed in clothing a few decades removed from our modern times. Right away, she managed to pick up on the fact that he was not a pleasant person—in fact, he wasn't a flesh and blood man at all. It's always easy to come to such a conclusion when the person in question enters your room and dissolves into nothingness in the process.

Well, this scared the lass out of her wits, her response bringing Mom up to the room for aid and comfort. Mae, good mother that she has always been, reassured her daughter that all was well and what she had seen couldn't hurt her. This kind of reassurance can be too little butter on the toast when such encounters begin to repeat themselves.

It wasn't long before the old ghost began showing up on a semi-regular basis. With each appearance he became a bit bolder. He began entering her room, sometimes in broad daylight, and remaining there until he was certain she was caught in the firm grip of fear. For some reason, he seemed to enjoy taunting her. Some nights he would come into the room and stand by her bed. At least once he pulled the blankets off her. Sometimes she would come into her room and find the pillows in a state of disarray, and she knew he had made one of his visits. She described him as being "mean," and she was always on edge when bedtime rolled around. She felt like he was trying to "get her." Soon, the visitations were of such frequency that she began to feel as though something bad had happened in the past in her bedroom, and she was uncomfortable sleeping there alone, so she began to take up residence in her mother's bed with dad off at his night shifts.

What our young lady didn't realize when she began tucking herself in with Mom, was that Mom's bedroom was also the scene of ghostly appearances and strange sights.

The master bedroom is on the main floor and is quite spacious. There's a short hallway inside the bedroom which leads to a closet on the right and the master bathroom on the left. Shortly after Mom and daughter began passing the night together, the two of them were snugly tucked in when Mom glanced across the room at the dresser. Reflected in the mirror she could see a man standing just inside the hallway, looking into the bedroom. She couldn't make out his features with only the nightlight softly glowing nearby, but it was definitely a man. Mae said that she watched him for a minute or two, relieved her daughter was asleep already. Then he turned around and headed down the hallway. When Mae got out of bed to make an inspection, which takes more courage than most people can conjure up in such a situation, the man was gone. That's when she remembered that before the home had been remodeled there had been a door leading into another room of the house where the hallway now ended. This shows that the changes we make in our homes don't seem to block former accesses recalled by our ghosts.

Another interesting feature in the house is the occasional light show. Mae says there have been times when she was alone in the house, and what she could only describe as colored electrical balls would sometimes waft through the room, often flying quickly across the room and then exploding in sparks of color. She has also seen them in her bedroom at night, different colors, quite small and usually very quick in their movements. There was even the time her daughter encountered them. It was when they were in the kitchen getting ready to make cookies. The youngster went into the half bath near the laundry room just off the kitchen to wash her hands. When she headed back to the kitchen, Mae saw her suddenly stop at the foot of the stairs leading up to the bedrooms and just stand there looking. When she came over to investigate, they both watched the colored balls of light flitting around the landing at the top of the steps.

When I was first contacted by Mae about the nature of her haunting, it was through a series of emails. Those emails eventually extended over a long period of time, and after a couple of years she asked if I could recommend a good psychic. I have always been one to look upon the purported psychic with a jaundiced eye, but I did a little research on the web and finally made the decision to contact a professional psychic named Wendy Piepenberg from Ann Arbor. Before I would make any recommendation to Mae, I decided it was necessary to convince myself of Wendy's talents, if she had any at all.

I emailed Ms. Piepenberg, expressed who I was and what I did in preparation for writing my books, and she said she would be happy to meet with me. I was pleased we were able to set up our meeting at a local McDonald's just two hours later. At that meeting we made our introductions over a Coke and iced tea, and in reference to Mae's haunted house all I told her was that I had been dealing with a family on the west side of the state whose house was home to spirits. I gave no names or addresses and no further information whatsoever. Immediately Wendy withdrew into a few moments of drifting silence and then began to tell me about the nature of the haunting as well as the real reason the house was being sold (I had not even mentioned to her that Mae and her husband had decided to sell their home), and she was spot on.

The next day I made arrangements with Mae for a visit from myself and my team as well as Wendy. We arrived a week later at Mae's home on a sultry July evening. We met all the family members except Sid, who was away at work, and then we did the mandatory walk-through of the home, snapping photos as we went. I was clear that I didn't want anyone in the family to tell any of my team members or Wendy what encounters they had experienced or where they had taken place. I like my team to go into a place cold, with no preconceived notions floating around in their subconscious.

Night fell late that evening, and the heat was relentless. Still we went about setting up our video cameras and recording equipment and breaking out all the other devices conducive to a thorough ghost search. Areas of the home were assigned to teams of two individuals, and the hunt began in earnest.

It wasn't until shortly after midnight we began to notice small indications that something was amiss within the walls of the farmhouse. While the heat upstairs was stifling (there was no air conditioning), one of the bedrooms remained cold enough to incite a case of the shivers. A few minutes later, my main level team reported hearing tinny music very faintly passing through the room. They described it as sounding like the type of music one would have heard on an old radio program of the 1920s. This was our first sign that paranormal activity was making itself known.

Around 1 a.m., our crew was ready for a break. Pizza had been delivered, and we enjoyed munching our treat and washing it down with copious draughts of cold pop. With the heat still oppressive and a summer storm approaching from the west, half of my team continued their break inside the kitchen. The other half went out onto the back deck, which overlooks an expansive yard, to see if the developing breezes could cool their sweaty demeanor.

They hadn't been outdoors long when one of them slipped inside and told me I needed to come out on the deck, and to do so slowly and quietly. I followed the instructions and took up a perch on one of the steps of the deck. One of my team members whispered, "Just keep watching the yard, over by the trees." What he was referring to was a line of trees, each about twenty feet apart from the others. The moon was bright, and an approaching summer storm was lighting up the sky in the distance, having not yet reached our part of the county. I didn't have to wait long at all before I became aware of what they had been encountering out in the July night. The black forms of several "people" would appear from behind the trees and quickly run from one tree to the other, hiding behind each as they proceeded. Sometimes, one or two of them would step out from behind their cover, and stand looking at the house. They were about one hundred feet away, solid black and shaped like any other human would be shaped, but most of them could only be seen from the waist up.

Desirous of a better look, I broke out my night vision scope, but the forms were too far away for its powers of illumination. We were so mesmerized by what we were seeing (and it's very unusual to have several people view such a paranormal activity at the same time), we hadn't thought about going back inside for our video equipment for several minutes. When we finally brought them outside, the event had passed. It made for an eerie night for us. It's one thing to sit in a house and look for ghosts; it's quite unsettling to be in a house while the ghosts outside were peering in. It's sort of like the hunter becoming the hunted and gives you an idea of how a ghost must feel whenever investigators show up.

At our 3 a.m. gathering in the kitchen to exchange information, it was time for Wendy, our Ann Arbor psychic, to give us her impressions of what was going on in the house. Without having heard the history of the haunting, she expressed her assurance that there was one ghost, and older man, who in life had been abusive of young girls. He used to hurt them and took particular delight in doing so. She also said he goes into the daughter's room and torments her. She is very tuned in to spirits, which makes it easier for him to terrorize her, but he is afraid of being around the adults. When she calls for her mother or when she goes down to sleep with her mother, he backs off.

That wasn't the only spirit Wendy picked up on. She also said there was the ghost of a young teen in the basement. He stayed there to avoid the ghost of the old man, whose energy was strong and abusive. She said he had lived in the home years after the old man, but their spirits existed in the home together and are fully aware of one another. Then Wendy looked at Mae and said, "tell me about the woman in the kitchen." It was an interesting query, since I had never heard anything at all about a female ghost haunting the house.

Mae confirmed that there was, indeed, a female ghost, and that she kept showing up in the kitchen. She had noticed her presence shortly after having moved into the house, as things she had put away in the kitchen would be found in different places later on. It was as though the ghost was upset about another woman being in her kitchen and was rearranging things. On at least two occasions, Mae admitted to having seen her—an older woman in the garb of a farm wife from what seemed to be the 1940s. Not only had Mae seen her, but so had a friend of hers who had stopped by the house unexpectedly, only to look through the window and see this elderly woman standing in the kitchen. She left when no one answered the door and related her experience to Mae later.

Wendy finished up her discourse by explaining that the house had experienced a long history of negative occurrences. She told of child abuse, drug abuse, and marital strife over a long period of time and on the parts of many different residents.

You may have noticed I haven't mentioned much about Sid, the paterfamilias of the brood. That's because he's a very practical thinking sort of professional and would always deny that anything amiss was taking place in his home. He finally admitted to the haunting very late one Christmas Eve, long after the family had returned from church services and the kids had been put to bed. He and Mae stayed up late wrapping gifts and placing them near the tree. As they were busily engaged, they suddenly heard loud stomping coming from the upstairs foyer. Their kids had never done this before, and Mae was convinced it wasn't the kids at all, so Sid headed up to see what was going on. He found nothing amiss and all the kids sound asleep in their rooms. Sid retreated back down the stairs, and a few minutes later the stomping activity began once again. That's when he told Mae, "I don't care what you have to do, make this stuff go away."

The "stuff" hasn't gone away. The family moved out of the home yet had several weeks in which they could return for cleanup and touch-up work. Mae would always find the window in her daughter's room, which she had always securely closed beforehand, open a few inches. Sometimes items would have been moved from one place to another, and she feels she encountered the abusive old man whenever she went into her daughter's old bedroom. It would become hard for her to breathe, and she felt an oppressive spirit all around her. Eventually, she would just run into the house, pick up some things she had left there, and quickly leave.

Having had a few days of my vacation to kill, I went back to the home after the family had moved out. I dragged along some of my equipment, a blanket to erase the cold chill of an October night, some snack food, and a folding chair. Oh yes, I also took along some reading material—Fitzgerald's *The Great Gatsby*. I settled in for an evening alone, or at least alone with the ghosts if they were willing to show up.

It was a long evening, with nothing happening until well after midnight. That's when my reading was violently interrupted by what sounding like a rifle shot echoing through the house. I got up, flashlight in hand, and inspected the house, finding nothing. Then the night continued in silence and boredom.

My contact with Mae, as you have by now surmised, has been long and extensive. I am convinced that she and her children, if not her husband, are extremely open to paranormal phenomena, and most likely will be regardless of where they choose to live. Thus far, nothing strange has reared its head in their new home, but I think interesting things are in store for them in the future.

*Update—just before this manuscript went to the publisher, I received an interesting story from Mae about the history of this haunting. It comes from an unexpected meeting she had with someone who had no idea she and her family had once resided in the home. What follows is an account of their conversation.

Mae was working in a classroom at her school with a substitute teacher I now refer to as Keith. Keith is a man in his late sixties to early seventies, and she overheard him talking to a student about his old farmhouse and barn. She joined the conversation and asked him whether or not he had raised animals and where the farmhouse was located. Mae was surprised to discover Keith's old farmhouse was within one mile of the home she had just vacated and told him she had once lived in a farmhouse near his but had recently moved out.

Keith went on to say that this was back in the 1970s. He had purchased the home so he could be near his best friend, a man named Gary, who had moved to the area a couple of years earlier. When he described Gary's house, Mae said she felt her heart freeze inside her chest, because it was her former home. She managed to play dumb and just let Keith talk, and what she heard fascinated her.

He went on to say that his friend Gary lived in the old farmhouse while building a new home not far away. Gary had invited Keith to come over and see the new home under construction but said when he arrived that Gary seemed "very dark" and distracted. He had only very recently moved into the new place but still owned the old farmhouse. Since Keith knew his friend was one to hit the bottle a bit too much at times, he passed the dark mood off as being related to his drinking.

After a tour of the new house, Gary asked Keith to go with him to the old farmhouse he had just moved out of and see if he would be interested in buying the place. It had been up for sale for quite some time, but no one seemed interested enough to make an offer. Gary said he would spin Keith a good deal on the place, and it would be a good move for him financially.

Keith told Gary he was familiar with the house. He and his wife thought it looked nice, and it was situated on a desirable piece of property, but they had recently purchased their own home. They couldn't afford to make a change, commenting that the price of the farmhouse was out of their financial range. That's when Gary suddenly made an interesting offer—he would simply trade houses with Keith, even up, although Gary's place was worth more money.

Keith and his wife decided to go ahead and check the inside of the place out, having only seen it from the outside whenever they had passed by on their way to Gary's new home. They realized it was a good deal for them since it had been recently remodeled. It was beautiful inside, and included a new addition as well as completely new kitchen and bathrooms. They loved the big rooms as well as all the new renovations and expansive property and outbuilding. Unfortunately, Keith said he found the place "creepy" but said nothing to his wife about it. For her part, she had been unusually quiet during their tour and offered no immediate comment about the place.

When Gary had finished giving his friends the tour of the home, they went outside to return to his new place to talk things over. On the way there, Keith's wife explained how she loved the new renovations. When compared to their present home, it was superior in many ways, but there was no way she could ever live there. When Keith asked her why, she said the house had a weird feeling about it, as though she had been followed and watched the entire time she was there. That's when he admitted to her that he also felt the place was creepy, and the two of them decided to decline the offer.

They went over to Gary's place and told him "thanks, but no thanks," and then Gary started acting very antsy. He shocked them by saying they could have the house for free; he would just write it off as a real estate loss. It was a great and generous offer, but Keith had to again say no to his friend, explaining that both he and his wife felt the house was too creepy—something just wasn't right inside the place. That's when Gary started rambling on about how the house was haunted and how he himself couldn't get out of it fast enough when he had lived there. He said that everyone who came to look at the place when it was up for sale said the place was beautiful, but he had never gotten a single offer.

Gary went on to say that since he couldn't sell the place, and since Keith and his wife didn't want it, he would turn it into a rental property. From that time—the early 1970s—until 1990, it was just that, a rental. Gary said he couldn't keep anyone in the house for longer than six months to a year. He said people would change after they moved in, as though they were becoming different people altogether, and many times they would start taking or dealing in drugs and having wild parties.

When Keith finished telling Mae his story about the haunted home he had almost taken possession of free of charge, she explained to him that it was the very home she had just moved out of and for the very same reasons. The place was definitely haunted. She and Keith shared a laugh about their strange connection and promised to get together some time in the future to swap ghost stories about the place.

Planning a Visit? Your attempt would be fruitless, as I have been creative as to the location of the house.

Still Haunted? Is there road construction in Michigan?

Chapter 18
Mr. Bastard

Place Visited: A nondescript old-frame house in the city of St. Ignace, sitting close enough to the waters of Lake Huron to hit it with a stone after just a couple of tosses.

Period of Haunting: The family has been occupying this home for a long, long time, and their extended family has been part of the community for generations. The ghosts tramping around their place have been a part of their family for just about the same length of time.

Date of Investigation: My first encounter with the residents of this home was back in 2002. Phone call follow-ups were conducted in a scattered manner over the next several years.

Description of Location: St. Ignace is one of the oldest settlements in all of Michigan, having been founded as a Catholic mission by none other than Father Marquette himself way back in the year of our Lord, 1671. That date, however, only refers to how long the first Europeans populated the area. There were Native Americans calling the place home long before Europeans showed up to inflict them with their strange religion and even stranger culture.

Geographically speaking, St. Ignace sits in a pristine part of Michigan. It's located at the eastern end of the Upper Peninsula looking out across the azure waters of Lake Huron toward the ever popular Mackinac Island. In fact, the first city you arrive at after crossing the Mackinac Bridge headed north is St. Ignace. It's a historic place and relies heavily upon tourism with all sorts of gift shops lining the streets. It also offers modern ship transportation to the "Island" and back. In recent years an Indian casino has been added in an effort to vacuum away even more cash from the pockets of residents and tourists alike.

I've always believed Michigan's Upper Peninsula to be the prettiest part of Michigan. The St. Ignace area is rocky and covered with tall pines and hardwoods. I once heard a tourist ask one of the locals what the weather is like around there, and the grizzled old boy answered, "Well, there's two weeks in August when the ice fishing is lousy."

Note: St. Ignace boasts a population of only about 3,000 persons. The vast majority of them have family roots going way back. Since this family didn't want the publicity, I offer no evidence of where they live or who they are, and offer you only a family alias as identification.

Haunt Meter * * * *

AFTER WRITING MY FIRST BOOK, *Haunted Michigan: Recent Encounters With Active Spirits*, I began receiving requests from libraries, schools, and community groups to give lectures about my experiences with Michigan's ghosts. Over the years I've given dozens of these lectures, with groups ranging from six to four hundred persons. At the end of these lectures, I sit—sometimes for hours—at a local restaurant with people who say they need to speak with me about their haunting. That's how I came to know the Evans family (as I said earlier, it's an alias).

The family had been visiting relatives near Lansing when they discovered I was to give a lecture about ghosts at a library in Jackson. They made the trip down, endured my droning voice for two hours, sat through another hour of questions and answers, or attempted answers, and then asked me if they could speak with me privately about the ghosts spiriting through their home in the Upper Peninsula. They seemed like normal folks, if there really are such folks, and I agreed.

We were sipping drinks at a local McDonald's as Mike and Terry Sue entertained me with tales from the dark side of human existence as experienced by them within the confines of their hallowed home.

It began, Terry Sue said, long before they moved into the house. She remembered visiting as a child when her grandmother lived in the home. When she would see the ghosts, her grandmother always passed them off as "harmless relatives from long ago."

Terry Sue vividly remembered encountering the ghosts on several occasions. Once, when she was about six years old, she had been playing in the living room with her grandmother's old dolls when an elderly woman walked into the room and sat down on the sofa. She said the woman watched her play and smiled at her every time she looked up at her. After a while, the pleasant old woman had remarked, "those used to be mine." Terry Sue said she often saw the old woman, and she always felt safe around her. At that age, she said, she just assumed everyone else could see her, too, as it felt perfectly normal to her.

It wasn't long before Terry Sue started to encounter other people wandering about the place. As she got a bit older, she realized that these people were no longer alive; she had been encountering ghosts. The wonderful thing about this, from this writer's perspective, is that she wasn't at all afraid of them, nor was she ever discouraged by her grandmother about the situation. Too often, we adults raise our children to believe ghosts are "bad" or even "evil." The religious community really does a number on their constituents by telling them ghosts are demonic. The stigma projected upon these youngsters causes them to reject these naturally occurring encounters. This leads to fear, and fear leads to the type of denial that shuts down a perfectly natural tendency to experience part of life which not everyone gets to be privy to. The more we do this to our children, the more boring the world becomes.

Terry Sue loved visiting her grandmother—grandpa had long been dead—and didn't mind the other spirits who started showing up during her time there. One of them was a young boy who would talk to her. From him she discovered that he had lived in the house "a long time ago." There was an older woman with him who wasn't his mother but who took care of him. She liked being around him; he was playful, sometimes hiding things from her grandmother. There was another woman, this one quite a bit younger than the older woman, who also would appear from time to time. Terry Sue said this woman was very pretty, with big dark eyes and her auburn hair in ringlets. She liked having her around because she always smelled like flowers and could usually be seen sitting in the family rocking chair reading a book while she played with Grandma's dolls.

It wasn't until Terry Sue was in her late teen years that she first became introduced to "a bastard ghost," as she refers to him. Interestingly enough, he had never once shown up until shortly after the death of her grandmother in the late 1950s. She had gone over to the house to help the family settle the estate and divvy out her grandmother's possessions, and she got her first bad feeling, like something was wrong in the house now. She had been in her grandmother's bedroom for about an hour, sorting out her jewelry and packing up her clothing, when she caught the scent of something foul. That stench was immediately followed by a severe sense of dread. Looking around the room, she spied, within the reflection of the antique mirror hanging on one of the bedroom walls, the image of a man. Immediately, she knew this was a negative spirit. It was strange, she said, because he wasn't an old man and was actually very handsome and neat in his appearance. All she could see of him was his image from the shoulders upward, and she said he had dark, wavy hair, a straight nose, and thin lips. She thought he looked perhaps to be about thirty years of age. When Terry Sue would look around the room, she couldn't see him, but when she looked back at the mirror, he would still be there, a sarcastic smile spread across his face.

Having experienced many ghosts in the house all her life, Terry Sue simply walked out of the room, not particularly frightened, but a bit concerned. Who was this guy? Why had she never encountered him before? These questions puzzled her all that day and for a few days afterward.

Terry Sue was not next in line to inherit the family homestead, but her folks were reluctant to give up their own home, so the old house found her to be the next occupant. All she had to do was take care of the utilities, upkeep, and taxes—and put up with the extra inhabitants who assumed they were part of the package as well. Since she worked locally as a waitress in the mornings and at a tourist shop in the evenings, she could afford the place on her own. She loved it because she could sense the presence of her grandmother and reveled in all the great memories she cherished about her.

Terry Sue knew the ghostly activity would be a common theme within those hallowed halls, but that was fine with her. Soon, she was seeing the older woman who used to watch her play when she was a child as well as the other spirits who came and went as they wished. Sometimes, they could actually be helpful, as in the time her water pipe to the washing machine ruptured while she was at work for several hours. Returning home, she went into the basement to toss the wet wash into the dryer, and that's when she noticed water on the floor. She called her father to come over and inspect the basement and locate the problem. When he found the split pipe, he remarked to her how smart she had been to shut off the water to the house.

Terry Sue hadn't shut the water off, and no one else had been in the house that day.

Nice things would happen from time to time, as the ghosts seemed to show their appreciation for Terry Sue having taken over responsibility for the house. Sometimes she would return home from work in the evening, dog tired from two jobs, and find the breakfast dishes she had left on the kitchen table resting peacefully in the sink. Other times she would pull into her driveway after a long day and discover the shades, which had been up to let in the sunlight, had been pulled down.

Still, Terry Sue discovered she would also have to deal with the bastard ghost. From time to time his handsome, sneering face would show up, turning the atmosphere rather foreboding in its tone.

Mr. Bastard, as Terry Sue refers to him, once turned a social gathering into a macabre setting. Terry Sue had invited several friends over to celebrate a couple of their birthdays which had been close to one another on the calendar. The evening went rather swimmingly, with refreshments and laughter and girl talk. After their meal together, everyone went into the living room for dessert and coffee. As is the physiological case with we human beings, it's liquid in and liquid out, and soon the ladies—one at a time—started drifting toward the bathroom.

Terry Sue still remembers vividly what happened that night. One of her friends, whose name I omit from this tale, walked in on someone already occupying that space. She began to offer her apologies when she realized it wasn't one of the other girls. It was a man, and that she was only seeing him from about the knees upward. He turned to face her and presented her with his trademark sneer, which sent her screaming bloody murder as she ran back through the living room and dove into the arms of one of the other women.

Terry Sue did her best to calm the woman's frayed nerves and led a tour of the home to assure the others that all was well. Pressed about the issue, she finally admitted that the home was haunted, a bit of information which came a tad too late for at least one of her guests but which intrigued a couple of the others. Those two, who wanted to know more about the nature of things inside Terry Sue's home, stuck around after the blighted birthday bash and made the request to nose around the place when all was quiet once again. Gracious host that she was, permission was thoughtfully granted.

According to Terry Sue, the nosing around didn't last long. Her two friends stuck to one another like glue as they traversed the house, room to room, nervously but anxiously peering into every nook and cranny. It was when the three of them were in the basement things came to a sudden climactic end. As they were nosing around near the laundry area, the friends noticed Terry Sue staring over their shoulders. Slowly turning around, they saw the young man off in a corner watching them. As nervous as a frog on a freeway with a broken hopper, they edged toward the stairs, shot straight up them, and then headed out to their cars. It's often one thing to desire an encounter with a ghost but quite another to actually stand in the presence of one.

Terry Sue married in the early 1960s, but it didn't last long, only a couple of years. Yes, they lived together in the haunted dwelling, but that wasn't the reason for the breakup and didn't even contribute to it. The marriage simply didn't work. As stressful as it was for her to go through the divorce, her ghostly friends—the pleasant ones—began showing up more frequently, as though offering solace in a time of distress.

For the next few years, Terry Sue lived with her ghosts, even with the bastard ghost, of whom she really wasn't afraid. Finally, she married Mike, who shared her values and was willing to share her spirits. She was up front about the ghosts in her home, and love has so far triumphed over the paranormal.

The haunting continued, of course, perhaps because it takes more than nuptial vows to exorcize the dead. Then again, the two of them weren't interested in getting rid of their ghosts. Terry Sue continued to see them regularly; however, Mike was only peripherally aware of the spirits—until, of course, he was introduced to the young man with the sneering look and attitude.

Mike had been out in the yard one winter's morning, shoveling the day's snow off the driveway, when he glanced toward the house and saw someone standing at the bedroom window looking out at him. Mike described him as a youngish man, slender in build and with dark hair and clothing. Tossing aside his shovel, he ran into the house to see who had broken into the place, as the back door was always kept locked, and no one had passed him by on the way to the front door.

Heading over to the bedroom, he found the room to be empty of any intruder. Certain of what he had seen, and expecting a burglar, he retrieved his shotgun from the bedroom closet, loaded it, and cautiously went room to room looking for the home invader. He found nothing out of order, and no one inside the home other than himself. When Terry Sue came home from her job at the restaurant, she assured her husband he had seen the bastard ghost. It wouldn't be a good idea to try to shoot the guy, as it would just end up making a mess of the walls.

Mike was all right with the ghosts moving objects and calling his name from time to time, but he didn't like the idea of this ominous man showing up at will. He became even more incensed when Mr. Bastard invaded the privacy of his wife's shower.

Terry Sue and Mike both worked hard to make ends meet in the first few years of their marriage, with both of them often holding down two jobs. Terry Sue always looked forward to a relaxing shower after her night job. One night she was letting the warm water flow across her aching muscles when she was suddenly pushed quite hard against the tiled wall of the shower, making her slip and fall down in the tub.

Mike heard her scream—after all, regardless of how comfortable one is with their haunting, a sudden physical trauma catches you off guard. He came running to her rescue, listened to her story, and decided something needed to be done about this guy. The two of them had heard about a psychic who lived across the bridge in Mackinaw City and decided to make contact. (I don't know why so many people in this book go running off to psychics, but a lot of them have done so.)

A few days later, the psychic lady showed up, sipped herbal tea with them (which she had brought to the home herself), and proceeded to "read" the house. It was no surprise at all when she spoke of how the house was home to many spirits, some who were there permanently, and others who came and went as they pleased. For the most part, she said, they were protective. She revealed, however, there was one spirit who was just plain nasty, who liked to frighten and intimidate people. He too, she informed them, would come and go because there were other homes he visited as well.

This psychic lady, whose name they couldn't remember and who has now taken up residence herself in the spirit world, asked for the lights to be trimmed as she attempted to make contact with Mr. Bastard. With elongated shadows covering the table where they were seated, a plea was made for the slender man of poor manners to listen to her. As she admonished his activities, she announced he was in the room with them and was very angry. She described him as having lived his first life around the late 1880s and had died young, in the wintertime, the result of some accident.

The psychic informed them this man's will was strong, and he was angry about how soon his life had ended. He was very much in love with a woman, and the accident kept them from marrying. As she informed him he would have to leave the house, a dining room chair suddenly slid out from under the table and fell over on its side.

Feeling his will was too strong for just her admonitions, she then summoned the other spirits inside the home for help. She told Mike and Terry Sue that the other spirits had been keeping Mr. Bastard from displaying even worse behavior and were willing to help force him out of the house. Sliding into a trance—or at least what looked like one to Mike and Terry Sue—she muttered a few words and then rejoined the "normal" world, indicating that with the help of the other spirits, he had been banished from the home.

Mike and Terry Sue had no further encounters with the bastard ghost. He would, however, appear to Terry Sue from time to time in other places, and still does. He has shown up where she works, at family outings, and in other spots Terry Sue has frequented. She says she still runs into him once in a while, and they've actually had a couple of stare-down contests with one another, but he hasn't come back into her house. It seems to me the psychic lady should have instructed Mr. Bastard not only to leave the house alone but to leave Terry Sue alone as well. Maybe then she wouldn't be bumping into him in other places, but Terry Sue says that's all right with her.

The haunting of the home continues to this day. Both Mike and his loving spouse have seen the old woman who has been with Terry Sue since childhood and assorted other entities. There have even been the occasional spirits who are seen only once as they passed through the house on their way to wherever spirits are going these days. Both of them feel secure in the home and appear to be quite happy and content living within a house filled with the dead.

Planning a Visit? You can't. Instead, visit one of the public places listed in my books. Better yet, talk to friends and relatives and find out about houses and buildings in your area that are purported to be overrun with spirits. Do a bit of investigating on your own.

Still Haunted? According to Mike and Terry Sue, it is.

Chapter 19
The Bedtime People

Place Visited: A private dwelling in a small town between Novi and Brighton.

Period of Haunting: This particular haunting has been going on for only the last four or five years.

Date of Investigation: We were first invited into this apartment for conversation and possible ghostly encounters in May of 2012.

Description of Location: This apartment is part of a large complex of apartments sitting near the downtown area of a small city in southeastern Michigan. It is a very well kept apartment complex, with neatly trimmed lawns and lots of friendly people. The woman involved in this haunting has not yet given permission to use her name and address.

Haunt Meter: * * (for the resident)

* * * (for those who visit)

VIRGINIA IS LOVELY WOMAN in her mid-sixties, who lives in a one bedroom apartment in a rather large complex consisting of several well kept buildings. Each building houses about sixteen apartments, an equal amount spread across two levels. The buildings are similar; the apartments are similar. That is, with the exception of Virginia's abode. Hers appears to be haunted in a very interesting manner.

Virginia is a dear friend of one of my team members. They worked together for several years, Virginia as a para-pro, and Claudia, one of the founding members of my team, as a special education instructor, now retired. Upon retirement, she and her husband, Glenn, another member of my team and also a retired special education teacher, moved to sunny Florida to live out their sunshine years. On one of their visits back to Michigan, Claudia made a point to visit Virginia, and the conversation turned to the old standby, "What are you up to lately?" Claudia remarked that she was going on a ghost hunt in Jackson with me and others in our group, and that was the first Virginia had ever heard of Claudia having interest in such things. Taking advantage of this new—found revelation, Virginia announced to Claudia that for several years now she had been experiencing the presence of ghosts in her apartment and hadn't said anything to anyone for fear they wouldn't understand.

When Claudia asked me if I'd be interested in interviewing Virginia and assured me of her honesty and clearheadedness, I readily agreed. An interview meeting was set up for the next night, and, all told, there were four of us present in Virginia's apartment to hear of her encounters with spirits.

Virginia, a most pleasant woman who lives alone and endures limited mobility due to health issues, began her tale in earnest. She told of how it isn't uncommon for her to stay up until two or three in the morning watching television in the living room. Around that time of the night, she would finally make her way down the hall to her bedroom, where almost every night her ghosts would show up.

I see what looks like a mass of shimmering stars hovering above my head near the ceiling. Then it drops down a little lower, and I can put my hand in it. It feels electric and makes my skin tingle. I call this my protective angel, and I thank her for coming every time I see her. Right away, I start to see people in my room, in the hallway, or the bathroom just off the hallway.

There's this one guy, he wears dark clothes and looks like he's from a hundred years ago, who comes and stands at the foot of my bed. He's there almost every night, and he just stands there like he doesn't see me. I figured he was from a different time period and was unaware of me because it's always like that. Then one night he raised his arm, pointed his finger at me, and then faded away. He still comes back, but that was the only time he actually seemed to notice me.

There are two ladies who show up to the right of my bed. They're always wearing Victorian style dresses, and they sit in chairs and talk to one another, but there aren't any chairs in my room, and they're sitting right where my dressers sits. I can never make out what they're saying because even though I can see their mouths moving, there's never any sound. They're young women and look very proper. I see them frequently, and I try to ask them what they want and what they're talking about. They don't pay me any mind; they just keep on talking for a while and then go away.

One time, I got up in the night to use the bathroom, and I always keep the night light burning in there for that reason. This time, I went into the bathroom, and I got a really strange sense that someone was in there with me. I turned to leave, and I could see a man standing in the hallway, just outside the bathroom door. He didn't seem to notice me and just stood there, really still. I went back to bed, and when I looked down the hallway, he was still there in the same position, just standing there.

I asked Virginia how long she had been having these late night—or early morning—encounters with the dead. She said it had only been for three or four years, and I found that interesting. Usually people who are that calm about ghosts rambling around where they are paying rent are people who have been encountering them most of their lives. That's when Virginia told me she had a psychic over to her apartment a few short years back and was told there were many spirits who were drawn to her. That's when they started showing up all around her, often and regularly. The power of suggestion? I don't know, you decide.

When I inquired if Virginia had run up against paranormal incidents as a child, she said "not really," but then told of how, as an adult, she started having many such encounters. She was born and raised in Hawaii and is of Hawaiian descent. She married a soldier, and in typical army fashion they moved around a lot from place to place. That was when she started to meet people who were interested in strange phenomena.

Being Hawaiian, it's part of our culture to accept the reality of ghosts and other strange events. We don't pooh-pooh it away when our children talk about seeing spirits. Instead, we let them know it's a natural part of life. That's how I was raised, so these things don't really frighten me.

My husband and I lived in Alaska for a while because that's where he was stationed. We made friends there, and one night we were invited over to one of their houses with some other friends we knew. We visited for a while, and later in the evening some of them decided to do some table tipping.

* For those of you unacquainted with this, table tipping is an old form of contacting spirits. As it has been explained to me, three or more people sit around a table, leaving one empty chair for the spirits. Everyone places their hands very lightly on the table, with the pinky fingers touching the pinkies of the persons on either side of them. Then yes or no questions are asked, and the table will lift up and tap one leg on the floor once for "yes" or twice for "no," or according to whatever arrangements were made with the ghosts ahead of time.

We had been working the table for quite a while, and it was the first time for me. That table actually lifted up and tapped the floor when you asked a question. Well, after a while I decided I needed to take a break and watch what was going on, you know, to see if anyone was manipulating the table somehow.

I went to the other side of the room and sat down to watch. They would ask a question, and I couldn't believe it; that table would lift up at one corner and tap out the answer. At one point, the table didn't tip—all four legs actually lifted up off the floor at the same time. I mean, they went up about a foot in the air. That made me a little leery for a couple of minutes, but I kept on watching. A few minutes later, they started going through the alphabet, trying to get the name of the spirit they were talking to. When they got the name spelled out, I told them that it was the name of a dead relative of mine. At that instant, the table slid across the room and right up to me.

Virginia went on to say she and some others had also used pendulums to contact spirits. They would tie something to a string, such as a heavy crystal or steel washer, rest an elbow on the table and hold it very still. A question would be asked, again of the yes or no variety, and if the object began to swing in a circle in one direction, it meant "yes," and if in another direction, the answer was "no." In short, Virginia had dabbled in several different forms and techniques of trying to contact spirits. She was careful to tell us that before every session, a prayer of protection would be offered for all those present in an effort to keep evil at bay.

As our evening together progressed, Virginia once again began to tell us of the spirits which visit her regularly. She spoke of seeing soldiers from different eras, from what appears to be the Civil War right up to those who showed up wearing camouflage outfits. She says they know they're dead, but for some reason she is yet to understand, they keep appearing in her bedroom or hallway on their way to who knows where.

I asked Virginia if she had ever encountered ghosts in places other than her apartment, and she said she had. She told of a recent trip to see friends in Arizona, where she stayed for several days and nights in their home. Every night ghosts would appear in the bedroom she was using. Usually they were Indians, mostly men, but sometimes women and children. Some of the men were older, and dressed in the sort of garb one would expect from times past. The younger ones would actually show up ready for war wearing the painted faces of protection. She would see them, but again, they were oblivious to her. The first night it happened, she had found herself shaken by the experience. After the third or fourth night, she got up the next morning and informed her hosts of what was going on. They said it was all news to them.

I asked Virginia how she could stand seeing so many spirits filling up her bedroom, bathroom, and hallway every night. She smiled and told us she had begun wearing a sleep mask so she could get some rest and not think about it. Still though, even with the mask she knows they are there and can "see" them clearly in her mind and watch what they're doing. When it gets too prevalent, and she needs sleep, she'll spend the night in her recliner in front of the television where nothing strange seems to happen.

In the course of the evening, I used my camera to take some photos of the haunted areas of the apartment. I have never had any trouble with my camera before, but nearly every other shot came out so blurry as to be rendered useless. As a result, I asked if I could set up my video camera and leave it there for the night. Permission was gracefully given, and I set it up where it was pointed down the hallway and into her bedroom. Before we left for the night, I gave Virginia a tutorial in how to turn the camera on and begin recording. She tried it out a couple of times and had no problems. She indicated she wouldn't turn it on until she was ready for bed. Even though the apartment lights are all turned out when she retires for the night (Virginia has stopped using the night light in the bathroom, as she's tired of seeing the same guy standing in the doorway watching her), my camera has a light of its own for night shooting.

The next day the video camera was returned to me with the message that Virginia had experienced a plethora of spirits that night. I couldn't wait to plug the camera into my computer and watch the results. There were none. In fact, even though Virginia insists she turned it on, nothing at all was recorded. All that showed up was the footage of the tutorial I had given her. Ghostly edits?

Because of my self-imposed deadline for finishing this book, I am only able to include this singular night's events. Further investigation will take place in the near future in hopes of capturing proof of the haunting of Virginia's apartment.

Planning a Visit? It's not something you'll be able to do.

Still Haunted? Virginia insists the ghosts appear almost every night.

Chapter 20
Roadhouse Ghosts

Place Visited: The Roadhouse—a neighborhood bar and restaurant in Jackson, Michigan.

Period of Haunting: This one has gone on for decades.

Date of Investigation: May of 2012.

Description of Location: The Roadhouse, a bar and grill establishment, sits on Jackson's north side at 4112 Lansing Avenue not far from the Michigan Correctional Facility, which was at one time the largest walled prison in the world and is itself an exceptionally haunted place.

The Roadhouse is an old-style neighborhood tavern, with many regulars snugging themselves up to the bar for something cold and a bit of friendly conversation. It stocks a full bar and keeps Killian's on tap (I only mention this because that's what I drink, and it's always best when on tap). The place has been around longer than any Jackson resident and was at one time a stopover spot for wagons headed to or coming from Lansing. At one time there was a large contingent of Native Americans living in the area, and it is said there is an Indian burial ground not too far down the street. There also used to be an artesian spring located a few hundred feet behind the place, but suburban sprawl has long since had its effect on it, rendering it unsafe to drink.

If you're heading over to check out the place, go there hungry. They serve darn good sandwiches. My favorite is one I raised my eyebrows at when I saw it listed on the menu and was given a description of it. It's called the "Sticky Burger" and boasts a large patty of ground round with onion, mustard, tomato, cheese, mayo, and—are you ready for this—peanut butter. It's really tasty, although very rich and quite filling. I washed mine down, accompanied by a basket of french fries, with an icy draft of Killian's.

The Roadhouse is owned by a genuinely nice couple—Alexander, and Leah. Leah grew up in the place spending a great deal of her youth there as her father owned it for many years. She and Alexander own and operate the business now. Leah is a local, but Alexander hails from Yugoslavia. Both are also artists in their own right, and some of their work adorns the walls of their business. The building sports a dining room with pool table and a long wooden table that seats a passel of people and looks as though it used to be part of a bar itself. Behind several attached doors is a large banquet room with a smaller video game room off to one side. The basement is in the style of the old Michigan basements with dirt floor and stone walls.

Haunt Meter: * * * *(There are plenty of ghosts, but they're not intentionally mean)*

I DROPPED IN AT THE ROADHOUSE for a real hamburger, having tired of those pre-formed, systematically produced clones one gets from the ever popular chain restaurants. Besides, McDonald's and Wendy's don't sell beer with their burgers. As I am always wont to do, I struck up a conversation with one of the waitresses and steered the conversation in the direction of ghosts. She unabashedly admitted the place was haunted and that just about every employee in the place has had an encounter or two of their own.

While wolfing down my Sticky Burger, I was introduced to Leah and Alexander, who stopped by my table to fill me in about the ghosts wandering around the place. It was an interesting conversation. Leah told me that as a child she would often spend the night in the building with her father, who would hang around after closing to do repairs and remodeling work. She didn't like those nights and sensed even then that they were not alone in the place. She mentioned it once to her dad who agreed there were both bottled and un-bottled spirits inside the building but that the un-bottled ones were friendly and even helpful at times.

When she grew up, she took over the business with her husband, Alexander. They soon encountered the ghosts for themselves. For Leah, it was usually in the form of a dark, shadowy man passing through the length of the bar or walking from the kitchen area to the front door. Alone in the place she would hear the sounds of someone skulking about and does admit it unsettled her from time to time. Employees would tell her about strange encounters of their own, and she was always inclined to believe them since they were either genuinely frightened or curiously intrigued. For his part, Alexander would laugh at their tales, dismissing them as over active imaginations on the part of the staff or slight inebriation on the part of the customers. That is, until he had his own wake-up call with the paranormal.

> It was a slow night, and a couple of the customers got on the subject of how our place was supposed to be haunted. They even told their stories about what had happened to them. After they left, I asked a couple of our employees if they believed all that stuff. They said they did, but I sort of made fun of it all. Well, I was seated in one of our chairs next to the half wall by the kitchen door. Just about the time I laughed about how they all had active imaginations, something pushed my chair forward with me in it. I mean, the back legs came off the floor and the whole thing leaned forward. That got my attention because you can see I'm not a small man.

That experience led me to build the ghost his own little bar, and it sits right next to where I had been sitting when I got shoved.

I noticed the strange little bar tucked away by itself in the corner. No one else ever sits at it. It does belong to the ghost and was built as a sort of tribute. It's rather cute, and I've included a photo of it for you to enjoy.

I should mention here that Alexander told me a story about something that happened to him when he was a younger man back in Yugoslavia. He and a friend, both art students, once headed up the side of a mountain to an old monastery to help out with some restoration work. The way up was difficult, as there were no real roads passing through dense forests just a narrow path. They were a long time trekking their way up.

When they arrived, they were treated generously by the monks who lived there and who, as Alexander puts it, were genuinely spiritual Christians. Having finished their day's task, they decided they needed to head back down to where they were living. However, night had fallen, and they had forgotten to bring along a flashlight or two. As they started their journey, they realized just how dark a mountainous forest can get, especially when the moon is just a sliver of silver in the night sky, blotted out by thick branches. In short, they found it almost impossible to stay on the path, unable to even see it most of the time.

Panic began to chill their spines and thoughts of getting lost or hurt out where no one may find them filled their minds with dread. But then, out of nowhere, literally millions of fireflies appeared in front of them, creating a blanket of light as they all flashed their inner beams on cue with one another. The two young men couldn't believe what was happening; it was as though a large neon light was pulsating in such a manner as to guide them down the mountain. They always stayed right in front of the two men, never deviating off the trail.

The little bar for the ghost

Those fireflies remained with them to the very bottom and then disappeared. As Alexander put it, it was a "spiritual experience," and he wondered if the prayers of the monks produced some sort of guiding protection for them on their journey.

One of the cooks at the Roadhouse, whom I shall refer to as Tim, has been on staff for several years. He has had more than one encounter with the ghosts. It's not uncommon for him to be working away in the kitchen and suddenly see a man walk through the kitchen doorway, head directly behind the bar, and then just evaporate. It unsettled him a great deal at first, but after a while he sort of got used to it. In fact, other staff members have seen the man coursing through the bar, usually exiting the kitchen and either going behind the bar or heading over to the front entrance.

It's not only the staff who encounter the ghosts of the Roadhouse. There's the intriguing story of a customer who came in late one night when the place was slow. Leah was on duty and stationed by the bar. The customer, a local man, thought he heard music coming from the banquet room which was closed off at the time and pitch dark. He opened one of the glass panel doors and peeked inside. As he glanced around, his eyes fell upon an old player piano that is inoperable but kept around the place to add to the atmosphere. Only this time, he spied an elderly woman sitting at the piano and could actually hear the tune she was playing. He naturally thought it was odd, since she was sitting in the dark and looked as though she belonged to a period of time quite removed from the present.

The customer quietly closed the door, then approached Leah and asked who the lady was playing the piano in the banquet room. Leah assured him there was no one there and that she couldn't hear any music. That's when his slight case of nerves turned into a full blown case of the willies. He knew what he had seen, realized it wasn't normal, and immediately left. It was a long time before he darkened the doors again.

The Roadhouse has been a place of business since its inception back in the 1800s. It has had many incarnations: a tavern where you could get a room if needed, a classy restaurant, a speakeasy during Prohibition, etc. In fact, down in that Michigan basement, there's a tunnel off in one corner with an entry low to the ground and easily covered up with just a few boxes. It leads to the house next door and was used to spirit illegal hooch into the building when customers were getting dry or out of the building when the law started to act serious about separating the clientele from their bathtub gin. In fact, it is said that the mob—read, "gangsters"—who controlled the flow of illegal booze made short work of a competitive gang's henchman sent to try to horn in on their territory. They did away with the poor dumb slob with a piece of hot lead and buried him under the basement steps. A little excavation could add validity to the story, but no one cares that much to dig up the past.

The old secret tunnel for transporting
liquor during prohibition

Alexander and Leah, like many others in their line
of business, like to offer their customers entertainment.
While they often have bands and dancing in the banquet
room, they once decided to have a psychic come in to do
readings for those inclined to part with a few dollars to
find things out about themselves they already knew or
to try to get a glimpse of what the future may hold.

The man they brought in came with very good
references, set up a table off in one of the corners near
the restrooms, and soon had a dozen or so folks sipping
beers and waiting for their turn to sit across from him.
Leah noticed that the guy started out just fine, but after
a few customers had received their readings, he began
to appear distracted and nervous. He finally called Leah
over and told her he was quitting early, leaving several
people in a lurch who had wanted to consult with him.
He explained that he had begun to see the ghosts who
resided in the building, and they were making him feel

uncomfortable and unwanted. It got so oppressive, he felt he simply had to get out of there; they were upset with what he was doing as though he were betraying confidential information. I've often thought it was pretty bad when a psychic couldn't take the heat from a few ghosts.

As my meal ended, I asked if I could make arrangements for my team to spend a night at the tavern/restaurant to check the place out and maybe run into a ghost or two in the process. Alexander and Leah must have been satisfied that I was normal enough to be trusted and granted my request. I informed them that whenever investigating a haunted place my caveat is that at least one person associated with the location be on the premises with us. It's just my way of making people feel comfortable we're not going to be disrespectful or cause any damage. After all, the Roadhouse stocks a full bar, and that can be a temptation whenever a ghost hunter gets a bad case of nerves in the middle of the night.

I arrived with only a partial team. When we take a look into a dwelling that is not expansive, we use fewer people. That way there's not too much activity to interfere with what we're trying to do. Alexander, a self-proclaimed night owl, joined us and was more than a gracious host. He allowed access to the entire building and interrupted us only to generously offer liquid refreshment of the soft sort. He was available for questions when they arose as well.

The four of us (five including Alexander) toured the establishment and got some historical insight from Alexander. Just as the tour ended, a customer had an experience with one of the resident ghosts. Her name is Lisa (the customer, not the ghost), and she and her husband live in the neighborhood within walking distance. She said that's handy when they wish to have more than just a drink or two as they don't have to drive home. They're regulars at the Roadhouse and enjoy the atmosphere and camaraderie. She and the others who were at the bar when we arrived had no idea why we were there, which makes the incident more delicious.

Having downed her first drink, Lisa stepped away from the bar to go outside to enjoy a cigarette—Michigan no longer allows smoking in public places, so smokers must take their chances with Mother Nature. At any rate, she was several feet away from the front door, still inside the building, when she put her cigarette in her mouth and reached for her lighter. As she raised the lighter to her lips, it was suddenly knocked out of her hand with enough force to send it scurrying across the floor. I heard her telling her friends about the incident after she returned to her seat at the bar. She became very excited when she learned why we were in the building.

Seated next to Lisa and her husband were two other regular customers of the Roadhouse. They both spoke of experiences they had run up against at various homes they had lived in, but all that is fodder for a future story and book. I bring it up only to point out that when one person shares a haunted experience, it gives others around them permission to feel comfortable sharing theirs.

After the Roadhouse closed for the night and the last customers issued their farewells, we went about setting up our equipment in various locations of the building. Two members headed down to the basement, where the Prohibition tunnel is separated by mere feet from the spot where the Prohibition gangster is supposedly buried. In the meantime I settled in to a spot in the banquet room with another team member, pointing our cameras from such a location as to encompass the bulk of the room and certain to include the old piano (we thought it would be great if we could capture some video of the old girl tinkling the ancient ivories, but alas, it was not to be). Then both teams settled in for ninety minutes of quiet observation and note taking.

At the conclusion of our first session, the four of us met in the banquet room to touch base on what, if anything, we had experienced. It wasn't much of a conversation, as nothing out of the ordinary wafted our way. As we were talking, Alexander walked over to offer us a soft drink. Then he asked us why we were concentrating on the basement and the banquet room when the bulk of the activity was in the dining room/ bar/kitchen area. We relocated our equipment, took up residence in areas adjacent to those positions, and began our second session of recording and listening.

The second session ended just as the first session had ended, with no cooperation from the spirits. Again, as we chatted, Alexander came over to join us and offer us yet another soft drink. As I sipped my cola and listened to the small talk covering the several minutes of our break, my eye was caught by a figure out in the entryway of the bar. Let me set up the scenario for you.

When you enter the building by the front door, you walk into what resembles an enclosed front porch, replete with beer signs, plants, and a dry erase board announcing the specials of the day. Standing in that area, you can look through a set of windows into the bar proper and vice versa. That's where I saw the figure of a man move from just inside the front door and pass two of the windows, as though heading into the bar. The figure was black in shape but clearly human—at one time at least—and definitely real. Guess where our cameras were not pointed at the time? Yeah, it's like that quite often.

We decided to begin round three of the investigation, wanting to stick around through the "witching hour." I had grown up thinking the witching hour began at midnight, but have since learned through research that it actually begins at 3 a.m. The theological theory here is that Christ was on the cross until 3 p.m., at which time he was declared dead and taken down. If something miraculous had taken place to benefit humanity at that

See a male ghost walking behind the bar

hour, then it was believed the powers of darkness make a point to enhance their presence at the reverse time—3 a.m.—when all is dark and foreboding.

Nothing happened during that hour, and our team was getting a bit fatigued, so we called it a night. We packed up our equipment, thanked our host for his generous hospitality, and drove off into the early morning hours for home and much appreciated sleep.

Planning a Visit? Please do. The help is friendly and the owners are perfectly willing to share their stories of ghostly encounters. However, be courteous enough not to waste their time, and show your appreciation by ordering a meal. They offer everything from prime rib to that great sticky burger.

Still Haunted? I'm told it always has been and always will be. Maybe one of those ghosts is a former owner of the building from way back in the day. Or maybe there's a Native American who leaves his resting place down the road to visit his old stomping grounds.

Chapter 21
Cold, Clammy Babysitter

Place Visited: A private dwelling in Battle Creek in a quiet and unassuming neighborhood.

Period of Haunting: According to the family paterfamilias, the haunting has been going on for about three years. He didn't know the folks who owned the home before him, so he's not able to say if it was haunted before his family moved in.

Date of Investigation: June–July of 2003.

Description of Location: Battle Creek is a familiar name to anyone who lives in Michigan and to a whole lot of people all across the country who happen to eat cereal for breakfast. It's the home of Kellogg's, Post, and Ralston cereal companies, which has earned Battle Creek the moniker "Cereal City." It's just off the I-94 corridor between Jackson and Kalamazoo.

When I was a child, I asked my teacher how Battle Creek got its name. She told the class it came about as the result of a great Indian battle in the 1820s (back when I was a kid, Native Americans were always called Indians). My imagination pictured hoards of painted fighters bearing bows and arrows and tomahawks fighting against the brave White settlers willing to sacrifice their lives to protect their families. I didn't know the true history of the events. A survey party of four to six men encountered two locals who tried to steal some provisions resulting in one Native American getting seriously hurt but no other casualties. Yet another great childhood legend bit the proverbial dust.

Battle Creek is not the tourist community it once was. Kellogg's no longer gives tours of its facility, and that was a big draw. Since then, a new draw attracts lots of folks on a once-a-year basis. It's the world's longest breakfast table, spread out through the downtown area for blocks. The other major event is the hot air balloon festival. Binder Park Zoo, relatively small but well kept, brings in lots of families, and Battle Creek now has its own casino.

Since the economy suffers from the closure of local industry, the population of the city proper has declined in recent years. However, the federal government chose Battle Creek as the location of a Veteran's Administration hospital, and the Hart-Doyle-Inouye Federal Center is also within the limits of the city, all of which helps the community economically.

Haunt Meter: * * * *

LEO STEWART (of course I'm not using real names here) and his wife Lena purchased the house in a nice south side neighborhood back in the late 1990s. At first, everything was hunky-dory, just an average couple living in an average home in an average Michigan city. The neighbors were friendly, they had found a church home they liked, and both of them had jobs that seemed to make their lives comfortable.

According to Leo, nothing strange had ever been noticed, or even thought about, until the birth of their daughter, Mackenna. That's when life as it had been became life as it was to be—more than a bit scary and very puzzling.

> Almost right after we brought Mackenna home from the hospital, odd things started to take place. She was a newborn, so she wasn't sleeping through the night. She was bottle fed, so Lena and I took turns getting up to

feed and change her. I remember like it was yesterday the first time I ran into the ghost. I went into her room to take care of her, and all the baby stuff we kept on the dresser was on the floor—diapers, oil, wipes, everything. They weren't tossed all over the place; it was like someone had just picked them up and set them on the floor. I looked around the room and thought to myself, "what the hell...?" I asked Lena the next morning if she had been cleaning up in there and laid the stuff on the floor, and she looked at me like I was crazy. She told me no mother who loved her children would ever do that.

A couple weeks later, it was my turn to take care of her again, and I went into her room and changed and fed her. We kept a rocker in there, and I rocked her and fed her until she went back to sleep. Then I put her back in her crib and turned to go back to bed. When I turned around, there was a woman standing in the doorway watching me. I was blown away; I mean, I just stood there staring at her for a minute and then said "who the hell are you?" When I did, she disappeared. She was there one second and totally gone the next.

I went back to bed and just laid there, picturing her in my mind. She looked to be in her sixties, and she was wearing a house dress like my grandmother used to wear when I was a kid. She was just standing there with her arms down at her side, and she had a real sad look on her face. At first it scared the living hell out of me, but after I got to thinking about it all, I sort of felt sorry for her. The next morning, before the babysitter came in so I could take Lena to a doctor appointment,

I told her what I saw and asked her if we should tell the babysitter about it. We decided not to, because good babysitters are hard to find, and she was a good one.

More incidents took place as the months passed. The click of high-heeled shoes would be heard moving across the kitchen floor, locked doors would be found unlocked, and closet doors that had been closed would be standing open. Once, as the two of them lay in bed, they heard the water in the bathtub start running. Leo went into the bathroom and found the water running at the right temperature for someone to take a bath.

*Note: I find the differences in the sexes amusing. Lena started to worry about their safety, while Leo worried about water damage to the house.

Little things continued to plague Leo and Lena, but they paled in comparison to the next added attraction, and it wasn't at the hands of the woman they'd been blaming for the odd incidents. This time, Lena filled me in, and even months after the event, I could still see the fear on her face and hear to quiver in her voice.

It was a Saturday afternoon, and Leo had to go into work that day, which didn't make me happy because we had to cancel some plans to get together with family for a picnic. Anyway, Mackenna was asleep in her crib—she must've been about six months then—and I had gone downstairs to toss some clothes into the washer. I hadn't been down there a minute when I heard this really loud screeching noise like some animal had been hurt or something. I mean, I could just about feel my blood freezing in my veins. The next thing I knew I was flying up the steps. It must have been my mother's instinct that propelled me because I was scared out of my wits, but my baby was up there.

I ran to Mackenna's room, my eyes bugged out and afraid of what I might run into on the way. I got to her room and she was still asleep, and that scared me even more. I started thinking, "how in world can this child sleep after that?" Then I just stood by her crib for a couple of minutes getting my nerve back. My heart was pounding so hard I could barely get my breath.

After I calmed down some, I started rationalizing—you know how it is, whenever we run into something we can't explain, we make up excuses for whatever it was so we can keep on going. Then I left Mackenna's room and very quietly shut her door. When I got to the living room, I literally froze in my tracks. Over in the doorway to the kitchen I saw this, thing. I didn't really see it with my eyes; it was weird, like I was seeing it in my mind. I was positive it was really there—I knew it was really there. That's the only way I can describe the sensation. It was really short, only about three feet tall, and it was shaped like a human only really grotesque looking and animal-like. It didn't seem to have eyes, just holes in its face, but it must have had eyes because I could tell it was looking at me. It was milky white all over with a patch of hair at its crotch, but I couldn't tell what it was. It had a wide mouth and it shook all over as it stood there. I have never been in the presence of anything so scary in my life. Then it ran across the kitchen, and I could hear the sound of it going across the floor. Right away I knew that those times we heard what we thought were high heels was really this thing. I guess it must have had hooves or something. I ran back to Mackenna's room, shut the door and just sat in the rocker next to her until Leo came home.

You'd think after an encounter as bizarre as that one they'd have packed up their belongings and caught the first flight to Paducah. When you're tied to a mortgage and have a new baby, it's not that easy. Leo and Lena spent the next several days and nights enmeshed within the stress of not knowing from one minute to the other what or who was going to suddenly disrupt their lives.

The ordinary was interrupted nearly a month later when Lena had put the baby down for her nap and then spread herself out on the couch to watch a favorite daytime television show. As most of us do in such a situation, she fell fast asleep, the warmth of the house and the soft cushions of the sofa having lulled her into peaceful bliss.

Lena's slumber was softly interrupted by something cold and, as she puts it, "rather clammy" against her wrist. Gently awaking and opening her eyes, she was surprised to see an elderly woman hovering above her and that it was this woman's hand pressing against her own.

Lena admitted she was startled at first, but the woman had such a peaceful look about her she immediately knew not to be afraid. The woman had kind eyes, and Lena felt as though she was trying to comfort her. Even after the woman faded away, Lena had a continuing feeling of protection. The whole experience gave Lena the assurance that everything was all right.

When Leo came home from work that evening, she told him all about what had happened, and when she described the woman, he knew it was the same lady he had encountered shortly after they had moved in. The two agreed that this was a protective spirit, something that was affirmed for them a few weeks later when she once again appeared, this time to both of them. Lena told me:

> We were watching the Letterman show and having a snack. Of course, Mackenna was asleep in her room. We heard her start to make those sounds babies make when they may be waking up, and we listened to see if that's what she was going to do. You know how it is, you don't want to rush right in there and really wake her up if she's just making sounds in her sleep; you want to see if she'll just settle down first.
>
> We sat there for a few seconds, and just when we thought she wasn't going to wake up, we heard her start to cry a little bit more. When she did, we both turned to look in that direction, and we saw the old woman sort of float down the hallway and into Mackenna's room. We just stared at each other, sort of froze, not knowing how to act or what to do. Then we realized Mackenna wasn't crying any more. We looked at each other like, "OK, which one of us is going in there?" but neither of us said anything. After a few more seconds, we both got up and went into her room. She was sleeping peacefully, and no one was in there with her.

The elderly woman kept appearing from time to time, mostly being attentive to the needs of Mackenna. Once, when Lena went in to check on her before going to bed herself, she stopped abruptly at her daughter's door and watched as the old girl sat in the rocking chair next to the crib, slowly rocking as though she were watching over the little one as she slumbered. Lena said she looked at the woman, then looked at her daughter, and stepped away from the door and went to her own room to think things over. When she generated enough courage, she tiptoed back to her daughter's room and once more peeked inside. The rocking chair was empty, and Mackenna was sleeping like you'd want your baby to sleep.

The old woman was deemed to be a protector of sorts, someone who was drawn to Mackenna, and as far as ghosts go, they weren't threatened by her floating around the house. The nasty little critter with holes for eyes was a whole different story. Lena encountered it once again.

It was a really nice day, so I took Mackenna outside for some sunshine and fresh air. We have a fenced-in back yard, and I took some toys out there for her to play with while I sat in a lawn chair reading.

We'd been out there almost an hour, I'd say, when all of a sudden I heard this banging around inside the house coming from the kitchen. It sounded like someone was slamming pots and pans around. I jumped up without thinking and ran inside, and there were broken dishes all over the kitchen floor. I looked up and saw the cabinet door where I kept the dinner plates was wide open, and I knew I hadn't left it that way.

I didn't want to leave Mackenna outside alone, so I rushed back out, picked her up, and took her inside. With all that glass on the floor, I put her in her crib, and she naturally started to cry—she didn't like it one bit. I didn't blame her for crying, but I had a mess to clean up. I went back to the kitchen, got out the broom and dustpan, and started cleaning up. All of a sudden it was like the whole room was filled with this awful presence. The place stunk like rotten garbage and was so strong I felt like I was going to puke.

I went to the back door to catch my breath, and when I turned toward the kitchen again, that thing was back, and I could sense that it went zipping across the floor and into the living room. I screamed like hell.

In just a quick minute, I got really mad and didn't want that thing near my daughter. I ran back through the house and into her room. She was still screaming mad at having been put back in her crib, but other than that she was just fine, and that nasty little demon was nowhere around. It took every bit of courage I could find to go back into the kitchen and finish cleaning up, but since the stink was gone, I could sense it was gone, too.

This time, Lena didn't wait for Leo to come home from work. She got him on the phone and let him know in no uncertain terms where he needed to be. Leo, of course, did just as instructed, and then the two of them decided it was time to do something—anything—about what was going on in their home.

They didn't want to tell their minister about what was going on, and they really didn't want him to know they were going to bring in someone who could help them out. They sat down at the computer and started searching, and they couldn't believe how many people claim to be psychic. There wasn't a way for them to judge who was legitimately psychic and who would take their money without offering a solution.

Leo and Lena finally found a woman with psychic proclivities who was associated with a nationwide organization of psychics. They conducted a telephone interview with her, met her for coffee at a local restaurant, and only then did they agree to hire her to investigate their home.

Author's note: they made their decision based upon things the psychic had brought up during their coffee meeting.

It seems she knew things about both Leo and Lena she couldn't possibly have known. That usually does the trick.

The psychic, whom I shall refer to as Anne, made arrangements to come over to the house the next evening. Leo and Lena had told her absolutely nothing about what was happening except to say they believed they had ghosts, and they were frightened.

Anne showed up a few minutes late, as she explained she had gotten a bit turned around on her way there and had to backtrack. It makes me wonder how psychic one can be if they can't find their way to where they're going, but psychics are human too. At any rate, she entered the home, enjoyed a few minutes of small chitchat, then got down to business. She told both Leo and Lena not to tell her what had been happening or where as it would interfere with what she wanted to tune into naturally.

Anne passed through all the rooms of the house, sometimes pausing as though lost in thought and sometimes coming to an abrupt halt as though running smack into something no one else was seeing. The run through of the home lasted the better part of an hour, and then Anne asked if she could go back to certain areas alone and sit quietly. Permission gratefully granted, that's what she did, while Leo and Lena sat in the living room sipping coffee and waiting for Anne's analysis.

After nearly another hour had passed, Anne announced she was ready to tell them what she had discovered and asked if they could go sit in the kitchen. Over a cup of coffee, she informed Leo and Lena that there was a great deal of activity in the home, and most of it was centered around their daughter. Not wanting to panic them, she immediately told them there was an elderly woman who watched out for her and was very protective of her. She said the woman was not associated with the house and was not related to either of them but was a protective spirit who had been drawn to the home by the energy of their daughter. That was the good news. The bad news was that this woman showed up to help keep a negative energy form away from the little girl. She explained that this negative energy form was an expression of the earth's natural energy. Certain places generate either positive or negative energy, and this energy can manifest itself in different ways. In this case, she sensed it was showing up as some sort of half animal, half human, and was trying to get to their daughter to possess her.

This wasn't the sort of information Leo and Lena found comforting, and they insisted on knowing what they could do to get rid of the nasty little critter. Anne explained to them that she would go into a trance and try to press the negative energy being back into the earth and try to seal it there. She said she had done such a thing before, but it may not be a permanent solution depending upon how strong an energy it was. There would be a whole lot of resistance on the part of the little creature. That being said, she also told them they should explore moving to another home somewhere else.

The long and the short of this uneven tale is that the psychic claimed to have sealed the negative energy, and both the critter and the old woman weren't seen for several months. During this time, the home was sold and the family settled into fresh digs in another part of town. The added attraction was that they were told their daughter had a strong spirit and a lot of positive energy. As she grew it should be nurtured to good use.

Planning a Visit? I know you'd like to, but unless you're psychic yourself, you won't have a clue where this house sits.

Still Haunted? Not at the time Leo and Lena packed up their belongings and set up housekeeping elsewhere. Who knows, maybe that negative earth energy will take on yet another grotesque shape and pop up again—or maybe it already has.

Chapter 22
The Lumber Baron

Place Visited: A spacious, Victorian lumber baron style home on Center Street in Bay City, Michigan.

Period of Haunting: It's been going on for many years now.

Date of Investigation: The early 2000s.

Description of Location: Bay City is just that, a city on the bay, Saginaw Bay to be exact. Because of its location and due to the vast forests of yesteryear which once existed coast to coast in Michigan, Bay City was one of the places where freshly cut lumber was hauled for shipment out onto the Great Lakes and off to places beyond. Back in those days, Bay City could be a wild and woolly place to make your home. The main street was one long strip of watering holes, with alcohol-sodden lumberjacks and stevedores tossing back whiskey and flailing out with fists. As I said in an earlier book, some of those bars had trap doors in the floors, and captains ready to steam off with a load of lumber often were short crew members. They paid a bounty to the bar owners who would steer a drunken sot over the hatch and drop him into the clutches of a boatyard crew.

Much has changed since those days, although one or two places in town still sport those trap doors. The downtown taverns are a lot classier, and it's a great place to find a good burger or steak. My suggestion is just to park your car and walk the downtown business area. You're certain to discover a non-chain restaurant you'll truly enjoy. The city is home to the River Roar, a high speed boat race that attracts lots of folks to the Saginaw River. You can also enjoy the summer Rib Fest down by the river, the yearly Civil War re-enactment, and every now and then the Tall Ships pull into the bay and head up the river, large sailing vessels reminiscent of days gone by.

The home in question is one of many so-called lumber baron homes, built by those entrepreneurs who made their millions denuding the forests and lining their pockets. Driving through this area, you can see for yourself the competition they had with one another when it came to building themselves new digs. These places are huge, ornate, and massively beautiful. Once a year there is a tour where, for a fee, you can visit several of these homes and marvel at how much money these guys sunk into these mansions. The home which concerns us sits amongst all the others, and there are so many of them I'm able to indicate which street it's on, but I won't disclose the exact address.

Haunt Meter: * * * *

ONE OF THE RESULTS of having written books about haunted places is that you find yourself meeting all kinds of people. Many are interested in the stories I write. Some want to share their ghostly experiences. Some are intellectuals who try diligently to understand, or even debunk, the stories I've written (which is all right with me, I'm not too concerned about whether folks believe me or not). Some folks are just plain nut cases, which explains some of the political elections we've experienced in our country.

At any rate, as the result of one of my lectures I was put into contact with a sincere young woman about her uncle's home up in Bay City. She and other family members have, according to her, had numerous run-ins with ghosts traipsing through the place. She offered to give me her uncle's phone number and told me to contact him about checking the place out. I suggested that she give my number to her uncle, and if he felt comfortable doing so, he could give me a call. Then, and only then, would I possibly pay the place my respects.

Sure enough, a few days later her uncle, whom I shall call Ernest Hantz, called my cell phone and introduced himself. He turned out to be a professional person (read: loaded to the gills with greenbacks) who had purchased the home years ago and made it his primary residence. He filled me in on some of the strange things going on, and then we made arrangements to meet in person and examine the interior for those pesky little spirits.

Ernest said that when he moved in, it was mid-winter, and the house needed certain repairs and renovations. The place wasn't in a state of disrepair, mind you, it was more in need of minor tweaking, and the renovations were of the sort to please the new owner.

Ernest says the first thing he had done was a professional cleaning and reconditioning of the thick oak woodwork lining the walls of the library and a refinishing of the library shelves. This resulted in lots of dust as much of the wood needed sanding. Then the smell of varnish also permeated the entire room and wafted out into others when the library door was open. At the same time, he contracted some plaster work for the master bedroom, which is also quite a messy task. As is wont to happen with ghosts, they started making themselves known when their abode was being messed with.

It started innocuously enough, as haunting's often do. The team employed to refinish the library reported that more than once their tools and equipment were messed with while they worked or when they would take a break or go to lunch. During one lunch break, they returned to their work to find the step ladder they had left set up in order to reach the ceiling trim was all folded up and lying on the other side of the room.

At first, they thought maybe Ernest had come into the room for an inspection of how things were advancing and had for some reason moved the ladder. Alas, the fellow who had been upstairs engaged in his plastering assured them that Ernest had not been in the home all morning. He had called to say he would be coming home late and to lock up the house when they were finished for the day. In the meantime, the woodworkers passed it off as though one of the two of them had taken the ladder down and just didn't remember doing it. That worked for a day or two when other interesting things started taking place.

Let's refer to our two woodworkers as Gene and Roger. Gene, the elder of the crew, began to notice his tools taking on a life of their own. For instance, his electric sander would be set on the floor while he inspected his work, and when he'd reach for it, it would be somewhere across the room and unplugged. That happened more than once to both he and Roger. There were times when their brushes, which they kept in a metal tool box, would simply be missing. They'd always find them but not always in the room in which they were engaged. Once, Ernest had come home to find several of those brushes lying in his kitchen sink, which displeased him quite a bit. Thinking they had been placed there for cleaning by his artisans, he intended to lecture them about wandering around his antique home with dirty brushes. They assured Ernest they certainly had not pulled such a stunt and explained to him some of the strange events they had been encountering while toiling away in that vintage library of his.

At first, Ernest thought they were making the stories up, so he headed up the stairs to the master bedroom for a quick conversation with his plasterer, a fellow I shall dub Bill. Ernest told Bill the stories Gene and Roger had related to him and waited for the type of response he expected—cynical laughter. He didn't get it.

In fact, Bill seemed a bit relieved to be able to relate to Ernest the odd things he had been encountering.

Bill went on to say he thought someone had been sneaking into the master bedroom when he wasn't looking and messing around with his batch of plaster. Several times he had prepared a small batch to just the correct consistency then set up his ladder to work on the ceiling. He was involved in creating an intricate design, only to retrieve his plaster and find it much too watery to work with. He went on to relate that he, too, had many of his tools mysteriously disappear, even those he had just momentarily set down as he inspected his work. Once, he said, a metal triangle he had been using to create his corner designs went flying off his step ladder and smashed against one of the bedroom walls putting a nick in the old plaster. He admitted that little incident made his nerves a bit queasy.

Gene, Roger, and Bill hung in there amidst all the uncanny events they continued to encounter. They finished their work, albeit a bit ahead of schedule, which may or may not be attributed to the inspiration given them by the ghosts. Things didn't so go well for the electrician Ernest brought in for what should have been only a couple of day's work.

Let's refer to our electrically endowed professional as Marvin. Marvin was hired to go down into the cavernous basement and replace the ceiling lights throughout those deep recesses. It wasn't work that was required to bring things up to code; it was just that Ernest didn't like the old overhead bulbs sticking out of the ornate metal socket plates and the exposed wiring tacked to the basement ceiling.

Good ol' Marv began in the morning, unscrewing the bulbs and prying off the old socket plates. He ended before lunch when he came up stairs, called Ernest at his office, and told him what had been going on down there. The first thing he had noticed was a strong sense he wasn't alone down there. Then he began to see tall shadows skirting from one side of the basement room he was in and over to the other. He described it as human shaped. He would see it for a brief moment, then it would be gone, and then it would show up again.

Marvin related that lights he had turned on would suddenly go out. He'd turn the switch back on, resume his work, and once again the lights would shut off. He could even hear the switch flip as they did so. Thinking, as any electrician worth his kilowatts would, there must be something amiss with the circuit breaker box, he began searching through the basement for the breaker box. He found it in another room of the basement, just off the stairway he had used. Entering that room, he discovered no lights would work in there at all, so he resorted to his flashlight. Examining the breaker switches, he came to the obvious conclusion there was nothing at all amiss with the electrical system. As he used his flashlight to exit the room, all the lights came on by themselves.

By this time, electrician Marvin had just about had enough but decided he would try to ignore whatever else was happening around him, and get the hell out of there. Eventually, however, he found getting the job finished was going to be something someone else would have to be hired to do. It seems that although he had actually managed to remove several old fixtures, he did so under spirit-filled duress. The final straw came when he decided to remove the old fixtures in the room with the breaker box—supposedly because it was closest to the stairway in the event that ghostly activity would overcome his courage, which had been waning fast.

Marvin went into the room and had just pulled a pair of pliers out of his tool harness when he once again sensed he wasn't alone. Slowly turning his head to one side, he found himself in the presence of, not a shadow, but a man—a man as solid and as colorful as any human, only he knew this was not a man of flesh-and-blood proportions. He described him to Ernest as being about five feet-ten-inches tall with medium brown hair and a full but neatly trimmed beard. He wore dark clothing with an old style jacket which buttoned high and appeared to be in the garb of an officer of some boat. He remembers seeing a watch chain hooked to a button of the man's vest and leading into a vest pocket. The man then asked in a rather stern voice, "What do you think you're doing?" and then disappeared. That disappearance was immediately followed by Marvin's disappearance. He quit the job, apologized to Ernest, and felt guilty enough about it to call it even—no bill for work already begun but not yet finished.

The renovation work lasted the better part of the year, with other workmen, and even Ernest himself, encountering the odd idiosyncrasies of the ghosts. At least the workmen could go home at night and leave the ghosts behind them. Ernest didn't share that perk. He was with those spirits long after everyone else would leave for the day and alone with them all through the night.

Ernest would hear strange sounds emanating through the hallways as he lay in bed. He enjoyed reading in bed while sipping a nightcap. The house would be as quiet as a tomb at that late hour, and every little creak and snap would catch his attention. Nearly all of those noises he could legitimately pass off as the groaning and creaking of an old wooden house, but not all of them were that easy to explain away.

One night, lying in bed with his book and his whiskey, his ears picked up the faint, yet distinctive, sound of footsteps. Laying the book aside, he slipped off his reading glasses and stared at the bedroom door, which was closed. As he stared, the footsteps became louder and closer. Let's allow Ernest to finish the tale.

> I just sat up in bed and listened. It was
> obvious someone was in the house with me,
> and they shouldn't be there at all. What was

strange was that I knew it wasn't an intruder because something within me sensed it was a spirit. Well, I'll tell you, that awareness didn't make me feel a damned bit more secure. You can call the police if someone is in your home who had illegally entered, but what do you do, or who do you call, when it's not human?

After a few moments, the footsteps came to a stop just outside my bedroom door. A moment later, the doorknob started moving, like someone was checking to see if the door was locked. It's one of those antique knob assemblies, the type where the knob is white porcelain, and you can lock the bedroom door from either side with an old fashioned skeleton key. I have the key in my night stand, but I never use it. Anyway, the knob moved from side to side, but the door didn't open. Then I could hear whoever it was walking farther down the hallway, past the other bedrooms. Then it stopped, and everything was quiet and normal again—except for my bladder!

This wouldn't be the only night Ernest would hear the footsteps, and the hallway upstairs was not the only place he'd encounter them. He began to hear them once in a while in the morning while he took his breakfast in the kitchen. The steps would move against the hardwood floor inside the dining room. Sometimes he encountered them when he came home for the evening. He would enter the home through the back door after having parked his car in the garage out back and would hear someone upstairs walking around, sometimes slowly pacing, sometimes angrily stomping about. Once, he even called the police. It was the first time the "normal" walking about seemed angry, and he could hear what sounded like furniture being shoved around in one of the upstairs bedrooms—a bedroom that was as yet unfurnished. The police arrived, checked out the perimeter of the home, and then did a thorough search of the entire premises, finding nothing. As they left, one of the police officers gave him a couple of phone numbers where he could be reached any time day or night. He explained that he had been called to the house many times by the previous owner for the same reasons, and he was determined to come face to face with the ghost he believed was in the house. This made Ernest feel secure on one level, yet insecure on another.

As time passed, Ernest experienced the strange phenomena many other persons experience when living in a haunted house. He became accustomed to it all. In fact, it started to feel quite natural, as though he was living with someone who was very private and quite harmless. Sort of like a brother who's a hermit by nature and who keeps strange hours and habits. While the haunting may have begun to feel normal to Ernest, it was not so to his guests.

Take the time Ernest decided to have some guests over around Christmas time, just some colleagues, their spouses, and one or two other dear friends. He had the downstairs parlor, living room, dining room and foyer professionally decorated, and a caterer friend of his supplied the Christmas fare: cinnamon cookies, plum pudding, a citrus punch, and assorted meats and cheeses. He even had a pianist engaged to perform carols and background music. Again, let's allow Ernest to add the color to our story.

> On the whole, it really was a successful evening. Everyone had a good time. The food was wonderfully prepared, and everyone was in a relaxed mood. I had even hired a man to dress as a butler, and he greeted the guests as they arrived, very adroitly ushering them into the home, taking their coats and directing them into the parlor. It was a fun and rather meaningful evening, but it did have its moments.

As my guests arrived, I enjoined them to partake of the Christmas fare, and they would fill their plates and help themselves to punch, coffee, tea, or something a bit stronger, if that was to their liking. Then we sat and listened to the piano as it was played in the adjoining room and enjoyed friendship and conversation. Every now and then, the fellow I had hired as a butler would step into the room to see if anyone needed anything. It was truly an old fashioned Christmas gathering.

After about the first hour, when the party was just getting going really nicely, one of my lady friends complimented me on how good everything looked and how she thought it was a great idea to have a butler and a servant girl in old fashioned clothing. Well, I knew I had hired the fellow to be a butler, but I also knew I had certainly not hired anyone to be a servant girl.

I didn't want to frighten her, or any of my other guests who may have seen the woman, so instead I thanked her, but then asked her how her memory was. I asked her if she could describe the clothing of the both the butler and the servant girl now that they were out of sight. She, of course, accurately described the butler, right down to the pinky ring on his left hand. Then she described the servant girl as well. She was about thirty years of age, and her hair was light brown, worn upward, and covered with a little square, white hat. Her dress was black, and her apron was white with gold trim, longish, draping down to her mid-calf area. I asked where she had encountered her, and she said she had noticed her standing in the doorway of the parlor from time to time, smiling as she watched over everyone. I asked if she had spoken to her, and she said she had done so only once when she had to use the restroom and asked for directions as she had stepped into the hallway. She said the woman didn't speak back but pointed down the hallway.

Well, about this time my friend became suspicious of my questions and asked me about it. I figured it was time to let her know the truth, and I informed her that I had not hired a servant girl, and that I had no idea who she was talking about. At first, she thought I was trying to play a joke on her but quickly realized that was not the case at all. Her eyes grew as wide as saucers, and she was absolutely speechless for about a minute.

Well, you know how it is with people, part of her didn't want to believe what she knew to be true. Then another of my guests, who evidently had heard enough of our conversation to add to the discussion, informed us that she, too, had seen the young woman. Well, right away I made a joke about the house being haunted, told them I would regale them with stories at another time, and then announced to them I needed to give our pianist permission to take his break.

I walked into the sitting room where he was playing and told him he could take whatever time he needed to catch his breath and to go into the kitchen and help himself to some of the goodies I had left in there for him. He went into the kitchen, and I returned to my guests.

Just a few short minutes later, he was back in the sitting room at the piano. He wasn't yet playing; he was just sitting there. I thought that to be odd, so I went to see if everything was all right. He then looked at me and said, as stony faced as you can imagine, "Did you know your house is haunted?"

Immediately, I informed him of the truth and told him I had become well acquainted with the ghosts of the house and that they were perfectly harmless. Then I asked him what had happened. He said he had gone into the kitchen and prepared himself a plate of cookies and a cup of cinnamon coffee from the carafe the caterer had left in there. He had turned around to sit at the kitchen table and enjoy his snack when he suddenly found himself face to face with a rather attractive young woman in what looked to be a servant's outfit from the old Victorian period. He was surprised to see her there, as she had not been there when he entered the kitchen and he hadn't heard anyone follow him in. As he started to greet her, he said she just smiled and sort of evaporated out of sight. He was really quite shaken. I assured him all was well and that others had seen her also. There was nothing to be afraid of. Still, his playing was not quite as sharp as it had been before his break, but I couldn't blame him. What intrigued me most was that I had never seen this woman before and haven't run into her since. I guess she just enjoyed Christmas, or maybe she had been an employee of the family who lived in the house over a hundred years ago and had served at their Christmas gatherings.

Ernest has lived in his home several years now, and the haunting continues. For a while he was hopeful he would encounter more than footsteps, shaking doorknobs, and the sound of furniture being shuffled around in the upstairs bedrooms. He got his wish about two years after having moved in.

They say summer colds are the worst, and sure enough, Ernest managed to catch one. He felt miserable enough to stay home from his office, fixed himself some chicken soup and a cup of tea, and headed into the parlor to sip them both and then take a nap. He says he was about three spoonfuls into his soup when he noticed a man standing just outside the parlor at the edge of the vestibule. He was wearing dark blue clothing, and he estimated him to be under six feet tall and about sixty years of age. He had a neatly trimmed beard and looked for all intents and purposes to be a sea captain, at least that's the impression he received from the man. Ernest says his spoon was halfway to his mouth when he just froze. The two of them looked at one another for several long moments, and then the man narrowed his eyes, nodded his head, and walked off down the hallway and out of sight. Was it our sea captain? Did a sea captain ever really live in the home? At this point, no one really knows.

Planning a Visit? I wish you could, but Ernest is a professional person who is very protective of his home, his acquaintances, and his personal space.

Still Haunted? Yes, the haunting of the historic lumber baron home continues.

Chapter 23
The One that Started it All

Place Visited: A two story frame farmhouse dating back to the 1820s located just south of Wooster, Ohio.

Period of Haunting: My association with the haunted home began in April of 1987 and continued through August of 1994. Through exhaustive and exhausting investigation, it has been determined that the haunting began shortly after 1910 and continues to this very day.

Date of Investigation: As stated above, off and on from 1987 through late 1994.

Description of Location: Wooster, Ohio, is a middle American town settled amongst the rolling hills of Amish country. The city is home to Wooster College, a fine liberal arts school with a very good reputation for academics.

The home in question is south of the city and just off Batdorf Road. The home is one of the oldest in that part of Ohio with the original part of the structure dating, as I have already indicated, to the late 1820s. Over the decades it has expanded, with an addition here and an addition there. Originally, it was built as a farmhouse. As it sits now, still in its original location, it overlooks a wide picturesque valley to the north. There is a full basement, and the ground floor consists of an enclosed porch of a comfortable size, kitchen, living room, dining room and small half bath. The second story offers three bedrooms and a very large bath, that room having at one time been another bedroom. Perhaps the best way to describe this house is to say it looks and feels haunted.

Wooster, Ohio, is located just a few miles east of Ashland, where I lived for three years while attending seminary in Delaware, Ohio. The city has an "All American" look and feel with a beautiful courthouse and many historic homes. It is also home to a famous potato chip processing plant and not far from Orrville, the home of Smucker's—the jam and jelly folks. If you decide to take a trip to the area, avoid the chain fast food joints and opt for a real meal at one of the many Amish restaurants dotting the countryside. They're the ones who actually make everything from scratch and aren't skimpy on the portions.

Haunt Meter: * * * * * *(This is the most haunted dwelling I've ever entered and by far the most chilling)*

AS THE TITLE INDICATES, this is the haunting that started it all for me. What do I mean by this? I mean that this is the haunting that began my active participation in hunting down spirits. Yes, I did grow up in a haunted home with myriad ghosts flitting about the old homestead, but none of those experiences were as intense as those I encountered while investigating this place.

I realize this chapter is going to be long but rightfully so. I also must tell you, my dear readers, that I have attempted many times to pen this tale only to be stopped by the spirit who has tormented the many owners and tenants of this home for decades. That is why I have not included this chapter in either of the first two books I've written about haunted places. You must also forgive me for including this chapter within a book about haunted places in Michigan, since this home rests comfortably—or perhaps, uncomfortably—in Ohio.

As I just indicated, my first attempts to research the home in hopes of writing a full book about its resident ghost were halted by the ghost himself. Each time I would begin typing away—or even thinking about typing away—he would show up, nasty cretin that he is, and make my dreams, and quite often my awakened moments, miserable. For years I had a pact with him, promising never to write about him if he agreed to leave me alone. From the moment of that agreement until the present, both of us have honored that agreement. I now break it and invite this vicious, sweat stinking, abusive ghost to take his best shot. I think I'm up to enduring his rage born of having suffered all these years from little-man syndrome (wow, I bet that gets him going).

I moved to Ashland, Ohio, reluctantly. I had just finished my Bachelor of Arts degree with a Religious Studies major at Albion College and had been accepted to do my Masters of Divinity at Duke University. Unfortunately, there were no churches available for me to serve in that part of North Carolina, so there was really no way to support my family while attending to my schooling. A last minute change of plans saw me heading down to The Methodist Theological School in Delaware, Ohio. It was my last choice as a seminary, but they did offer a church, a parsonage, and a salary just large enough to keep the family fed, so off I went.

My first semester there, in the autumn of 1987, I met many other students in the same situation as I, and we naturally formed a bond. Many times we would meet early in the morning, before classes, in the seminary coffee lounge and discuss theology, philosophy and all those other topics which lead to a career where you can earn enough money to eat at McDonald's once a week. It was always good conversation and time, we all felt, well spent.

During one of those conversations over donuts and tea (I'm not a coffee guy, I'm a Scotsman), one of the participants pointed out how one of our professors had made a statement in class wherein he stated, "I just can't believe there are still people who believe in haints" (haint is an old fashioned word for ghost, and this instructor was an old fashioned type of guy). I then admitted to my discussion group that I believed in ghosts because I had grown up in a haunted home and had encountered them many times throughout my life.

After that conversation, as I headed to class, a fellow student approached me and asked if I'd ever helped people understand how to handle a haunting. I answered that I had done so on many occasions. He then informed me that he was serving a church in a small, rural community, and he and his wife had become friends with another couple. They visited their home on a few occasions and were told the place was haunted. The family wasn't, at that time, particularly frightened about it, although they had their moments of fear. However, they wanted to know if there was anyone who could give them a hand dealing with it. My colleague asked me if I would take a shot at it. I asked my friend why he didn't do it himself, especially in light of the fact that they attended his church, and he responded by telling me he didn't believe in all that nonsense. I told him I'd be glad to visit with the folks in question and asked if he could tag along to make the introductions. He shook his head and said, "No way, I'm not going in that house again."—a strange and telling remark coming from someone who insisted he didn't believe in all that "nonsense."

Later that week I had the opportunity to give those folks a call and introduce myself. They turned out to be a wonderful, eclectic, and entertaining couple named John and Flo, just about my age. Since they didn't sound as though their marbles were dropping out onto the floor, I made arrangements to visit them the following week and asked if I could be given a tour of the home and bring along a friend who shared my interest in things paranormal. They quite charmingly approved my request, and on the date agreed upon the two of us showed up—myself and my buddy with the two first names, John Dennis. Now let me explain, John is a one-in-a-million sort of guy. One time at Annapolis Naval Academy, he was left alone in a dinghy on the

Atlantic and told to navigate back to port using only the stars. He was also a registered nurse and a very stout fellow with biceps the size of cantaloupes.

We arrived around ten in the morning on a Friday. Our hosts, John and Flo, (hang in there folks, there are two Johns in this part of the story), had delayed going into work so that they could give us the tour. After they showed us around and made certain we felt free to raid the refrigerator, they headed off to work. We would have the house to ourselves until six o'clock since their daughter was modeling in New York and their son had high school athletics practice until early evening.

At that time, John and I were fledglings to the ghost hunting game, but we did make a point to take along a couple of cameras—35 mm since there were no digital cameras back then—and a couple of cassette tape recorders since there were no digital audio recorders either. Alas, I miss the days of old-fashioned ghost hunting. At any rate, we decided to do a walkthrough of the house on our own first. The idea was to stay together, visit each room individually, snap several photos, and make notes as to their condition. We were very methodical because, well, we were both Methodists.

We began with the basement, which is not unlike most other basements—a bit damp, cement floor, but a good place for kids to play. Then we covered the rooms on the main floor and afterward headed up the stairway to the second level. Heading down the hallway, the first room we came to was the main bath on the right-hand side of the hallway. It used to be a bedroom, and now it had a short hallway leading into an expansive bathroom that was tastefully decorated with antique accents. The next room was the master bedroom, and it was a charming and comfortable looking room. An antique high-boy dresser stood against one wall, and it faced a gorgeous four poster bed adorned with a heavy Amish quilt. Paintings and photographs hung on the wall from ribbons attached to antique nails. It was the type of room one would photograph for a magazine about country living.

Having finished snapping photos of the master bedroom, we trod down the hallway and took shots of their daughter's room. Her name was Heather, and as I mentioned, she was out of school and in New York working as a fashion model (yes, she was that stunning). Her room looked about like one would expect a young woman's room to look, feminine and delicate with a place for everything and everything in its place. At the head of the hallway was the son's bedroom, and it was everything one would expect of a teenaged high school male, which means it was the complete opposite from his sister's room. Rock posters on the wall, clothes on the floor, musical instruments and athletic gear strewn about in a haphazard way.

After photographing every room upstairs, we headed down the hallway to go back to the main level and retrieve our recorders. As we passed by the master bedroom, we both froze solid in our tracks. That lovely, picturesque room, fit for a magazine spread, was now askew. The highboy dresser had all its drawers pulled out, and clothing was scattered across the floor. The paintings and photos on the wall were now all hanging crooked from their nails, and the Amish bedspread was lying all crumpled at the foot of the bed. We hadn't heard anything. We hadn't seen anything. Someone had paid a visit to that room in an effort to get our attention, and it worked. John's first remark was something religious about excrement, and I agreed.

After taking new shots of the room, we descended the stairs and decided to settle down for a bit with a cup of tea. Sipping our tea and munching on some cookies pilfered from their cookie jar—the expensive sort neither of us usually spent extra cash for—we engaged in light banter as we sat in the living room surrounded by built-in bookcases and overstuffed furniture.

As we indulged ourselves the room seemed to drop in temperature several degrees. We both noticed the change, and John remarked how some folks believe that a change in temperature, especially when the temperature drops down to outright chilliness, is indicative of the presence of a ghost. He chuckled about that and then added, "In an old house that would be pretty poor proof a ghost had just entered the room." But as he made that remark, the family cat, just a good old fashioned tabby, walked out of the kitchen and began to cross over the living room carpet. Passing by one corner of the room, the cat paused, stared into the corner for several seconds and then, back arched and hair raised above its spine, hissed at something we couldn't see. Then the feisty little feline continued its walk and headed onto the covered front porch to lay in the sun. To say we were impressed is to put it mildly, and you've got to love cats, as they take no guff from anyone—living or dead.

The bulk of the afternoon was spent sitting quietly in the living room after having set up our cassette recorders in the upstairs bedrooms. We simply remained silent, John opting to do what he had been practicing for years, a form of yoga meditation, while I read a magazine. Around four o'clock, we decided to collect our recorders, plug in our respective headphones, and listen to the tapes. We recorded absolutely nothing. When John and Flo returned home, we filled them in about our escapades, apologized for the condition of their bedroom, assuring them we had nothing to do with the mess, and then headed off for home, promising to return in a week or so if that was amenable to our hosts, which it was.

With the demands of work and school weighing heavily upon both of us, John and I didn't return to the home for nearly a month. This time we arrived on a Saturday morning, around eleven o'clock, and spent an hour or so talking to John and Flo. We shared what we had experienced on our previous visit, and they were pleased it hadn't been a waste of our time but weren't surprised at all by the nature and tone of what we had encountered. For them, it was pretty much run of the mill stuff, right down to Sparky the cat and his hissing.

Flo then told us the story of her first encounter with their ghost. It wasn't long after they had moved in, and the kids were both in elementary school. She said John was at work at the potato chip company, and she had not yet begun working outside the home. She had spent the bulk of the day alone in the house, unpacking boxes and putting things where they needed to be. About the middle of the afternoon, she decided to take a relaxing bath before the kids came home.

Flo ran the bath water, adding perfumed bubbles and lighting candles, and then went into the bedroom to tune in the radio to her favorite classical station. She returned to the bath, immersed herself beneath its scented water, and closed her eyes. Just as she was starting to feel relaxed, the classical strains of Bach took on a different form as she listened to the radio dial slide through station after station, finally coming to a rest on a station that offered country music. Not being a country music fan (this lady has class), she stepped out of the tub and returned to the bedroom where she moved the dial back to where it had been. Sliding back down into the warm water, she had just placed a wet washcloth over her eyes when she again heard the radio dial slowly passing by several stations and coming to rest on the same country station.

Flo told us she thought that was odd but wasn't particularly frightened. After all, it was a new place for them, and there were probably quirks that needed to be worked out and dealt with. Little did she know how right she would be.

After Flo and John left to do some shopping in Akron, we were again given the run of the house, as their son was spending the day at the home of a friend.

This time, we had arrived with a bit of a plan, which is always handy when checking out a haunted house. We had decided to run our tape recorders, but this time we would ask questions in an effort to see if we could contact the ghost who had made such an impression upon us. We decided the questions needed to be "yes or no" in style and should be spaced about twenty seconds apart. Since we didn't think our apparition would give us verbal answers, we began by asking him to answer with one knock meaning "yes" and two knocks meaning "no."

We stationed ourselves with me sitting halfway up the staircase between the main and second floor and John stationed about halfway down the upstairs hallway. Since the stairway was flush against the side of the house, it meant the hallway shot out at a right angle at the top, and I wouldn't be able to see John. The idea was to sit quietly for several minutes with our eyes closed in an effort to center ourselves and maybe open up a bit psychically.

The first question made us both break out in laughter right after it was asked. It was, "Is there anyone here?" I mean, if there's no one there, how could they answer with two knocks for "no"? We had to start the whole process of centering ourselves once again. That took about fifteen minutes, and then I began asking questions that are usually asked during a ghost hunt: Is this your house? Are you alone? Did you die in this house?

We must've asked questions and run our recorders for about an hour with the idea of listening to them later when we would have more free time. Curiosity, however, got the better of us, and we decided to at least listen to a few minutes of our attempt to contact the dead. Our very first question was, "Can you see us?" and we were blown away when we heard a distinct knock on the tape, as though someone had rapped a knuckle on the hallway wall. We hadn't heard it with our own ears as the question had been asked, but there it was on the tape. Just to see if it was a fluke, maybe a glitch in the recorder, we moved on to the second question, which was, "Is it all right for us to be here?" and immediately there came two firm knocks. Again, this answer only showed up on the audio tape as we hadn't heard it at the time we had asked the question.

A few of the questions received no answer at all. Several of the questions were responded to with the appropriate knock or two. We discovered through our questioning that the ghost was a man (which we had suspected) but that he wasn't alone. There was a woman and a child with him. He went on to indicate it was his house, and he wanted the current residents, along with us, to get out. He also informed us that he hadn't died in the home because he didn't consider himself to be dead.

It was the middle of the afternoon when we had finally finished with the tape and all of our note taking associated with it. We were hungry, so we left our equipment in the house, jumped into the car, and headed down to the nearest fast food joint. Over sandwiches, fries, and soft drinks, we made the decision to try some more recording when we returned and made a new list of questions to ask. Then we drove back to the house.

We set up our gear to communicate with the dead in the same places and returned to our familiar posts. I wasn't two questions into our experiment when I suddenly heard and felt a deep exhaling of breath on the side of my face, not once but twice. I was about to call out to John when all of a sudden I could hear him scrambling to stand up. He fairly ran over to the top of the stairs, looked down at me, and said, "He just went into the daughter's bedroom."

Have you ever felt drawn to some event yet repelled by it at the same time? That's how both John and I felt at that moment. Still, we cautiously crept down the hallway and over to the room where John said he had seen the ghostly figure go. Except for the furnishings, the room was empty, which was both a disappointment and a relief to us. A split second later we heard the sound of my tape recorder as it bounced down the stairs, coming to rest upon the landing. At that point, John and I headed downstairs, retrieved my recorder, and cooled our heels at the dining room table. We had come to encounter the ghost of the house and discovered that we'd had a bit too much interaction. It was time to go home.

On the way home, John described to me what he had seen. He had been in his position part way down the upstairs hallway and was listening to me asking my questions as our recorders were running. He felt a slight rush of cool air blow against him but thought nothing of it since it's such an old house. A short few seconds later, he caught movement ahead of him and looked up. He said he saw the image of a man who looked to be in his mid-forties, stockily built, with a short, reddish beard. He was wearing dark clothing the resembled the era of the of the early 1900s. John said the man stood there looking at him for the briefest of moments with his arms folded, then turned and walked into the girl's bedroom.

Author's note: I informed you earlier, dear reader, that every time in the past when I would start to write about this haunting, or even speak of it to groups, the ghost would start interrupting my life and making things difficult. The last couple of paragraphs are evidence to me he still means business. In those paragraphs I constantly had to correct misspelled words, and I found I had actually typed words I didn't want to type, my mind intending one thing, my fingers typing another. At one point my entire manuscript simply disappeared from the computer. I couldn't find it anywhere in any of my files or even on the memory stick I use when typing. It was gone without a trace. Then, it turned up again several minutes later after much colorful language on my part.

We called John and Flo later that evening and filled them in on our experiences. Again, they were not surprised. They informed us that they have often seen him, as had their children and other relations, and that he has been seen by scores of other relatives and friends. In addition, they told us that everyone in the family, as well as many friends, have often heard a baby crying. The crying comes from, of all places, the stairway leading to the second floor. That's pretty good confirmation.

I made arrangements to sit with John and Flo and talk about the experiences they've had in their home. Flo, a very calm person in whose presence you feel relaxed and comfortable, told me of one of the first hard and fast encounters anyone outside the family was privy to:

> We had been in the house just about long enough to get settled in and were finally comfortable having a small house warming party. It was in the fall, and there were probably ten or twelve good friends over. It wasn't a real dinner or anything like that, but we had everyone arrive around 7 p.m. for finger foods and wine—John and I love to serve nice wines. Everyone took a tour of the home as they arrived, and then we all sat around the living room talking and sipping our wine.
>
> That late in the year it gets dark early, so it must have been about 9 o'clock, and I was chatting with a couple friends from work. I kept noticing another circle of friends talking, and one of them kept glancing over to the entryway of the dining room. We'd already eaten, and the lights were out in there, but I thought maybe she was still in a munchie mood, so I mentioned to everyone there that if they were still hungry there was plenty of food in the dining room. This woman—she was a friend of John's from his work—knew I had seen her looking in there. A few minutes later, she came over to me when she could

get me alone, and she asked who the man was who kept showing up in the dining room watching everyone. I asked her what man she was talking about, so I could maybe introduce her, but she told me, "No, he's not one of us; in fact, I don't know if he's real."

I stepped aside with this woman and asked her what she thought she had seen. She said that off and on for over an hour this man would show up and stand in the doorway, just far enough inside the darkness so as not to be seen by everyone. She said she knew he wasn't part of our gathering because he looked mean, and he kept looking at her like he hated her being there. From what she said, he was well under six feet tall, sort of heavy set but muscular looking, and he wore old-time clothing and had a beard. She said he would catch her eye, then smirk at her for a few seconds and step back inside the dining room where she could no longer see him.

I told her that we'd had some strange things happening in the house since we had moved in, but we'd pretty much chalked it up to the nuances of moving into an old house. I was able to share some of our stories with her because I could tell she wasn't afraid. Instead, she seemed very interested and asked if she could go through the house again, which we did. I've always wondered since then if anyone else saw him that evening, but I guess I'll never know.

As you've certainly figured out by now, this in-your-face ghost figures prominently in this tale of the haunted house outside Wooster. In fact, he seems to be in control of all the paranormal activity taking place there, and he doesn't really give a tinker's damn who he picks on—even if they are children. Let's allow Flo to continue:

Our daughter, Heather, was probably in the third or fourth grade, and we decided to have a birthday party for her at the house. She was all excited and invited a bunch of her friends over. When you're having a party for kids, with ice cream, cake, and pop, you don't need them running through the house spilling things, so we decided to hold the party in the basement.

We played games and opened up her presents and had ice cream and cake, then just let the kids run around and have a good time. I went upstairs for something—I don't remember what it was—but I was only gone for a minute or two when I heard screaming, and all of a sudden it was like a stampede coming up the stairs.

I thought something terrible had happened, like maybe one of the kids got hurt. All I could think of was what in the world I was going to tell the parents because I wasn't even downstairs at the time. No one was hurt, but everyone was scared to death. From what I could gather, because it's not always easy to get a straight story from little kids, one of the girls kept seeing a scary looking man. She told a couple other kids what she had seen—a mean looking man standing off in a corner behind one of the big columns. Some of the other kids made a game out of it because they thought she was making it all up. They started running around the room, jumping out at each other, and saying "boo" and things like that. While they were having a good time and teasing this girl, this guy just popped out in front of everyone and scared the hell out of them. It was so bad that no one would return to the basement, and several of the kids wanted to go home. It sort of killed the party, and I felt really bad for my daughter.

It's interesting to note that the kids who saw the ghost pretty much described him the same way the lady at the housewarming had done. They said he was big (remember, these are little kids, and just about any adult will look "big" to them) and had a beard. A couple of them said his beard was red or "sorta reddish," and they said he wore black and was mean looking. After this incident, John and Flo knew they had a bona fide ghost on their hands.

Flo went on to say that as the years passed they would encounter this spirit many times and in many ways. Sometimes he would make himself known without actually showing up in person. For instance, there was the time when Flo decided to spend a warm autumn afternoon making cookies while the kids were in school. She mixed up the batter, preheated the oven, greased the baking sheet, and slid it into the oven, setting the timer for the appropriate baking cycle. Then she went into the living room with the idea of reading between batches.

When the timer went off, Flo said she went into the kitchen to remove the cookies from the oven, but they were only half baked. Her first thought was that she hadn't set the oven temperature properly, but looking at the dial she saw that the oven itself was turned off. Well, you know how it is when odd little things like that happen; you tell yourself you must have forgotten to actually turn it on in the first place, even though you know better.

Flo reset the oven temperature, set the timer for just enough minutes to finish baking the first batch, and then returned to her reading. A few minutes later the oven timer went off, and returning to the kitchen, she found the oven was again turned off. It wasn't that the temperature had been messed with; the dial itself had been turned to the off position. Flo spent the rest of the afternoon playing this silly game until, finally, she was able to bake the cookies without incident, but only after staying in the kitchen to read until each batch was finished. As long as she remained in the kitchen, nothing was messed with.

After several years in the house, Flo decided it was time to find out if any former owners of the home had been victims of a ghost. It's not easy to call a previous owner and ask such a question. How would you like someone you don't know calling you on the phone and out of the blue asking you if you see ghosts? Flo did just that.

The first person she called was the most recent past owner, who was rather curt with her and made it clear she didn't wish to speak about such silly things. After speaking with some neighbors, however, she was given the name of an elderly woman who had lived in the home for a couple of years back in the 1950s. She was told this was a sweet old lady who everyone liked. Flo looked her up in the phone book, saw it was a local call, and dialed her number.

Flo introduced herself, apologizing ahead of time for the nature of the call, and then went on to describe just some of the strange little incidents the family had experienced since moving in. She then asked the lady if there had ever been any strange things going on in the house when she had lived there. The lady basically said, "Oh, thank you for calling—I thought I must have been going crazy." She continued by telling Flo that she had indeed seen the ghost of a man, and she described him almost exactly the way everyone else had described him. She said all sorts of scary things would happen—lights would be burning that she knew she hadn't switched on, doors would open and close by themselves, and electrical appliances would work only intermittently.

But what had really frightened her was the ghost of the man. He would appear in her bedroom, sometimes at night, sometimes during the day, and stand in the doorway watching her. After a couple of years, she said she couldn't take it anymore, and she sold the house and moved out.

This bit of information led my buddy John and I to decide to check the local newspaper archives and county records to see what we could find out about the house. It was a long and rather tedious search, one that would start and stop according to our work and school schedules. We managed to compile a listing of all the folks who had owned the home going back to the early 1900s. We stopped there because the ghost was described as wearing clothing from that particular time period. It was interesting that the home had been sold so many times throughout the years. In fact, up until John and Flo bought the house, no one had lived in it for longer than three to five years. That gave us cause to wonder just how many people had bumped into this character and just how miserable he had made their lives.

My buddy John and I decided to spend another day alone together in the house, running our recorders, sitting quietly and meditating, and hoping to run into something worth telling our grandchildren about in our golden years. Arrangements were made, and on the appointed day we found ourselves enjoying a chance to check out this genuinely haunted home again.

Only one ghostly occurrence took place that day, and we had to wait hours for that to happen, but it was well worth the wait and, in a way, rather amusing. It seems that for some reason John was a bit nervous, the way one feels when they know something is present and something is going to happen but not knowing when it will happen.

We helped ourselves to several cups of tea as we let our recorders run, and had sipped the brew and quietly read magazines until the tapes ended. When the tapes had run their course, we downed even more cups of tea as we sat in trance-like moods listening under individual headphones for anything strange.

Having completed that task with nothing out of the ordinary to show for our time other than full bladders, John announced he had to make use of the bathroom facilities. I waited for him to get up to go, but he just sat there looking at me. I said something like, "You go first and I'll wait here, then I'll go," but John said, "No, I don't think that's a good idea." Then I knew what he was getting at; he wanted me to go with him.

Going to the bathroom together is something women have no issue with. They're always doing it, much to the fascination of men. We always think, "Why together?" or "What are doing together in there?" If men were to say to one another, "Hey, let's go drain our radiators," everyone would raise an eyebrow. With women it's different. I knew John was under extreme pressure to relieve himself, because I felt the same way. I also knew he didn't want to go upstairs to the bathroom alone, so I relented and followed him up the stairs.

As I said earlier, the upstairs bathroom used to be a bedroom in years past. I also explained that when you go through the bathroom door, you enter a short hallway which spreads open into the bathroom proper. Not only did John want me to follow him upstairs, he preferred I go into the bathroom with him, so I did. As he honored his body's call of nature, I stood like an idiot pretending to admire the wall decor.

After John dutifully washed his hands, he retrieved a hand towel that hung from a brass fixture in the shape of a lion's head with a hook beneath its jaws. He dried his hands, hung the towel back on the hook, and followed me out of the bathroom. Just as we got to the bathroom door, the hand towel flew past our heads. Now, that's a distance of about six or eight feet, so it's not like it just fell off its hook, it was more like someone had thrown it.

Women, when suddenly frightened by something, generally scream and run for cover. Men, when suddenly frightened, react quite differently. We have our manly honor to preserve and often react with a type of anger that is really a way of hiding our fear. Such was the case with John. He went into a rage, picking up the towel and cursing whoever in the house had thrown it at him. Then he stomped back into the bathroom and with massive biceps bulging tied that towel onto the brass hook as tightly as he could. Then he said, "There, now let's see you do it again," and turned to walk away.

We made it all the way out into the main hallway and had headed toward the stairs when we heard a soft thump. Looking behind us, we saw the hand towel lying on the floor just outside the entry to the bathroom. At that point John's complexion turned a few shades lighter than normal, and he said to me, "Gerry, the next thing that happens, don't be between me and the door." Then we returned downstairs to the living room, where we sat quietly for about an hour, ears set in the alarm position to detect any sound out of the ordinary.

At this point, I glanced at my watch to check the time, not wanting to impose upon the residents of the house by being there when they came home from school and work. I was surprised that my watch had stopped at a few minutes past 1 p.m., and I knew it had to be much later than that. I figured the battery had finally died, so I asked John what time it was. He looked at his watch, and it too had stopped—at the same time as mine. We knew this was more than a coincidence, and John informed me that he knew exactly what time it was; it was time to go home.

We grabbed our recorders and cameras, rinsed out our tea cups, and headed out to the car. About half way home, I glanced at my watch again and was more than a bit surprised to see it running just fine. If that weren't strange enough, it was also showing the correct time. I pointed this out to John, who looked at his watch and discovered the same thing. For several minutes of the ride home, the car was silent.

The summer before we began our first investigation of the haunted house owned by John and Flo, they had one of their nephews fly in from New Mexico for a visit. A teenager in high school, his plans were to visit with his aunt and uncle over much of the summer, having lived in the area while growing up. It didn't work out as planned.

He was all excited about spending his summer vacation with us, and we picked him up from the airport and brought him back to the house. He decided he wanted to sleep on the sofa bed in the living room so he could watch late night television, so we let him. The next morning he didn't look as though he'd gotten much rest, but we just passed it off as jet lag or something like that. The next morning he still looked out of sorts, and he didn't seem as happy as he was when we had picked him up. We just figured that in time he would let us know if something was wrong. We thought maybe he was having second thoughts and was getting homesick.

After the third night, he came to us and said he wanted to go back home. Well, the plan was for him to stay most of the summer, so we knew something must be terribly wrong. We asked him what was up. He was hesitant at first, then he told us how every night for three nights he would be awakened by a man who would shake his shoulder. He said that when he woke up from it, the man would just stand there, looking down at him and smiling a mean kind of smile. He said the guy stunk from sweat and wore a beard.

He'd fold his arms and just stand there, like he was taunting him. Our nephew said he would close his eyes for as long as he could stand it, then peek to see if the guy was still there. Each time, the man would be gone. He just couldn't take it anymore and wanted to go home, and I really can't say I blame him.

An effective deodorant could have solved his odor problem, but there was no cure for his misogyny. While he loved to torment the kids, he was also the kind of guy who would prey upon women. Flo had this figured out early in her acquaintance with the spirit when she began to hear a woman crying from time to time. It was a deep, mournful crying, like someone with a broken heart. Once while she was heading upstairs to her bedroom, she heard the woman crying and stood silently on the steps and listened. She said the crying seemed to move from one end of the upstairs hallway to the next, and she could also hear the rustling of a dress, sort of the sound satin would make when someone wearing it would be walking. She listened for at least a minute, and a couple of times she thought the woman would actually reach the top of the stairs and she'd run into her.

Author's note: those stairs begin at the bottom with a landing two steps up. Then you must turn right to go the rest of the way. At the top, you must turn right to go down the hallway.

Flo didn't run into her that day, but her daughter caught a glimpse of her when she was home alone one afternoon after school. She was in her bedroom when she began to hear someone crying, very lightly, then a bit more obviously. At first, she wondered if her mother had come home early from work and was upset about something. She hadn't heard her come into the house, however, and she thought the crying seemed "otherworldly like."

The teenaged girl tiptoed to her doorway, where she, too, heard the sound of a rustling dress. She could tell the woman was moving back and forth down the hallway. When she got up the courage to cautiously peek around the doorway, she caught the image of a woman about thirty years of age wearing a purple dress that flowed to the floor-—her hair in long ringlets. She didn't see her face clearly as the apparition was walking away from her. She said the woman walked to the far end of the hallway, as though she was going to head downstairs, and then turned around and looked at her. Heather says the woman was pretty but had the saddest expression she had ever seen. She said it broke her heart to look at her. Almost as soon as their eyes met, the woman disappeared.

I digress, and it's time to validate my claim that the male ghost is a misogynist. Let's allow Flo to make my point for me.

I think George (this is the name the family gave their sweaty ghost) was the kind of guy who used women, who didn't really like them, and maybe just used them for his pleasure. I sense he was a real bastard. Anyway, I say this because one day I was in the shower, and all of a sudden I felt a man's hand grabbing my butt. It wasn't something I imagined; he grabbed really hard. It made me jump and look to see who had sneaked in and grabbed me, but nobody was there. I was alone in the bathroom. Another time, I was in the shower—this must have been a year or so after the first time it happened—and he grabbed me again. Only this time, the bastard grabbed my breast and he really squeezed hard. I screamed that time, and John came running upstairs to see what was going on. I shut the water off and told him what had happened. You could even see the red marks where his fingers grabbed me.

Flo had decided not to tell her daughter about her shower incident for fear it would unduly frighten the poor kid. As it turned out, that was probably not the best approach. Heather, who was well into her teens by then and a beauty queen in her own right, was in the tub taking a shower and getting ready for a date with friends. As she soaped up, she felt someone's hand press against her back, and she froze in terror. She said the hand then slid down her back and stopped at her rear. That sent her screaming for help and running down the hallway to her room. Mom had to sit with her for a long time, explaining that it had happened to her as well, and that everything would be all right. Still, it was a long time before the junior beauty queen would take a shower alone in the room.

The bathroom shenanigans reinforced the idea that their ghost was mean spirited. They also began to wonder if he and the woman and baby they would hear from time to time were somehow connected to one another. These were the only ghosts they had knowledge of until one day when Flo was cleaning up the house, adrift in a sea of dusting, vacuuming, and all those mundane chores that come as part of the mortgage.

She had come down from the upstairs bedrooms with an armful of laundry and was on her way to the washer down in the basement. As she passed through the living room, she had to go past the open entryway of the dining room. As she did, she saw someone standing outside the dining room picture window, which looks out at that deep panoramic view of the expansive valley I mentioned very early in this chapter.

It was a man, and he was much older than the ghost in question. He was quite old, with sunken cheeks and white hair, and he wore a high collar and a black hat. He was just standing there, outside the window, looking out toward the valley. Naturally, Flo was puzzled and walked into the dining room for a closer look. As she did, the man turned slowly until he faced the window.

He didn't seem to notice her, and after a few seconds he walked past the window and out of sight. Flo knew there was no point in trying to go outside and track the man down because it couldn't have been a flesh and blood human being. You see, just outside that dining room window the yard drops off into the valley. The guy would need to be twelve feet tall to look into the window.

One usually associates ghosts with stormy nights, the wind howling like a banshee and rain slicing against the windows while thunder explodes like intermittent cannon shots and lightning pierces the sky to illuminate skeletal faces in the dark recesses of another room. Maybe that's how it is with some ghosts but not with this guy. Although ghosts aren't usually expected on ordinary mornings when the summer sun radiates through open bedroom windows and all is bright and beautiful, George has never cared about the time of day or what the weather is like.

Heather, then sixteen and a junior in high school, had slept in that morning, then breakfasted and showered, and was in her upstairs bedroom sitting in front of the mirror of her antique dressing table finishing her makeup. She suddenly felt as though she was no longer alone, that someone had come into the room. Turning around to look, "he" was there, he being the red-headed ghost she accused of having groped her in the shower. He stood in the doorway, and the two of them had a stare-down of sorts which lasted, in Heather's estimation, a full two minutes.

As they examined one another, Heather made a point of getting a good look at him. She even made a point of where the top of his head met the frame of the door. He was short for a man by modern standards, about five feet six, and she estimated his weight to be around 180-plus pounds. He was wearing dark pants and a dark jacket, which reminded her of what may have been dressy clothing for a hundred years ago, and a white shirt. His beard and his hair were both red, and he had small, dark eyes. He was very aware of her, as he stood with his arms crossed, smirking at her as though daring her to react to his standing there.

Heather, the essence of femininity and class, decided to stand her ground. She would not cry out this time; she would not cower away or close her eyes in fear. Instead, she did what many others would consider unthinkable. She made up her mind to go downstairs, which meant she had to pass through the very door in which he stood. With a deep breath for courage, she kept her eyes locked on his and headed toward the doorway. As she approached, the bearded man turned aside, watching her as she passed. Heather could hear the rustling of his clothes as he moved and could smell the stink of his sweat. Having gone partially down the hallway, she turned to look back, and he was gone. The impression she got from him was that he loved to frighten and pick on women. He was, in her words, "A very mean person."

As a teenager living in a haunted house, you're never sure whether or not to confide in your friends. Heather chose not to. However, some friends found out for themselves that something was amiss. For example, there was the day one of her friends drove her home from school after having worked on a project together. They pulled into the driveway that beautiful autumn afternoon, and Heather intended to invite her friend inside for a snack. Before she had to chance to do so, her girlfriend, who had been looking at the spooky old place from her position behind the steering wheel, asked, "Who was that man who was standing in the upstairs window?"

Heather knew the jig was up because she knew no one was home, and the ghost was prowling around the place like he owned it, which he pretty much still believed. She told her friend there wasn't supposed to be anyone at home and, out of curiosity, asked what she had seen. She was told that as they pulled into the driveway and came to a stop, she noticed an upstairs curtain move to one side, and beheld a man looking down at them. It was only for a brief moment or so, but he looked middle aged and had a beard.

Having heard the description, which seemed to perfectly fit their ghost, Heather informed her friend that their home was haunted and that she had just seen a ghost. Then she apologized to her and made the comment that she would invite her in, but she understood if she refused. Heather was surprised when her friend insisted on going inside for the proffered snack, adding that her aunt's house was also haunted and she had often seen the ghost of a young woman floating around the place. The two girls teamed up over carrot cake and milk, regaling one another with tales of their ghostly experiences.

At this point in the story, I make what may seem to my readers to be an unnecessary divergence from our tale. Yet, what I'm about to relate to you is connected to our story. Hang in there, it's worth my telling, and I hope worth the time it takes for you to read.

Back in December of 1987, the same year of my encounter with this haunted home, my brother Glenn suddenly died of a brain aneurysm before having reached the age of forty. Needless to say, it was tragic and traumatic for our entire extended family, and I was deeply hurt by his passing. At the same time, I had been working with the haunting of John and Flo's home.

As a result of a book I had been reading at seminary, I came across the name of someone who was supposed to be the world's most gifted psychic. His name was Alex Tanous, a man whose level of education was more than simply impressive. Dr. Tanous had completed a classical education program at Boston College, then had gone on to receive his Masters in Philosophy from that institution as well as an M.A. and Ph.D. from Fordham, an M.S. from the University of Maine, and a Doctor of Divinity from the College of Metaphysics of Indiana. He had gone on to teach theology at Manhattan College and St. John's University, both in New York, and was currently teaching at the University of Southern Maine. This was no academic weakling.

*Author's note: Years later, I discovered that none other than Kahlil Gibran, the celebrated author and mystic, had told Tanous' mother, while pregnant with him, that her son would be a man of exceptional gifts and exceptional sorrows.

In addition to his academic accomplishments, Tanous was closely associated with the American Society for Psychical Research in New York City, where his psychic abilities had been and were being thoroughly tested. He was amazingly proficient in the diagnosis of illnesses and had the ability of "leaving" his body to examine a targeted address across the country, accurately describing the home's interior and furnishings. He had done this on many occasions while in a locked room and under the supervision of the ASPR. On at least one occasion, while locked in the room in New York with many eyes peering in at him, he had been seen by the people at the targeted address way off in another state, where they said he entered the house, sat down at the piano, and played a tune or two before leaving once again, having never said a word to anyone the entire time.

I thought maybe Dr. Tanous might be able to give me a hand understanding the haunting of the home in Wooster. Feeling a bit bold, I picked up the telephone one afternoon and called him at home (yes, the book actually listed his home phone number). I was surprised and nervous when he answered, however, Dr. Tanous was very gracious in receiving my call, his voice gentle and demeanor inviting. When I apologized for having disturbed him uninvited, he assured me no apology was necessary and that he was glad I called.

At this point, I informed him about my involvement in a nearby home where the occupants believed they had a ghost present amongst them. I did not name names, give an address, or offer any details about the nature of the experiences. I indicated I simply wanted advice on how to approach the situation and what to do about helping the family deal with their active spirit. What he did next was something totally unexpected.

Alex (he insisted I call him by his first name) stopped me as I neared the end of my explanation and request and said that first he wanted to talk about me. That set me back a bit, as I had no intention of talking about me; I was only interested in how to deal with the haunting. He wanted to know about my "call" to ministry. Now, you must understand that a "call" to ministry means you had some sort of mystical or transitory experience which led you to believe God was calling you to become a member of the clergy. In the past, whenever I had been asked such a question, and it is a question a clergy person is asked frequently, I gave my standard answer. A traumatic time of unemployment and destitution at about the age of thirty showed me I no longer had control over my own life and destiny. I needed to turn my life over to God. Alex said to me, "I don't want to hear the story you give others; I want to hear the truth. I want to hear about the time when you were a little boy and were overcome with a horrible fever and died—when you had left your body and met relatives for the first time who had passed away well before you were born."

To say I sat at my desk stunned is an understatement of epic proportions. I had never told anyone of that experience. In fact, it had taken place when I was five years old, and I had indeed met deceased relatives for the first time and had seen what life after death was like. It was that singular experience which gave me the insight that going into the ministry was exactly what God intended me to do.

I told my story to Alex, and if that weren't enough, he went on to tell me I had just experienced a terrible loss. Without having been given a shred of information from me, he told me I had recently lost my oldest brother (oldest was a word which added to his credibility as I was born number three of four boys), and that my brother felt responsible for giving me encouragement. He was always with me and was standing behind my chair as we spoke. As those words came from Alex, I suddenly felt three strong tugs on the back of my shirt, and Alex said, "Did you feel that? It's your brother."

Eventually, our conversation returned to the haunted Wooster home, and Alex explained to me that ghosts are simply human beings who either have not crossed over or who have returned with some sort of message for someone. He told me to simply meditate before and during my visits to the home and invite the spirit to communicate with me.

Author's note: Alex Tanous passed away several years ago, however, you can go to Google and simply type in his name. A wealth of information, and even a website devoted to the continuance of his work, will be at your behest.

During my final year of seminary, I returned for yet another encounter with the ghost of the manor. This time, I brought along my nephew David, a young man very interested in things paranormal and who happens to be a police officer. According to the arrangements I had made, the evening was supposed to include the two of us, and maybe Flo, the owner of the home. However, when we arrived early that evening, the driveway was full of automobiles.

Upon entering the home, we discovered Flo had invited several guests for dinner and a seance. All this was news to me, but when one is a guest in another's home, one must go with the flow of events in the most congenial of ways. We partook of homemade veal parmigiana, spinach salad, roasted asparagus, and glasses of vino accompanied by entertaining conversation. After dinner, most of the guests left, and I discovered that only one of the guests, a close friend of Flo's whom I shall refer to as Daria, was to remain for the "seance."

Dishes washed, glasses refilled (as a rule I never let my team members drink before or during a ghost hunt, but rules are made to be broken in the name of civility), we retired to the living room to begin our attempt to contact the spirit or spirits flitting about the domicile. That's when Flo did something I advise others to avoid, she broke out her Ouija Board. I immediately suggested we avoid its participation in our endeavors, but she and her friend were insistent, assuring me they had used it many times over the years and that it was always an active conduit to the spirit world. I told her that was exactly why I avoid it, because it is a portal through which other spirits, some of whom may have ulterior motives, move. Still, she was insistent, so I told her David and I would simply be observers and note takers.

Flo and Daria spread the board atop her coffee table, lighted several candles, turned off the electric lights, and then stationed husband John at the top of the stairway where he would have a good view of the upstairs hallway. David and I sat on the living room floor, several feet apart, but with a good view of the board, our eyes at table level. I told him to particularly watch the planchette and to later give an opinion as to whether he thought it was guiding them or they were guiding it. Then they began.

There were a few moments of centering, during which time the two friends sat quietly with their eyes closed and meditated. Then they placed their fingertips lightly upon the planchette, as the directions indicate, and one of them began asking questions. Almost immediately, the board seemed to respond to their touch, and the planchette began to move. When asked,

"Is there anyone who wishes to speak with us?" the planchette slowly headed on over to "yes." When asked if the spirit happened to be female, and if the spirit had lived in the home, both answers were once again in the affirmative. When asked if the woman was the only spirit in the home, the answer was in the negative, and when asked who was with her, it spelled out "child."

The two friends were on a roll. Every question was met with an answer as the planchette almost seemed to scurry from letter to letter. David, sitting near me on the carpet, busily jotted down the questions and answers in an effort to keep up with them. Soon it became apparent that they were communicating with the wife of the red-headed spirit. Flo and Daria paused at least twice, on the verge of tears and commenting aloud how they both felt so sad that they could sense the woman's grief.

As it turned out, the woman was about twenty-six years old, her name was Anne. She had lived in the home in the early 1900s and was constantly looking for her child. The child, indicated the board, had died in the home shortly after birth. When asked if she could see the child, the spirit answered negatively. When asked if she could hear the child, she answered positively. Then she was asked again if anyone else was with her, and this time she spelled out "husband." Through more interrogation, it was determined she was afraid of her husband. He wasn't letting her leave and was keeping her from finding her baby.

Near the end of this round of questioning, Flo and Daria, suddenly and at the same instant, cut loose with a frightened gasp and raised their hands away from the board. At that moment both David and I watched as the planchette very quickly moved to the left several inches and then shot to the right and left the board, landing on the floor. Needless to say, that little event was impressive—even more so at the time than the information they were gathering.

The women asked for a couple of minutes to compose themselves and then began round two. More questioning revealed the woman had been "beeten," as the board spelled the word, and she had followed her child in death by a matter of only days. Around this time, the living room suddenly became aromatic with the scent of lavender, a fragrance not too many modern women use in today's world. Once again, the teammates at the board let out another squeal and pulled away from the planchette, which entertained us all by shooting off the board and onto the floor again. Still, troopers that they were, they continued with the questioning.

David and I missed this round of questions as we found ourselves distracted by a swirling, white mist wafting into the living room from the enclosed front porch. It was about eighteen inches high, a couple of feet wide, and several feet in length. It moved slowly over to where we were sitting, as though it had a mind of its own, and when I reach my hand out and touched it, it was very cold. I admit that David and I were a little bug-eyed at its arrival, and we continued to watch as it approached the board then turned away and moved off into the kitchen. The women, having spotted it as it came near to them, stopped their questioning and joined us in our observation. Then they declared the whole Ouija board event ended.

Flo snuffed out the candles, switched on the electric lights, and called her husband down from the top of the staircase. As John entered the living room, Flo very excitedly told him they had contacted a woman. Before she could even go into detail, which she was champing at the bit to do, he responded with, "Hell yes, you contacted a woman. I've been watching her walking up and down the hallway for ten minutes."

John went on to describe the woman as being in her late twenties or early thirties, rather pretty, with her hair up in a bun and wearing a long, dark green satin style dress. He said she kept walking the hallway, lightly crying and looking lost and afraid.

David and I remained at the home until midnight, when things seemed to slow down and everyone began feeling exhausted from what they had bumped up against. As we stood at the front door saying our good byes, David peered through the living room and over to the stairway leading up to the bedrooms and playfully hollered out, "Goodbye, George!" Immediately there came a loud cracking noise, like a piece of wood had exploded over by the staircase. Flo nonchalantly looked at David and said, "George says good night."

My friend John and I spent a great deal of our free time researching county records and the local newspaper, trying to discover information pertinent to the haunting. Finally, we found a couple of stories from the early 1910s which told of how a man and his wife had moved into the house soon after their marriage. It seems that right away he couldn't get along with his neighbors, suggesting he was a difficult person to deal with. He had left the area for an extended business trip, returning months later to a wife who presented him with a newborn baby boy. There was some question as to the timing of the birth, and very soon after his return the baby had "slipped out of its mother's loving arms" and had fallen to its death on the stairs. The woman, evidently brokenhearted, had taken her own life by, according to the paper, taking a dive out an upstairs window. If it all sounds suspicious to you, you're in pretty good company.

Full of pride in our research, we immediately phoned John and Flo to tell them what we had discovered. We managed to tell Flo, who answered the phone, that we had found the name of their ghost. Before we could tell her what it was, she said, "We know his name—we used the Ouija board last night and it spelled out 'George.'" It was the exact name we had discovered, and humorously, the name he'd been given by the family all along.

Just after the discovery of what had happened in the house, my time was up in Ohio, and I was off to Michigan to begin ministry in my first church. Not wanting to forget my experiences in the midst of George the ghost, I decided to write a brief story about what had been going on and sent it to the Akron Beacon Journal, a local newspaper. To my surprise, they made it the cover story for one of their Sunday weekly supplements, and word quickly spread about the ghost hunting preacher. That news spread all the way up and into Michigan. It wasn't long before I started getting calls and letters from folks in our neck of the country asking for help with their ghosts. Those adventures led to the writing of three books about Michigan hauntings.

Planning a Visit? Batdorf Road is long and winding, but with a little clever investigation you'd probably be able to figure out which house it is. Don't go knocking on any doors. People are very clannish in that area and likely to help you along on your return trip.

Still Haunted? I think it's safe to assume George, his wife, and his child are still inside the house—she still looking for her murdered child, and he still making life miserable for her and anyone else poking their noses into his business and his house.

Encore, Encore!
The Ghosts of the Michigan Theatre

*What could be more suited as an encore story
than that of a haunted movie theatre?*

Place Visited: The Michigan Theatre, 124 N. Mechanic
Street, Jackson.

Period of Haunting: It's hard to say. Rumors of ghosts
flitting about the place go back several decades, and
those spirits can still be spotted from time to time in
various places throughout the theatre.

Date of Investigation: June 2012.

Description of Location: Back before the internet,
email, social media, video games, and video streaming,
the theatre was the center of entertainment for the
local community. Walking into the dark recesses of that
cavernous edifice was to be transported to new worlds
where you could fly to Mars, shoot it out at the OK
Corral, or pick up tips on how to come on to a girl.

When I was a pup, my dad would slip my brothers and
I fifty cents and drop us off on Saturday afternoon at
our local movie house. It cost thirty-five cents to buy a
ticket, and I usually spent the remaining fifteen cents
for a giant sack of lemon drops. Then we'd settle into
our seats for a passel of cartoons, previews of coming
attractions and two—count 'em two—full length feature
films. Those Saturday matinees were always horror
movies. All us neighborhood kids would sit together,
entranced and wonderfully terrified by such epics

as *Horror of Dracula* or *House on Haunted Hill* or *The Tingler*. It was a whale of a treat for 50 cents.

One of those magnificent theatres (no, I'm not misspelling the word, I'm simply presenting as it has appeared on their buildings for decades) is the Michigan Theatre in downtown Jackson. Construction began in the late 1920s with the idea this would be the most ornate and magnificent movie house in mid-Michigan, and it is, in fact, opulent. No expense was spared in its construction, yet it fell afoul of that cataclysmic event, the Great Depression. That's why, when the Michigan Theatre opened in April of 1930, there was no money for the magnificent pipe organ they had planned to install.

This place is a wonderful example of how movie theatres used to look in the infancy of the medium and puts all the new antiseptic looking movie houses to shame. Words cannot express how ornate this place is, so I invite you to view the photos I've provided for this chapter. I will say the place is huge, with an auditorium rising three stories above the sloping floors. It boasts two levels of balcony and a full sized stage, as in its early days live performances by such artists as Groucho Marx, Al Jolson and many other famous folk made the circuit.

I recall my first visit to the Michigan Theatre. I stood in a line which queued down the street and around the corner, waiting more than an hour in the rain to could see Charlton Heston's Moses match wits with Yul Brynner's Pharaoh in *The Ten Commandments*. As the years passed, I often sat in the balcony for such films as *The Big Country*, *To Kill a Mockingbird*, *Bullitt* and *The Godfather*. Sadly, with the popularity of VCRs and network television, most large movie houses went the way of silent films, or were partitioned off from one giant screen into a multiplex of several smaller screens. The Michigan Theatre couldn't afford to remain open, and it was forced to close its doors for several years until 1993 when it came under new ownership, and a massive restoration program began. Slowly but steadily, the theatre is being returned to its initial grandeur. Today, it boasts a yearly attendance of around 40,000 people, as well as several ghosts.

There are several dressing rooms—one behind and below the main stage, where the most important performers awaited their curtain call, and four more, one atop the other, all reached by a winding staircase. There was also the requisite orchestra pit, now protectively covered up. Down below there are two separate basements, and tucked away three stories above the ground floor are the administrative offices. This building must have been the shining star of the blue collar Jackson, and the community is proud of it restoration work.

As always, I toss in a place or two where good grub can be had when visiting the area. Just around the corner from the Michigan Theatre is a place called "The Pickle Barrel," where great sandwiches, coffees, and designer soda pop can be had. This is not a fast food joint but an old style deli with top notch ingredients. If your taste is for something more formal, across the street from the Pickle Barrel you'll find two of Jackson's finest restaurants—"Darryl's" and "The Bella Notte." You'd be hard pressed to find finer food anywhere in the city.

Haunt Meter: * * * * *(the ghosts are mostly pleasant, but it can be unsettling when they appear without warning)*

I HAD OFTEN HEARD TALES of the haunting of the Michigan Theatre and was anxious to have a chance to visit the place for myself. It was easy enough to arrange. I simply picked up the phone and spoke with the director of the theatre, Steve Tucker. Steve is a retired school teacher and musician and is fiercely dedicated to the restoration of his historic building. After our phone conversation, we met in person so I could assure him I

Michigan Theatre

was not some nutcase trying to exploit the theatre. Then I paid the requisite $125 to reserve the building for the day. (This is the only time I've ever paid to investigate a haunted place, but it's justified since the money is used to restore the theatre I grew up loving.)

During that initial visit, I was given a tour of the premises and shown where we could go and what parts of the building were off limits. With the exception of the negative pressure wind tunnel in one of the basements, we were to be given virtually free reign of the building. I was fascinated by the progress being made in restoring the place and felt as though I could smell the history wafting through the corridors and into the auditorium.

When the tour was completed, I spoke with some of the staff members, inquiring into the purported haunting of the building. Steve, the director, indicated that he was too new to his position, hadn't had anything paranormal happen to him thus far, and that he was

Michigan Theatre entrance

really quite skeptical about such things. I then trekked on up to the administrative offices to speak with Marilyn Guidinger, who works as the office manager and has been associated with the theatre for many years. Marilyn is a soft spoken, friendly and intelligent woman, holding a Ph.D. in Chemistry from Penn State and an MBA from Northwestern University. She is no lightweight in the intelligence department, and loves her association with the theatre dearly.

I asked Marilyn if she ever experienced anything paranormal in her years spent within the theatre. She indicated that she had not had anything unusual happen to her personally but had heard stories from time to time about the place being haunted. She told of an event they held a few years earlier when several psychics were invited in to entertain the public. One of these individuals had stationed herself on the second floor to conduct her readings, and when asked if there were any ghosts hanging out in the place responded,

"Oh, yes. There's actually a young woman sitting on the stairs behind us. She's been watching us all evening."

There are many volunteers helping out at the theatre. They come and they go, but they all contribute to restoring the historic building. Marilyn told me about a teenaged boy who helped out one summer cleaning up the place and running the occasional errand. He had been in the auditorium finishing up one of his chores when he happened to look up into the balcony. Seated about half way up, he saw a man and a woman looking down at him. Since it's kept relatively dark in that area, he couldn't make out what they were wearing or see their faces clearly, but it was obvious to him it was a couple. He finished his task, looked into the balcony once again, and they were still sitting there, as though waiting for some movie or program to begin. The young man left the auditorium and ran into one of the office staff. He asked who the people were in the balcony and was told that, at that time, they were alone in the building and the doors were locked. When he went back to see if the man and the woman were still seated inside the auditorium, they were gone. A psychic who had visited the theatre months earlier had ascertained there were three spirits roaming through the cherished building and that two of them always remained in the balcony, a man and a woman.

Among the treasured stories about the haunting of the Michigan Theatre concerns one about "the lady who sings." It seems a former employee of the movie house, named Allison, had spent a night inside the locked building and at times heard a woman's voice singing. It was soft and a bit distant but quite beautiful. A short while later, Allison received a phone call from the granddaughter of the first manager of the theatre. When informed of the nocturnal soloist, the granddaughter told Allison that her grandmother had loved singing and aspired to become a professional singer. During that conversation, Allison mentioned how there had been talk about workers and guests occasionally spying a man walking through the auditorium dressed in an old usher's uniform. The granddaughter assured Allison they had not been deluded because she had often seen the man as well when visiting the Michigan as a little girl.

Marilyn isn't the only person to have given me a tale of strangeness about the theatre. A couple of years back during one of my lectures about haunted places, I met a middle aged man who was an electrician. He told me his company had been hired to do some wiring work when the restoration of the building was in its infancy, and that he was downstairs in the west basement plying his trade. As he went about his business, he saw an elderly man dressed in 1930's clothing start walking across the room. The old man paid no attention to what he was doing, walked past him, and then faded away before reaching the other side of the basement. When I asked what affect this had on him, he told me he packed up his tools and refused to work in the theatre. His boss had to send in a coworker to finish the job.

Our group of paranormal investigators (as indicated elsewhere, we refer to ourselves as the Bogles) arrived at the theatre on a hot and sun-soaked Monday morning. Upon entering the foyer, we were pleased to be informed that Steve had given us permission to use the soft drink system at the refreshment stand throughout our visit. It didn't take us long to indulge in his offer. We set about unloading our equipment, and, that accomplished, I conducted a tour of the building so all our members could become adequately acquainted with its layout. Tour completed, we divided into groups of two and picked out where each team would be stationed for a couple hours at a time.

Taking our positions throughout the building, each team sat quietly, running their audio recorders and snapping digital photos from time to time. As instructed, they asked questions, hoping for ghostly

Michigan Theatre Auditorium — Where spirits are seen

responses, but it appears the ghosts were a bit shy. These initial sessions were met with virtual silence. We received nothing from the auditorium and nothing from the backstage area. All the dressing rooms, the basement, and the projector room were quiet as a ghost.

Lunch time rolled around, and we decided to stroll over to the Pickle Barrel for sandwiches and cold drinks. Sitting around a common table, we discussed our next attempt to contact the ghosts we had been hearing about. Several of the team members said they wanted to do a seance, and I was all for it and willing to participate until they mentioned they had brought a Ouija board with them. Since the use of a Ouija board during my very first ghost hunt years ago in Ohio had led to some negative experiences, I opted out.

We returned to the theatre, bellies full and all refreshed, and once again headed into the auditorium. There's a wide space between the stage and the first row of seats, so a card table and several folding chairs were set up there, and the Ouija board was spread out between two team members.

Before the session began, Jim Cummings, a fellow Bogle, produced a very sensitive floor microphone and set it up next to the card table. He then attached it to some sound recording equipment he had brought along from his recording studio. (Jim has been a professional musician all his life, and has played with some famous artists in his day.)

When all was in readiness, two of our team members, Claudia and Roberta, began working the board while Sarah sat nearby taking notes and the rest of us watched quietly from our individual perches. Their session was pretty much a blow-out, so it was eventually decided that others give it a try. Again, things were slow going, that is, until Jim and Roberta took a shot at it. That's when the board decided to respond and quite rapidly at that.

When asked if there was anyone who wished to speak with them, the planchette shot up to "yes." Soon, through a series of questions, it was discovered that the spirit was that of a thirteen year old boy who had once lived in the area. Further conversation revealed that he had been abused and killed back in 1951. He gave his name as "Eddie," and indicated that he loved being at the theatre. It reminded him of the good times he had spent there while still alive. He said he didn't know his attacker and had been lured to his death. When asked if his killer had been discovered, he explained, through a series of questions, that he had been caught and put in prison and that he was also now deceased.

Eddie the spirit seemed to enjoy his conversation with Jim and Roberta but grew quiet when they took a break and two other team members gave the board a shot. After several minutes, they relinquished their seats, giving them up to Jim and Roberta once again. Eddie seemed pleased to have them back and answered

Second floor where they encounter a young woman

their questions rapidly and willingly. When asked if there were other spirits in the building, Eddie had the planchette point to "no," but after some admonishment corrected himself and said "yes." When asked if they could speak to the other spirits, Eddie was very reluctant to let go and was told that if he would allow another spirit to speak, they would get back to him afterward. That seemed to work, and in a moment's time Eddie backed away and the spirit of a man seemed to make his appearance.

If the Ouija board is to be believed, this next spirit turned out to be Eddie's father. Through "yes" and "no" questions, he filled us in about having served time in the military during World War II, and that he was now with his son. Together they were enjoying their time at the movie house. He indicated he did not personally know the man who had killed his son, but that his spirit was elsewhere and not around the theatre.

The rest of the afternoon was spent wandering through the cavernous building, snapping photos and running our equipment. None of us ran into any disembodied spirits, although one of our team members, Sarah, did snap a few interesting photos. She had climbed the winding stairs behind the stage, going past all the dressing rooms stacked one upon the other, until she reached a landing high above the stage. From that perch, one can look all the way down upon the stage and view everything going on down there.

Up on that concrete expanse there sits a storage cabinet. In one series of photos, Sarah noticed something unusual associated with that cabinet. The first photo clearly shows just the cabinet, but in each successive photo there appears a black mist. In each shot the mist moves in more fully until it obscures from sight at least half the cabinet. Then the mist moves away again. In trying to recreate the event, I failed. A shot of the mist is included with this story.

When five o'clock rolled around, we packed up our equipment, filled our cups with the free soda we'd been offered, and headed home to spend hours upon hours reviewing audio and video. That very evening I received a call from Jim Cummings. He had been reviewing the audio and video of the Ouija board session, and when he had asked Eddie the question, "Are you in pain?" he received a clear "no" in response.

Late Breaking News!!!

As indicated within this story, one of my colleagues in the ghost hunting adventures we undertake is Jim Cummings. Jim owns and operates Soundstage1 Productions in Climax, Michigan, a professional recording studio which also happens to be the largest such studio in western Michigan. He has been in business for nearly thirty years and specializes in sound recording and high end commercial production. Past clients have included the likes of Honda, Pepsi, Ford

Motor Company, Amway, Archway, Whirlpool and Disney. His is a world class recording studio (actually, it's four studios under one roof), and he has recorded some very famous musicians in his day. He also provides services to law enforcement agencies and private detectives. By the way, he has been a professional musician with his own band, the Jim Cummings Band, most of his life, and still tours. Why do I tell you all this? So you can be as amazed as I was at what he discovered as a result of our ghost hunt at The Michigan Theatre.

Do you recall that Ouija board session I referred to in that story? Jim had set up his high tech microphone near the table where the board was being used. He asked a series of questions, and during the session no voices were heard. However, he took his expensive audio recorder back to his studio, where he picked up a few answers to those questions. For example, at one point he asked the little boy they had contacted, "Did you suffer when you died?" and the answer was an audible "no."

It's both strange and exciting to receive answers like this, but that's only the beginning of the strangeness. In order to explain what I'm talking about, I'm afraid I must first get a little technical.

Jim tells me that all sounds have their own frequency, and that those sounds can be isolated and enhanced. In an effort to do just that, Jim ran his audio from the Ouija session through his spectrum analyzers, which measure these frequencies. He also engaged the use of his high end thirty-one band graphic equalizer, as well as his parametric equalizer, which expands band width, adjusts frequencies, and eliminates frequencies which interfere with the sounds he wished to isolate. An example of what I'm saying is this: if you're recording your mother singing and someone walks across the floor while another person rings the doorbell, all those sounds would be recorded together, and each would have its own frequency. However, you only want your mother's singing without the accompaniment of other noises. You would isolate Mom's voice, the footsteps, and the doorbell individually, and then eliminate all but Mom's voice. Simple, right? The results of Jim's efforts, though, were downright eerie. The voices on his tapes could not be isolated. They didn't have a frequency of their own. You ask, "What's strange about this?" Well, every sound has its own frequency. Again, these voices had no frequency of their own. When I asked how that could be possible, Jim told me, "it isn't possible." This means we can only speculate that the voices were coming from some source or dimension outside those known to us. Creepy? Oh, yeah. But it gets even better.

For those of you who have read my first book, *Haunted Michigan: Recent Encounters With Active Spirits*, you are acquainted with the story of the haunted home in which I spent my misspent adolescence and early manhood. In that story I wrote of how I had recorded video and audio of the stairway leading from the ground floor of the house upwards to the second level bedrooms. Well, I finally sent that videotape to Jim for him to professionally analyze, because I had recorded various voices—at least one of which recited two poems in an old man's croak.

Just a day before I shipped this tome off to my trusty publisher, Jim called me to give me the results of that audio (there was nothing of substance on video). All I wanted him to do was isolate the voices, enhance them without background noise, and send the results back for me to enjoy. Guess what? That's right, none of the voices had a frequency of their own. None of them. They couldn't be isolated, only amplified. Again, that just isn't possible.

Intrigued, I sent Jim a copy of the audio I had picked up from a recording I had made at the Historic Fort Wayne, a tale included in this book. It was the audio recording of approaching footsteps and one voice announcing he was closing the door. The story was the same. The voices on the tape could not be isolated from ambient noise as they did not have their own frequency.

How do I explain all this? Ghost voices must reach us through a mode of communication beyond that of our own.

Planning a Visit? Why not? They still offer great programs, such as classic and contemporary films, musical concerts of all types, and other forms of entertainment. They even rent the place out for weddings! My advice is to support the theatre by buying a ticket to one of these events. You can also become a member of the theatre by making a donation. The more you donate, the greater your perks as a member. Go to their website and check them out.

Still Haunted? I believe the ghosts still float around, sometimes perching in the balcony or wandering through the halls. Is ghost hunting great, or what?!

About the Author

Gerald S. Hunter has always possessed an affinity for storytelling and his work has appeared in the Detroit Free Press, the Akron-Beacon Journal, and the Michigan Christian Advocate. He became interested in the paranormal at a young age when his family moved into an old farmhouse in the Village of Brooklyn, just south of Jackson, Michigan. It was the intense ghostly occurrences there which whetted his appetite to investigate the nature of hauntings. Gerald is an ordained United Methodist minister. He currently resides in Hillsdale County with his wife and cats. This is his third book about haunted places in Michigan.